MEMORY LANE

PINE COVE BOOK FIVE

HJ WELCH

Memory Lane
Pine Cove Book Five

PROLOGUE – SIXTEEN YEARS AGO

JAY

THE DAY JAY COAL FELL IN LOVE WAS ALSO THE DAY HE ALMOST died.

He never did anything by halves.

"Don't look down!" his best friend, Angel Shields, yelled. Jay clung to the railings of the bridge over the railway line, the wind rushing through his hair as he trembled in fear.

He was going to kill Kenneth Brooker. That was, if he didn't fall to his death right then and there.

"Angel," Jay whimpered. His arms felt like jelly as he kicked his legs through the air, dangling like a worm on a hook. He and Angel shouldn't have been messing around on the bridge. He knew that. But he'd been safe with Angel. It was only when Kenny had jumped out and scared him that Jay had lost his footing and slipped.

In the distance, a train horn blared.

Jay snapped his head up, meeting Angel's terrified gaze. "Angel!" Jay cried out again. Somewhere on the bridge, Kenny and his cohorts were jeering, but all Jay could think about was Angel.

"I've got you, okay," said Angel firmly, sounding strong

,even though his eyes were wide. "I'm going to pull you up. The train won't hit you. It's too far below."

The horn sounded again, this time closer. Much closer. Jay gripped on to the railing as tight as he could, feeling like a complete idiot. Images of his family – especially his twin brother, Robin – flashed before his eyes.

He was never going to see them again.

Except Angel was there, crouching down beside Jay on the wrong side of the bridge. They'd done this silly stunt a dozen times, thrilling themselves with the adrenaline from the height while the train thundered below them. But usually they stood on the lip that was just wide enough for their feet, and clung to the rails. Jay had been a fool not to realize how dangerous it really was, how easily one of them could fall.

With one hand, Angel held on to the railing, and with the other he pulled at Jay's elbow with a vise-like grip. "You can do this, Jay Coal!" he barked as Jay inched his hands up the rails, hauling his body higher. "I'm right here! Don't look down, and don't stop!"

The train blasted its horn again, the sound vibrating through Jay's bones. The driver must have seen them by now and was trying to get them to hurry up.

Jay didn't need telling twice.

He kicked his legs in the air, as if the momentum was helping him climb. He wasn't going to die on this damn railway line. He was going to make it back onto the bridge with Angel, and they were both going to start high school that fall. They had it all planned out. Their future was side-by-side, just like they'd promised each other so many times. Jay wasn't going to wreck that all by doing something so dumb as dying.

His arms were shaking, and for a terrifying moment, Jay slipped a couple of inches back down. Both the boys cried out, but Jay managed to cling on to the railings, and Angel was there with his steel-like grip. Jay knew Angel would never let him go. Jay took from his strength, gritting his teeth as he swung his knee up, trying to get some purchase.

"That's it, just a little farther," Angel encouraged him, pulling on his arm. "You're *not* going to die on me like this. Come on, you can do it!"

Jay let out a guttural moan, his bare knee scraping against the rusty metal as he pushed with everything he had. Finally, mercifully, he got some purchase, and managed to pull himself up. Clinging to the railings, he got back up on the edge of the bridge, panting for breath.

He was safe. But still, Angel clung to his arm, maybe just to make sure he didn't fall again.

"What do you think you're playing at?" Angel yelled to the boys on the other side of the bridge through the railings.

Kenny and his cohorts looked white and ashen, but Kenny elbowed the ones next to him, and then sneered at Jay. "How was I supposed to know you were gonna jump off the damn bridge?" he said with a smirk. "Not my fault you ignored the safety signs." Shame washed through Jay. Kenny might have been a bully, but he kind of had a point.

"Morons," Angel growled as he hugged Jay to him.

"I'm sorry," Jay whispered as he clung to Angel, inhaling his oh-so-familiar scent. Angel smelled like home and fun and comfort. Jay knew that no matter what happened, he'd be okay with his best friend by his side.

Even if he had almost fallen off this rickety bridge.

The train screamed one last time, its horn rattling Jay's teeth. And then the locomotive was hurtling underneath, shaking them as they clung to the bridge railings. Jay moaned as he hugged Angel. But now he was safe. He wasn't going anywhere.

It took him a moment to realize that the train had eventually passed, but that he was still clinging on to Angel as well as the railing. Jay's heart was pounding in his throat as he breathed deeply.

His body was reacting to the fear, yes. But it was also reacting to having Angel's strong arms wrapped around him.

Which was crazy. He and Angel had known each other since kindergarten. Yes, Jay had recently come to realize that he was gay, but he didn't have feelings for *Angel*. That was nuts. Angel was his best bud, his bro. Of course Jay had noticed that Angel had started getting bigger from football lately – more manly – but that didn't mean Jay felt any differently about him.

Right?

It had to be the adrenaline making his shorts feel so tight.

He looked up at Angel and managed a trembling smile. "Thank you," he whispered.

Angel chuckled and shook his head. "You idiot," he said with deep affection, ruffling Jay's hair. That felt *nice.* "Don't ever do that to me again. I like you walking around, not splattered."

Jay laughed and hugged his best friend tightly. "I promise. I won't."

"Do you two need some privacy, you fucking fairies?" Kenny jeered from the other side of the railings. His gang laughed nastily and made loud kissing noises against the crooks of their arms.

Jay's face flamed, and he tried his best to hide behind Angel. He and Robin didn't quite feel ready to come out yet, and had talked about maybe doing it at the start of high school. Except Jay knew he couldn't hide something like that from Angel, so he'd made his confession at the start of the summer with his heart in his throat.

It had been terrifying, and Jay had dreaded Angel walking away from him in a heartbeat. But Angel had acted like it was no big deal at all, and sworn to Jay he'd keep his secret until

Jay was ready to come out to the rest of the school. Jay was lucky to have such an amazing friend, and he'd hold on to what they had for as long as he could.

But still, being in the closet hadn't stopped the likes of Kenneth Brooker teasing them mercilessly, probably guessing the truth. But Jay had Angel to watch his back.

"Shut the fuck up before I make you," Angel snapped. Then he rubbed Jay's arm and jerked his head. "Come on," he murmured kindly to Jay. "Let's get off this bridge before anything else happens."

Jay nodded sheepishly. Of course *Angel* wasn't gay. But for some reason, he hadn't abandoned Jay yet. It was like Jay was watching a ticking clock, waiting for the day when his best friend realized that he was better off without him. But so far, that day hadn't arrived, and Jay kept believing Angel when he said they'd always be side-by-side.

Until then, Jay would try not to worry. But his insides were squirming as he followed Angel, desperately hoping that no one could see the confusing boner he was sporting in his shorts. He didn't have a crush on Angel. He *didn't*. That would be a disaster. There was no way that wouldn't ruin everything between them.

So Jay willed his dick to calm down and behave.

The summer heat beat down as the two boys carefully made their way to the end of the old, rusty bridge. Cars might once have driven along this road, but now it was just a dirt track that led into the woods. At the end where the bridge met the bank, one of the railings was missing, creating a gap just big enough for two mischievous boys to slip through. Not that Jay felt like doing this again anytime soon.

Angel insisted that Jay went first, getting him to safety before Angel himself forced his way through the hole. And then he was barreling toward Kenny. "That wasn't funny," he

5

yelled, jabbing his finger in Kenny's face. "You could have killed him!"

Kenny rolled his eyes and swatted Angel's hand away. "Maybe you shouldn't have been dicking around on the wrong side of the bridge, hmm?" he said, folding his arms. "Not my fault you're idiots."

"Come on," said Jay, pulling on Angel's T-shirt. His bleeding knee was stinging, and his T-shirt stuck to his body with sweat. He felt small and stupid, and didn't want to see Kenny and his goons laughing at him any longer. "He's not worth it."

Part of Jay was ashamed. He knew that Kenny was right. He and Angel shouldn't have been on that side of the bridge. But Angel always made things so exciting. He had this way of getting Jay to want to try and be a daredevil like he was, always chasing an adrenaline rush. Angel made Jay believe he could do *anything*.

Jay's rush was being on stage. He was a drama geek and Angel was a football star. It didn't matter how much they promised each other that they'd always stay side-by-side. Perhaps this was the wake-up call Jay needed to realize that one day, Angel was going to leave him behind. Jay could follow him onto the railway bridge, but that didn't mean he wouldn't fall off it.

Was he going to get himself killed to try and keep up with his best friend?

Yes, a small voice whispered in his head. *I'll hold on to Angel for as long as I can.*

Jay bit his lip and glared at Kenny, who was squealing and making silly faces, supposedly imitating Jay and Angel on the bridge. If Angel kept hanging around with Jay, he'd be tarnished with the same brush, like right now. Jay didn't want that.

Acid squirmed in his belly as he pulled Angel away.

Angel's popularity would plummet if Jay didn't distance himself from him soon.

If only it were that easy.

"Come on," he mumbled. "I don't want to embarrass you anymore."

That finally seemed to cut through Angel's rage. He tore his gaze away from Kenny and his cohorts, who were still laughing themselves silly on the footbridge.

"What?" Angel said incredulously. He hugged Jay to his side as they stepped off the bridge and found themselves back inside the cool pine forest their town was named after. "Dude, no. You never embarrass me. Kenny is the one who should be mortified. He's a total dumbass who can't even admit that he almost got you killed. What a loser."

Jay bit his lip and peeked up at Angel. He'd been taller than him since sixth grade, and when they hugged like this, Jay tucked perfectly under Angel's arm.

It did feel pretty great.

Oh, no. There were those *feelings* again. The flutterings in his tummy and the throbbing between his legs. *Nope!* That wouldn't do.

Jay laughed and untangled himself from Angel's grip, punching his arm like they always did. "Yeah, but...they aren't..."

Angel frowned at him. "Aren't what?"

Jay sighed and kicked a rock. *"Gay,"* he spat out. "They've worked out I'm different, and hanging out with me is going to drag you down."

Angel blew a loud raspberry and ruffled Jay's hair. Jay blinked and looked up at him in shock.

"They can try, but nothing's gonna drag us down if we've got each other, right?" he said, shaking his head. "You're my best bud! Side-by-side forever! Who else am I gonna do dumb shit with and eat cheese straight out of the spray can and watch the best movies with? It's you, Jay Coal. Nice try, but you're stuck with me."

Jay bit his lip, ashamed at how relieved he was to hear that. "Okay, fine," he grumbled, shoving his best friend playfully. "But you still have to come see me in A Midsummer Night's Dream next month."

Angel groaned and covered his face with both his hands. "Oh no, not Shakespeare, dude! I take it back! Friendship rescinded!"

"Nope!" Jay declared happily as they walked along the forest path. "You're stuck with me, so there," he declared, repeating Angel's words back to him. "I'm going to come to every one of your football games next year with huge embarrassing signs to support you. I was thinking of painting 'You can do it, snookums!' on the next one."

Angel threw his head back and laughed, hugging Jay to his side again. "I can't wait," he said, grinning broadly. "What would I do without you?"

There was no denying the way Jay's stomach flipped as Angel looked into his eyes, the sunshine dappling on his golden skin through the trees, the gentle breeze ruffling his blond hair and carrying his unique scent into Jay's lungs.

Years later, Jay would appreciate that this was the exact moment he fell head over heels in love with his best friend.

And then he would spend the next sixteen miserable years trying desperately to fall back *out* of love with him.

1

JAY

"QUIET ON SET!"

Jay bit his lip and looked around, feeling like he was in a wonderland. After all the time he'd spent on stage growing up and then teaching high school drama, he'd never actually been on a film set. He'd occasionally thought about doing work as an extra, as so many film and TV shoots passed through Pine Cove. But he'd always been so busy with work.

Until now.

The main road that cut through the town's pine forest was crawling with people who all seemed to know exactly what they were doing. There were trucks everywhere with signs on them for catering, wardrobe, and production. Thick black cables trailed all over the forest floor like writhing snakes. Massive lights had been set up between the trees, and they even had huge paper lanterns strung over the road, presumably to simulate moonlight. Artificial smoke was being pumped in, giving the set a hazy effect in the dark January evening.

"That's the director," Jay's friend, Kamran Amir, explained, pointing at the stern-looking woman overseeing all the action. Meryl Jones. She was who Jay had technically come here to meet with – her and the casting director, Libby Meskin.

But they weren't who Jay was looking for.

His eyes trailed over the set as the camera assistant clapped the board in front of the lens, calling out the scene and take numbers. A hush had fallen over the forest as Meryl spoke in her clear, booming voice again. "Very quiet and still everyone…aaaand *action!*"

Jay would have thought he'd been more starstruck at being mere feet away from Bella Dalton. The British actress was certainly striking as she launched into the scene, delivering her lines standing by the shiny red sports car Kamran was going to be driving for the film later. But Jay's squirming belly had nothing to do with being in the presence of one of Hollywood's finest.

It had everything to do with the fact that after several years, he was finally going to see Angel again in person.

It was ridiculous. The two of them spoke almost every single day, texting and calling and FaceTiming. But Angel had been off traveling the world since college as a stuntman, and when he wasn't filming all hours of the day, he'd been living in LA or visiting his parents in Florida for the holidays. Jay hadn't seen him since they'd both been twenty-three, almost seven years ago.

When Angel had first started seeing Lisa.

Jay bit his lip and pushed down the automatic jealousy that wanted to rear its ugly head at the thought of Angel's long-term girlfriend. But that was ridiculous, especially since they'd been broken up for well over a year now.

Jay had always made himself be happy for Angel when he was in relationships. At least his high school girlfriend had been a sweetheart who'd insisted that Jay come to Senior Prom with her and Angel. But Lisa had always been kind of awful, and Jay was glad he didn't have to pretend to like her anymore.

Jay shook his head and watched as Meryl yelled, "Cut!" and they reset the scene for another take. He knew he was mulling over Angel's ex-girlfriends because he didn't want to face the real truth.

He was just as in love with his best friend as he had been throughout high school, and now they were going to be together again in real life for the first time in forever, without the protection of either of them being in a relationship.

Jay was dreading it as much as he was longing for it.

As they'd planned, the boys had been inseparable throughout high school, even after Jay had come out. But then Angel had gotten a football scholarship while Jay had gone to teacher training college. He'd always kind of realized that Angel was going to go away, but when a series of events had led him from football into the world of stunt work, his life had moved further and further away from Jay's, who came right back to Pine Cove and started teaching in the very school he and Angel had walked the halls of.

Side-by-side wasn't quite the same through a phone, but at least they'd tried. But Jay couldn't help but feel that his deepest fear had come true eventually. Angel had left Jay far behind.

Except fate had stepped in, and Angel was working on a film that was going to be shooting in Pine Cove for the next few weeks, bringing him back home to Jay, finally.

Was Jay going to be sick? Laugh hysterically? His poor heart couldn't help but latch on to the idea that Angel and Kamran working on the same film had to be more than just coincidence, right? What were the chances, after all?

But to what end? What did Jay hope was going to come of seeing Angel for a few weeks? Sure, they might get to hang out a bit between work, but then Angel would be gone again, leaving Jay with a possibly even more broken heart.

Jay rubbed the back of his neck as Meryl declared the scene done and they began setting up for the section of the car chase Kamran was going to be working on.

With Angel.

"Shields is traveling," somebody called out before replying something unintelligible into their walkie-talkie. Cherry pickers began to move with loud beeps to alert people not to walk in front of them. Jay's heartrate picked up.

"Shields?" he repeated to Kamran. "That's Angel."

Kamran nodded, looking around. "That means your buddy's on the move, heading to set. The costume trailers are in the woods thataway." He waved his hand vaguely. "They'll have dressed him up in the same clothes as the actor he's driving for."

"Right," said Jay. He was sure that usually he'd be fascinated to get an inside look at a working film set. But right now, his belly felt like it was full of drunk butterflies, and his mouth went dry.

So of course that was the moment that Meryl came marching up to him with a brown-skinned woman who could have been Libby, the casting director.

"Mr. Coal," Meryl barked with a curt smile. Her handshake was like a vise, but her hand was surprisingly warm. "So kind of you to meet us here. I'm glad Mr. Shields put us in touch. Ms. Meskin here is eager to meet your kids."

"Call me Libby," she insisted as she also shook Jay's hand, confirming his guess as to who she was. "I love working with local extras when we can. I understand you've spoken to the gay-straight alliance at the high school where you teach?"

Jay's nerves took a brief hiatus as he beamed at her. "I run the club, yes. They're ecstatic at the chance to maybe feature in a scene," he confessed with a chuckle. "I have to say I'm excited to see a big-budget action film with a queer lead and romantic storyline."

Libby nodded as Meryl got called away, leaving them to it. "You and me both," Libby said with a happy scoff, shaking her head. "I jumped at the chance to work on this project, and I've been reaching out to queer groups in all the areas we're shooting in to source extras. I know what this means to the community."

Jay had gone to see *Fallen Angels Club* a few years ago with his brother and a couple of their other gay friends. They'd all been absolutely convinced that Bella Dalton's co-star, Sabina Max, had been playing a queer woman. But Jay hadn't expected the production company to go all out and give the character a girlfriend in the sequel. It made him so proud to think that kids these days were growing up with so much more representation than he'd had as a boy.

He'd been over the moon when Angel had told him he was going to be working on the film, but Jay would never have imagined that the production would come to Pine Cove. It was usually horror films and supernatural TV shows that used their picturesque mountain backdrop and sprawling pine forests. But now here Angel was, back in Jay's life, if only for a short time.

Or would be any second now.

The nerves came back with a vengeance, dancing in Jay's stomach. This was ridiculous. After all these years, he'd thought he'd gotten a handle on these feelings. It had been tough in high school, but he'd managed to keep his crush a secret and protect his friendship with Angel. Jay had dated several nice guys during his twenties, but they'd all faded out eventually, never comparing to the love Jay held for his best friend.

He couldn't blame his exes for getting jealous when Jay and Angel were still glued at the hip through their phones.

When Jay had gone for his teaching interview, it had been Angel he'd called for a pep talk. When he had a good or a bad day, it was Angel's number Jay's thumb rang without pause for thought. Even when Jay had been screwed over by the plumber who'd remodeled his bathroom, it had been Angel who'd eventually sorted the whole mess out, not only saving Jay money but a huge amount of stress and worry.

It wasn't like Jay couldn't function as an adult without Angel. But Angel had this natural way of protecting Jay from crappiness in the world, even through the phone. It was like Angel was an addiction that Jay couldn't kick, and eventually he'd just stopped trying to date a couple of years ago. Why bother when nobody ever measured up to Angel?

But this was *crazy*. Nothing was ever going to happen between them, and Jay needed to stop torturing himself. Maybe seeing Angel in person would finally get him out of Jay's system, and he could try to seriously find a guy who would make him happy, like Jay's brothers, Robin and Swift, were.

But that would mean finally letting go of Angel, and Jay hadn't been able to do that since they'd met in kindergarten almost twenty-five years ago.

Jay was going to be thirty this year, and he needed to move on with his life and stop pining. He wasn't that same helpless kid dangling from a bridge anymore. He was a grown man with a career he loved and a wonderful family. If he wanted to marry and have kids of his own someday, only he could make that happen.

It was time that his poor, neglected heart accepted that the dream wasn't going to become a reality with Angel. It just wouldn't. He needed to stop comparing every man he met to his best friend, and live in the real world.

It was just a bit difficult when Angel stole Jay's breath away every damn time he saw him.

He didn't realize he'd gasped until Kamran and Libby paused in their conversation to look at him. But he hardly registered their stares. All his focus was on the man who had just emerged from the tree line, dressed in simple jeans and a T-shirt that looked like they'd been sprayed on his muscular body.

Social media and video calls didn't do Angel justice. Jay practically whimpered as his body reacted to seeing his best friend in the flesh for the first time in several years. He was talking earnestly to a young woman who was walking beside him, so Jay got the chance to drink him in unobserved for a second.

It was like Jay had a homing beacon within him that activated when Angel was close. It had been that way all throughout high school. Every nerve seemed to fire, his skin tingled, his fingers twitched, and his cock ached. Jay could usually hide it well enough, but when he was caught off guard, there was no stopping his entire being lighting up when his best friend – his soulmate, his other half – was close.

As happy as he was to see him, sadness also washed through Jay as Angel finally looked over and spotted him. Angel's face broke into an excitable grin, and he waved enthusiastically.

Jay had spent the last sixteen years trying to fall out of love with this man. And yet one smile told him that he was just as doomed as he ever was.

2

ANGEL

Wow. Jay looked great. *Really* great.

Angel always felt a hundred times better when Jay was around, but over the past several years, that had only been through his phone. Seeing his best bud again in person was like the greatest adrenaline rush, something Angel considered himself an expert on with his line of work. He felt like a total goof as he ambled over to where Jay was standing, his grin so big it was almost hurting his face.

"Dude!" he cried, throwing his arms around Jay in a bear hug. Damn, it felt good to have him in his arms again. "It's really you!"

"It's really *you*," Jay said with a laugh, patting Angel's back. He pulled away quicker than Angel would have expected, but maybe he felt weird hugging for the first time in front of all these people. A set was a crazy place if you weren't used to it, after all. "I can't believe you're home after all this time," Jay added.

Angel clapped Jay's shoulder and smiled at him. "I know, right? It's been too long."

Jay stared at him and bit his lip. The moment seemed to

stretch out, but not in a bad way. Angel just felt mesmerized as he drank in his best friend. Talking on the phone wasn't the same as being face-to-face. He knew that. But even so, he was kind of shocked at how happy seeing Jay again was making him feel.

"What are we here? Chopped liver?" Kamran said with a smirk, nudging Libby in the ribs.

Angel blinked and looked over at his co-workers. He'd been so focused on Jay he'd almost blanked out his new friend, Kamran, and Libby, the casting director.

Angel had barely been back in Pine Cove for two days. However, Kamran had made a beeline for him as soon as he'd arrived on set, apparently knowing all about him from Jay, and the two had become fast friends. Angel had asked Kamran for everything he could tell him about Jay over the past year or two he'd known him, hoping to get a little insider info on his best bud. He'd almost felt jealous of Kamran getting to see Jay all the time, but here they were now, all three of them together.

Angel couldn't keep his gaze off Jay for long. He'd started wearing his dark curls a little longer, and it really suited him. And – this was kind of nuts – but Angel swore that Jay always smelled really good. It was different from when they were kids, when Jay always seemed to smell of sunshine, no matter what time of year it was. Now Angel got a whiff of fresh soap, but there was a kind of spicy musk too that was uniquely Jay. That certainly wasn't something he could get from their hours of calls and FaceTiming.

It was kind of an odd thing to notice about another guy, and Angel heard that little voice in the back of his head that he'd tried so hard to ignore. *That's the kind of thing you'd notice about a hot woman.*

Angel scrunched his nose, then quickly smiled at Jay as he raised his eyebrows at Angel.

Angel had been broken up from Lisa for a year now. Her former snide comments about Jay rattling around his head were irrelevant. If Angel thought his best friend smelled good, that wasn't anyone's business but his own. In fact, with Jay's scent filling his lungs, it was as if Angel was back in high school again, feeling invincible with his best friend by his side.

"You ready for the scene?" Kamran asked Angel, pulling his attention back to work. Kamran was one of those stunt workers who lived in a shooting location and let the work come to him. Obviously, it wasn't nearly as steady as what Angel did, but as he hugged Jay to his side, he could definitely see the appeal of not being away from your friends all the time.

"Yeah," Angel replied with a nod, "it should be a pretty simple chase. We can go over it with the coordinator again if you like?"

Kamran scoffed and waved his hand. "Nah, I got it. I will go give the car a once-over, though. See what I'm working with." He punched Jay's arm and winked. "I'll give you guys more time to catch up."

"Thanks," said Jay, looking back at Angel.

"So you two went to school together?" Libby asked as she looked between them.

Angel nodded and ruffled Jay's hair. The scent of his shampoo drifted through the air. "Yup. We met in kindergarten. He keeps trying to ditch me, but I always come back."

Jay snorted and poked Angel in the ribs. "Like a bad penny," he agreed.

Libby's smile was warm, but she bit her lip, like she was thinking something else. She didn't elaborate, though. Then her face darkened as she looked over Angel's shoulder.

"Oh, here we go," she muttered as she unclipped her

walkie-talkie from her belt. "Can we get security on set, please?"

"What?" Angel asked, immediately pulling Jay closer to his side.

"Is there a problem?" Jay asked, looking between her and Angel.

Libby shook her head and began walking. On instinct, Angel followed. He and Jay naturally parted from their embrace, but Angel still kept Jay close by.

Libby pointed. "I think that guy over there – the one yelling at Meryl – is the same prick who's been harassing the production team since we announced we were going to be filming here. We've had a few protests from hate groups who think our gay film is going to blind children or some shit, but he and his group have been one of the loudest."

Rage boiled through Angel, and he felt Jay shrink beside him. Angel rubbed his back.

"Don't worry," he told him, all his protective hackles rising. Damn, they hadn't been reunited for more than a few minutes, and Angel was already prepared to throw himself in the way of homophobic crap for Jay again. Angel didn't mind it. In fact, he kind of relished being Jay's protector. But he wished they lived in a world where he didn't have to.

Angel had always absolutely hated anyone giving Jay or his brother crap over being gay when they'd been at school, and Angel had taken it upon himself to act as a kind of human shield when he could. It was as natural as anything to slip back into that role all these years later, despite the fact that they were both grown men now.

The brute currently brandishing his fist at Meryl was balding and wearing a beige trench coat. Angel narrowed his gaze as he looked closer at him. It had been more than a decade, but there was no mistaking those squinty eyes and sneering mouth.

"Oh no," said Jay, stepping away from Angel's hand on his back.

Angel's instinct was to pull him close again, but they *were* adults now, and Jay could probably take care of himself.

Even against this douchebag.

"Why am I not surprised?" Angel said in disgust as they approached Meryl and the protesting man.

Libby turned to look at them and raised her eyebrows. "You don't know this clown, do you?"

Angel rubbed his hand down his face and sighed as they got closer. The man's nasal voice was managing to carry over the hum of the film set. "It's *just* not good enough!" he was bleating.

"I'm sorry to say we do," Angel said with a sigh. Angel had hoped to see other familiar faces during his stay back in his hometown, but not this one. "Fucking hell," he murmured under his breath.

It wasn't all that surprising, though, that the man who was protesting the film's presence in Pine Cove was the man who had always given Jay and Angel an absolute shit of a time.

"Kenny Brooker," Angel said, shaking his head, looking down at Jay. "Can you fucking believe it?"

Jay sighed. "Actually, I can. Kenny took his dad's position over on the town council, and well, let's just say he's put up a fair number of fights over the years."

Meryl was looking stony faced at Kenny as he continued to rant at her. As they got closer, Angel caught a few words like 'morality' and 'outrageous.' In the hand Kenny wasn't using to shake in the air, he was holding a manila envelope. "Over a thousand signatures," Angel heard him spit out at Meryl, who had her arms folded over her chest and was peering at him through narrowed eyes.

Libby scoffed. "The last I heard, he barely had a hundred names. I bet he's bluffing."

"What's going on, exactly?" asked Jay.

Libby shook her head and glanced at them. "A bunch of parents and busybodies have been protesting the use of the town for the filming due to the LGBT content. They want us to move elsewhere. But we're already here, and we're not taking any bullshit."

"Damn fucking right," agreed Angel. "None of the others actually gatecrashed the set until now, though. What's wrong with these people, anyway? Do they have nothing better to do?"

"They live very unhappy lives?" Jay suggested, gritting his teeth.

As they approached, Kenny glanced over, and recognition lit up his face. "Of course you're here, Coal," he said in Jay's direction with the same lack of respect he'd had throughout high school. "You're a teacher, for god's sake. You should know better."

Jay clenched his jaw. "I'm not having this argument again," he said firmly, and Angel felt a surge of pride toward Jay for standing up for himself. "Is this something I can help you with?" Jay asked Meryl.

She sighed and looked between Jay and Kenny. "No, thank you, Mr. Coal. I believe I have it all in hand."

Kenny scoffed. "You're not even listening to my very reasonable complaints," he said in a hoity-toity tone.

He'd always thought himself to be a bit better than everyone else in Pine Cove because his dad owned a lot of properties around town. The funny thing was, Bryce Brooker was actually a pretty decent fellow from what Angel could remember of his youth. But he had a very large family, and apparently some of the apples had fallen very far from the tree.

"Oh, I've heard all I need to, Mr. Brooker," said Meryl. "Thank you for your concern, but I have a schedule to keep to."

"None of the romance scenes are even being filmed here," added Libby indignantly.

"That's not the point!" Kenny cried. He had a scruffy couple of days' growth on his chin, and he rubbed it angrily. "The whole movie is morally bankrupt."

He brandished the envelope again that presumably contained the signatures of people so bothered by a lesbian subplot in an action film they'd taken time out of their days to write their names on a damned protest. Angel ground his teeth, wishing he could look every single one of them in the eye and ask them just what their fucking problem was.

"Our town didn't agree to this, and we want you gone," Kenny continued to rant. "I'm on the council, and I have the signatures of many concerned residents in my hand. Mainly parents, who don't want their children endangered by this rotten, seedy garbage."

"Seedy garbage?" Libby sputtered in indignation.

"Actually," Jay said, raising his eyebrows, "the town did agree to it. And I know you're not happy with it, but that's your problem. It always has been," he added in a mutter under his breath.

Kenny shook his head. "I should have known that your sort would have agreed with this, Coal," he said in disgust. "But we've got families to think of. You should be ashamed of yourself. I've heard they want to involve kids in this debauchery!"

"Yes," said Jay proudly. "My GSA kids, and they're very excited about it." He laughed. "You're just jealous that you didn't get asked to be one of the extras as well."

Kenny's face went purple. "I wouldn't be in this thing if you fucking paid me. It's disgusting," he snarled. "It's not right. We have standards, and we don't consent to this. Of course *you* wouldn't understand this, Coal. You're not a parent and you never will be. Those school kids aren't yours. They're *ours*."

"Your son is three months old, and no one is suggesting he be in the film," said Jay, shaking his head. "You're just an angry bigot, and nobody involved with this production owes you a damn thing."

"Yeah, so beat it, Brooker," Angel said, jerking his thumb over his shoulder. "If anyone's a danger to children, it's you. If I were your wife, I'd keep your kid away from you and any bridges, if you know what I mean."

Kenny glanced at him, then his eyes widened as he did a double take. Apparently, he hadn't deemed Angel worthy of his attention until that moment.

"Shields," he sneered. "Good god. I have no idea where you came from, but I should have known that you'd be involved in this as well. I'm amazed that you haven't come crawling back to your boyfriend's side before now. Where there was one of you, there was always the other trailing not far behind."

Jay definitely stiffened beside Angel. He always felt so unnecessarily bad when people tried to insult Angel by calling him Jay's boyfriend. Like that was any kind of insult. Angel stepped closer to Kenny, narrowing his eyes.

"Nothing's changed since high school," Angel said, looking Kenny up and down, taking in his grubby coat and pot belly. "Well, maybe a few things," he added with a chuckle. "But you still don't get to talk to Jay like that."

Kenny smirked. "What you fucking perverts do in your own time is your own business," he said. "But you don't get to drag the whole town into your woke, PC bullshit. I'm here to register our complaint, and now I've done so."

He thrust the manila envelope at Meryl, who looked at it

with disdain and certainly didn't make a move to take it. Libby sighed and took it off him, tucking it under her arm.

"Thank you for bringing your concerns to us," Libby said politely with a tense smile. "But we do have a filming schedule to keep to, and I would ask that you leave the set now." She glanced over at the security boys who had emerged from the crowd and were watching everything that was going on.

Kenny huffed and put his hands on his hips. "Oh, there's no need to be dramatic," he griped. "I've said what I wanted to say, and now I'll be going."

"Don't let the door hit your ass on the way out," Angel called happily, waving him off as he stomped away from this film set into the darkness.

"Oh my god, on behalf of the whole town, I'm *so* sorry," Jay said to Meryl, looking mortified. Angel wanted to hug him again, but he didn't want to make him look weak. He had nothing to apologize for as far as Angel could see.

Luckily, it seemed Meryl agreed with him. "Nonsense," she said, looking around as she spoke. People had glanced their way, but it was such a well-oiled production, everyone had kept on setting up the next scene while Kenny had been ranting. "He's a buffoon. He's not the first we've met in the course of this film, and he won't be the last."

Jay didn't look convinced, though, and wrung his hands. "I just want to make it clear that the school board and the town council all voted on the matter, and the support for the film was overwhelming. We're a very diverse community in Pine Cove, and I don't want you feeling unwelcome."

Libby rubbed his arm through his coat. It was cold enough that their breath was coming out in curls of smoke. "In my experience, there will always be a small but loud minority. Don't let it bother you."

"Yeah, fuck that guy," said Angel, patting Jay's back. "He always was an asshole. Don't let it spoil anything for you."

He was referencing the kids' chance to be extras in the film, but there was definitely a part of him that was also furious that Kenny had sullied Jay and Angel's long-awaited reunion.

"Spoil what?" said Kamran as he jogged up to the group. He stopped and looked between Jay and Angel. "Aw, I miss all the fun. What happened?"

"We're filming this take before I grow old and die, is what's happening," Meryl snapped and turned away to deal with something else. There wasn't any actual malice in her words, though, and Angel knew she just wanted to get back to work. Kenny wasn't worth delaying production for.

"Come on, I'll tell you all about it," he said to Kamran with a wink. Then he took Jay by the shoulders and rubbed his thumbs against his coat. "You'll be waiting here when we're done?" he asked.

The anxiety finally melted from Jay's face, and he smiled at Angel. "There's nowhere else I'd rather be," he said.

Warmth flooded Angel, and he put Kenny from his mind. He was a douchebag who could complain all he wanted. The only thing that mattered was that Angel had his best bud back by his side, and he was going to keep him there as long as he possibly could.

Angel had driven this 1974 Chevrolet Nova several times already during the course of filming, so he had no need to familiarize himself with its inner workings. He just got himself belted in and the in-ear receiver set up so he could hear Meryl, then waited for the cry of "Action!"

Angel's heart slammed in his chest and his dick throbbed as he threw the car into drive and raced along the road toward the main belly of the set. He'd never get tired of that adrenaline rush, he was sure. Kamran was chasing behind him, then Bella's female stunt driver was hot on their tail. Angel had a very specific point that he needed to pass before he hit the brakes and swing the car dramatically right where the camera would be waiting to grab the shot.

He fucking *loved* his job. He was the luckiest son of a bitch that he got to play around like this and call it a living. But what made today even better was that for the first time ever, Jay was watching him work. Angel had always got the biggest kicks showing off his daredevil stunts for his best friend when they'd been kids. When he'd gotten older, the thrill had kind of reminded him of the feeling he got when a pretty girl smiled in his direction, in a weird sort of way.

So he grinned like a maniac as he sped up to where the mark was glinting on the road for him to slam on the brakes and swing the car like he'd done a hundred times before.

Except this time when his foot hit the pedal...nothing happened.

Angel only got a split second to register that he'd yanked on the wheel but the brakes had given him zero. Then gravity wasn't where it should have been, and for a moment, he was weightless.

In the next second, the spinning car crashed and rolled, shaking Angel around like a rag doll until suddenly, everything went dark.

3

JAY

"Dude, you're going to wear a hole in the floor,"
Kamran said. He stood up and squeezed Jay's arm, and Jay
blinked himself out of the trance-like state he'd been in.

"Sorry," he muttered, glancing at the other people in the
Pine Cove ER waiting room. An older woman gave him a
kind smile as he sat his ass down next to where Kamran had
been waiting. "I'm just losing my mind here," he muttered to
his friend as he bit his thumbnail, looking around their
surroundings for the millionth time.

The lighting was a soft buttery yellow, and the chairs
were reasonably well padded. Not the fluorescent-lit plastic
hellhole Jay might have expected. A TV was playing a football
game on mute with subtitles so as not to interfere with the
regular announcements over the PA system paging various
members of staff, and a vending machine hummed gently by
the wall closest to them.

It might have been kind of soothing, except the air
smelled *too* clean, there were faint beeping noises coming
from all directions, and every now and again, a doctor or

nurse would go sprinting past them like someone's life depended on it, which it almost certainly did.

Jay closed his eyes and tried to block everything out.

It's going to be okay. Angel's going to be okay.

Jay felt like he hadn't taken a single full breath since that heart-stopping moment when the car had flipped. For a fraction of a second, Jay had thought it was a part of the stunt, so the adrenaline that flooded him had been the good kind. But within a blink of an eye, all hell had broken loose on the set, and he'd known something was seriously wrong.

Meryl had screamed *"cut!"*, ripping her headset off and rocketing to her feet from the director's chair. The other two cars had skidded to emergency stops before they crashed as well. People had swarmed Angel's car as it spun to a halt upside down. And Jay…

Jay had frozen.

He couldn't process what he was seeing. He couldn't accept that his best friend might have just died. It felt like seconds, but it must have been minutes until Kamran was there, shaking Jay by the shoulders and yelling his name.

It was as if life had flooded back into Jay, and he'd broken into a frantic sprint to the crash site, screaming Angel's name as Kamran tried to hold him back.

But Angel had still been breathing. By the time Jay reached him, the crew had put the fires out, and the medical team had been gently extracting Angel from the car in time for the ambulance to arrive.

Jay swallowed a sob in the ER waiting room, remembering how weak Angel had looked. His injuries didn't appear terrible to the naked eye, but he'd been unconscious.

He was still unconscious as far as Jay knew.

Kamran batted his hand away from his mouth where he was still gnawing at the cuticle and frowned at him. "Don't do that, bro. It's unhygienic. Look, your boy didn't have any compound fractures and the only reason there was a lot of blood was because he banged his head. Head injuries bleed like a bitch, okay? That doesn't mean anything awful. I'm sure Angel is *fine*. He's tough as shit, right?"

Kamran laughed and nudged Jay with his shoulder. Jay managed a small smile. That was true. Angel was made of steel. He just bounced when other people would break. But...

"I just keep picturing the car spinning and crashing into the trees," Jay moaned quietly, dropping his head into his hands, his stomach plummeting all over again. "I thought he was *dead*."

In a rare moment of compassion, Kamran rubbed Jay's back. "I know, man," he said heavily. "That was some scary shit. But we just have to wait for the doc to come out and give us the lowdown, but I'm telling you, it's going to be okay."

"I don't understand what happened," Jay said, shaking his head. "Angel's never had a crash before. He's amazing at what he does."

Kamran nodded and patted Jay's back before clasping his hands between his knees. "It could have been a problem on the road no one noticed or a fault with the car. They'd just been checked over, but these things do happen."

"I just..." Jay began, biting his lip and straightening back up to look at Kamran. "I literally just got him back. If something happens to him—"

Fear lanced through Jay like a sharp knife. Angel was his *everything*. His rock, his comfort. This was why it had been impossible for Jay to move on from loving him for so long, but Jay swore to the universe he'd accept that Angel could never be his boyfriend just so long as he *lived*. Jay would do anything, he *swore*.

"Just let him be okay," he whispered, tears spilling over his cheeks again as he covered his face. "Just let him live, *please.*"

"Hey," said Kamran sharply, making Jay gasp and look at him. "None of that. The only thing that's going to happen to him is he's going to get a big hug from you when you're allowed to go in and see him, all right?" Kamran insisted with a raised eyebrow. "Look, it's not like you to freak out like this. I'm getting kind of unsettled by it, if I'm honest. Can you please go back to being the Mr. Coal who can silence a whole class of unruly teenagers with a single glance?"

Jay chuckled weakly. "Sorry," he said, shaking his head. He took a few breaths and scrubbed his face as he tried to compose himself. Even if he had to fake it. Panic wasn't going to help anyone, let alone Angel. "You're right. Getting myself in knots isn't going to do anyone any good. I just wish his parents were still in town."

That was stupid, though. Angel's folks had retired down in Florida not long after he and Jay had gone off to college. Angel had been a miracle baby, so Mr. and Mrs. Shields were closer to Jay's grandparents' age. But without family in Pine Cove, that had been another reason why Angel hadn't made it back here for so many years.

If Jay lost him on the very night he'd only just got him back in his life...

No. Kamran's right, Jay thought as he tried to stop his knee from bouncing and resisted the urge to bite his thumbnail again. There was no point in dwelling on that train of thought. Angel had looked pretty banged up when they'd pulled him from the car wreck, but there hadn't been any compound fractures, like Kamran had said. He was going to be fine. They just needed to be patient.

"Oh em *gee!* We came as soon as we heard!"

Jay jerked his head up, and he couldn't help but smile in relief at the threesome that spilled through the door to the waiting room. Most people turned their heads to look at them, in fact. Emery Klein had that kind of effect on people.

"Oops, sorry, everyone," Emery whispered apologetically as they went back to their quiet conversations or scrolling anxiously on their phones.

As always, Emery's own phone was glued to his hand as he rushed over to Jay in his heeled boots and scooped him up in a tight hug. He smelled like cherries, probably from the shiny lip gloss that he left on Jay's cheek after he kissed him, and Jay swore that glitter drifted off him as he moved to embrace Kamran as well.

"How is he?" Jay's twin, Robin, asked as he took his turn to hug Jay as well. It was awkward as he held two coffees, one in each hand. "I brought caffeine," he explained as he let Jay go.

Kamran waved his hands and grabbed both cups. "This boy doesn't need any more jitters. I, on the other hand, would marry you if you weren't already taken."

"Did Angel's car really explode?" Ava, Jay and Robin's older sister, demanded as she rubbed lip gloss off his cheek.

"No," said Jay, shaking his head, suddenly feeling so tired. But Kamran was right. Coffee might send him into another dimension right about now. "There was a fire. But only a little one and they put it out right away."

"That's what you get when Kamran tells Scout who tells Emery who tells me," said Ava, rolling her eyes. "So – the lowdown. Other than the head trauma, what's Angel's deal?"

Jay swallowed and looked to Kamran. "The head trauma could be a big worry," Jay said, but Kamran raised his eyebrows. *Right. Positive thinking.* "There weren't any compound fractures. They're checking him out now. Kamran drove me here. I called Angel's parents and left a voicemail. I assume they're asleep. Florida is three hours ahead."

It was like he could only think in short statements and

then say exactly what was on his mind. Try as he might, he was so overrun with worry, there just wasn't much room left for other brain functions.

Ava looked very grave as she held her bike helmet in one hand and then gave Jay a single-arm embrace. That was how she always looked, though. If she'd been smiling, Jay would have suspected the world was ending.

"He's going to be fine," Kamran insisted, but Jay shook his head.

"We're waiting to hear from the doctor," Jay told his friends. "It was awful. The car went flying. I don't know…"

He was mortified as his words broke off thanks to the sob that escaped his throat. People would expect him to be upset, but if he let them know how terrified he really was, how much his heart was threatening to break, then his closely guarded secret might come to light.

"Oh, poppin," said Emery, hugging him again. "It'll be okay, I'm sure. We'll sit here and wait with you, okay?" He tapped the backpack Jay realized Robin was wearing. "We brought plenty of reusable water bottles, energy bars, fruit, oh, and, um, a travel pillow for you, Jay, in case you need to stay all night. What else…" He unzipped the bag and began rummaging. "Oh, both kinds of phone changers because we couldn't remember what you had…"

Jay smiled at his friends, feeling very wobbly. "Thank you so much, all of you," he whispered. "I appreciate it a lot. But you don't have to stay. I can—"

"Nah, bro," said Ava with a scoff, lightly punching his arm. "We're here for you. Em, you got any sodas in there?"

Jay watched as they all found seats in the corner Jay and Kamran had been occupying, gratitude overflowing his heart. Emery dished out snacks, and Jay allowed his friends to fuss over him, distracting him from his bone deep dread just a little.

"Where are Dair and Scout?" Jay asked Robin and Emery, referring to their partners.

"I thought three of us was enough," said Robin with a sympathetic smile.

"Scout wanted to be here, but he's teaching a class," Emery explained, his thumbs flying over his phone.

Scout owned and operated his own boxing gym that offered classes to people of all abilities as well as regular matches for amateurs, semi-pros, and charity. As for a coincidence, Jay was pretty sure that he leased the building from Bryce Brooker, Kenny's dad. *Urgh.* Thinking of Kenny showing his ugly face on set made Jay's blood boil. At least he hadn't seen Angel's accident. He probably would have gloated.

"I'm giving him minute-by-minute updates for when he's done," Emery added, pulling Jay from his reverie. "He was very glad to hear you were unhurt, Kam."

Kamran had become good buddies with Scout under slightly mysterious circumstances the summer before last, right around the time that Emery and Scout had started dating. Jay was sure there was more to the story than they let on, but had never pried.

"Me?" Kamran said, then blew a raspberry. "Nah, I'm fine. I've just been keeping this one from spiraling out of his mind." He clapped Jay on the back. "He's convinced Angel's dead back there and they're just not telling us for kicks or some shit."

"Kamran," Jay mumbled in protest, rolling his eyes. He appreciated his friend's humor most days, but not in that moment. "Can we not say stuff like that? Not even in jest. We don't know anything until we speak with someone."

Ava cuffed Kamran over the head. "Yeah, dude. Don't jinx anything. Jay's heart might explode."

Fear rushed through Jay. "What do you mean?" Did they suspect his feelings were more than just platonic for Angel?

Robin huffed and narrowed his eyes at their sister, then gave Jay's knee a firm rub. "Just that he's been your best friend forever, and you're so close you talk every single day. It must be killing you that the person you'd normally turn to when you're worried is the person that you're worried *about*."

Jay sighed. Everyone deserved a twin. It made life so much easier with someone on his wavelength. He just wished that Robin hadn't drifted away from him in high school when he was dating that enormous creep, Mac. If it hadn't been for that loser, Robin might not have run off to Seattle for ten years. With Robin around, maybe Jay wouldn't have relied on Angel so much.

Perhaps Jay wouldn't have fallen hopelessly in love with him if he'd had his twin close by to talk some sense into him.

Well, there was no use dwelling on that. The past was the past. Anyway, there was every chance that Jay would be in love, even with his twin around to steer him right. Angel was just that amazing, so the point was moot.

However, Angel *had* become the one who Jay relied on, like Robin said. And without him here to calm Jay down, he was struggling. He really needed to depend on Angel less, though, if he ever hoped to let him go when he found a new girlfriend or got married or whatever. But Jay didn't have the capacity to think about that now. All his energy was focused on wishing for Angel's good prognosis. He sipped some water from the metal canister Emery had given him and tried not to let his thoughts run wild.

"Oh, hey, everyone," someone said, breaking Jay from his thoughts. "What are you all doing here? Is everything okay?" Jay spun around to look, hoping it was a doctor with an update on Angel.

It wasn't.

It was, however, Robin's best friend from Seattle, Peyton. She'd moved to Pine Cove not long after Robin and Dair had, and was a nurse here in the hospital. She'd paused in her rushing through the ER with a clipboard hugged to her chest, her eyes wide. She obviously didn't have an Angel update, judging by her question, but it was nice to see another friendly face.

Or so Jay thought.

"Peyton!" Ava cried, sounding alarmed as she jumped to her feet. "I didn't know – I mean – you're here. With me. *Us.* I mean – of course you are – this is where you work."

Peyton chuckled and rubbed her hand through the back of her short pixie-cut hair. "Yep. I just arrived for a night shift. You look, um, nice."

Ava looked down at her bike leathers. Objectively speaking, Jay could see his sister looked pretty badass. Maybe even hot, but – *eww* – he did not want to think of his sister like that. It was okay for Peyton to look, though.

Any idiot could see that Peyton had a thing for Ava. In fact, Peyton's cheeks had gone a little pink after giving the shy compliment.

So of course his dummy sister backed into the vending machine against the wall, rattling it and dislodging a bag of chips. "I, uh, left the stove on," she blurted out, then practically ran for the door. "I hope Angel's okay, Jay!"

Once again, the majority of the room looked toward Jay and his friends as the door swung back and forth in her wake.

"Sorry, everyone," Emery said again with a grimace. Apparently, he'd become the group's spokesperson for their disruptive behavior.

Jay sighed and shared a look with his brother and Emery. Peyton looked crestfallen.

"I'm sorry about our sister," said Jay, shaking his head. "She's just so…"

"Thick skulled," Robin finished crossly.

Jay got that Ava was so besotted by Peyton it turned her into a total klutz. But it was pretty heartbreaking to see Peyton try to be friendly, only to have Ava run off every damn time. He was starting to feel like Ava had missed her chance and they'd *never* get together.

"Oh, it's fine," said Peyton, although Jay could hear the catch in her voice. She waved her hand and shook her head. "I've got a ton of work to do. Anyway, you never said why you were here. Is everything okay?"

Jay stood and wrung his hands. "We're waiting for news on Angel Shields. I don't suppose you know anything?" he asked hopefully. "He was brought in after a car accident over an hour ago."

"Oh, the stunt driver," Peyton said with a smile. "Dr. Lee should be with you shortly. I don't know if he's my patient yet, but from what I saw, he's doing all right. He's awake now, at least."

Relief washed through Jay, and his legs almost went out from under him. "Thank you," he said gratefully. "That's fantastic news, thank you."

Peyton waved them off, then hurried back to work. Jay was able to sit a little less fidgety this time as they waited for official news, but he mostly tuned out his friends' gentle chatter.

Angel was going to be okay. That was all that mattered. But a crazy idea popped into Jay's head, and he sat fiddling with his coat zipper.

Angel could have died.

Should Jay tell him how he really felt?

Jay knew that Angel would – could – never feel the same way about him. He was straight, and that was that. Jay had never, ever wanted to ruin things between them by making Angel uncomfortable. But the idea that Angel could have left this world not knowing that, to Jay, he was the most important person in it, shredded him up inside. Was that completely selfish, though? Probably. Jay just needed to sleep off the shock of the accident. Then he'd get his head back on right.

"Mr. Coal?"

"Yes?" said Jay and Robin together, jumping to their feet to look at the woman in the white lab coat who'd just called their name. Then Robin shook his head and pointed to Jay. "You probably mean this Mr. Coal, right? For Mr. Shields?"

The woman approached them, and a quick glance at her name badge told Jay that she was Dr. Lee. "My notes just say Mr. Coal. I assume you registered at the front desk. What relationship are you to Mr. Shields exactly?"

"Boyfriend," Robin said at the same moment Emery blurted, "Fiancé!"

Jay looked between them in horror as Kamran snapped his fingers. "They just got engaged. Sorry for the confusion, Doc. Jay is totally Angel's fiancé. How's our boy doing?"

"No, that's—"

A lie, Jay was going to finish, but Emery jabbed his ribs so hard that Jay gasped.

Apparently, Dr. Lee was too busy flipping through her chart to notice their terrible ruse. She was probably also exhausted and at the end of a twelve-hour shift from what Jay knew of medical workers. Still, he didn't feel okay with lying to her, and honestly pretending to be Angel's fiancé was a little too close to home, considering the secret he was hiding.

But...he wanted to know what was happening. Angel *needed* him. And Angel's only family was currently asleep in

Florida. She might not tell them much if she didn't think he was next-of-kin.

Jay cleared his throat, hoping Angel hadn't said anything to contradict the lie. "Yes, I'm Angel's – Mr. Shield's – fiancé." Heat flushed through him even just saying that out loud.

Dr. Lee nodded and looked back up from her chart with a tight smile. "Well, I'm happy to tell you that your fiancé's injuries are mostly superficial, aside from a rather nasty bump to his head."

Dread rushed through Jay all the way down to his toes. "His head? Isn't that important? He needs his head. It's got his brain inside it."

"Whoa, breathe, buddy," Kamran said, squeezing his shoulder.

"It is important," Dr. Lee agreed, her voice kind, "and we've run some scans to assess the swelling. It's my hope that within a few days we should see a great deal of improvement. But..."

Jay swallowed, groping for Robin's hand. "But?" he repeated. 'But' wasn't good.

Dr. Lee took a deep breath. "You said your name was Jay?"

"Yes," Jay confirmed. "Has he asked for me?"

"A lot," Dr. Lee said kindly. "As he was coming round."

Jay's heart ricocheted from broken to ecstatic in an instant. *He* was the person Angel had been asking for? Not horrid Lisa? Petty as it was, Jay couldn't help but feel triumphant as well as just relieved Angel was awake.

"That's good, isn't it?" he asked.

"That *is* a good sign," Dr. Lee continued. "I want you to remember that when I tell you that Mr. Shields is showing signs of short-term memory loss. *But,*" she rushed to say before Jay could lose his shit, "it's almost certainly linked to the brain swelling from the crash, and I'm as confident as I can be at this point that he'll make a good recovery in time once the swelling goes down."

Jay let go of the breath he'd been holding, and Emery grabbed his other hand to squeeze it.

"He's got memory loss?" Jay asked. *"Amnesia? Are you sure – how can you tell? What has he forgotten?"*

Panic was rising in Jay, although that could also have been bile. He fought the urge to swoon and pass out. Angel couldn't lose his memories. Those were what made him *him!*

Dr. Lee held up a hand and gave him a firm but not unkind look. "He has no memory of the accident and didn't know he was in Pine Cove, although he seemed to know the town. He guessed he was in LA or London, which are two wildly different options."

"He filmed in London last summer," Jay said, trying not to let his voice tremble too much. "His apartment is in LA."

Dr. Lee nodded again and made a note. "I'm going to want to keep him in for at least twenty-four hours for monitoring. We'll know more by the morning, I'm sure. Head injuries and memory loss are tricky things to diagnose precisely, and each recovery is unique. But the fact that Mr. Shields is already awake and talking is a good sign."

"See," Robin said firmly. "It's okay."

"Yeah, baby, please don't cry," said Emery, rubbing Jay's back. It was only then that he realized that a couple of tears had run down his face. He hastily wiped them away.

"Right, okay," said Jay, trying not to tremble. "So there's every reason to be hopeful, yeah?" he asked, willing it to be true.

Dr. Lee gave him a tired smile. "Yes, Mr. Coal. The best thing for him now will be around things that are familiar. It says in my notes that Mr. Shields was staying in a trailer for the duration of the filming he was part of?" Jay nodded.

"Well, seeing as he won't be working for the next few weeks at the very least, I recommend that he move home again."

"Home?" Jay spluttered.

To LA? That seemed like a terrible idea. He'd be all alone, and—

Emery squeezed his hand. *Hard.* "Yes, home to *your* apartment. That you share. Because you're engaged, and Angel moved in with you. From LA."

He widened his eyes at Jay as his words slowly sunk in. Right. They were pretending to be engaged.

And of course Angel should come stay with him to recuperate. Jay could look after him while he was recovering. There was no one else who would care for him more attentively.

Even if being in that close proximity sounded like an utter disaster for Jay's poor, tormented heart.

But if it was what Angel needed to get better, then Jay was going to have to deal with it. It wasn't even a question.

"Yes, home," he said, nodding fervently at Dr. Lee. "I definitely want him home with me. If you tell me what to do, I'll take care of him."

"We'll know more over the next few days with regard to the head trauma," said Dr. Lee. "But the rest of his injuries are mostly bruising, small fractures, and pulled ligaments. Easy enough to tend to." She rubbed her forehead. "But Mr. Shields might have a little trouble creating new memories to begin with, so there's a good chance he'll need help to take medications regularly, that sort of thing."

Jay swallowed, glancing at his friends. "But that will just be temporary, right?" The idea of Angel's mind being messed with was disturbing him deeply.

But there was also a small part of him that was selfishly clinging to the fact that Angel had memory loss, but he still remembered Jay. 'Jay' was the first word Angel had said as he regained consciousness. He'd even said it more than once. Surely that meant Jay was important to him on some profound level, even if it was just platonic. They'd been best friends forever, but the last several years apart meant that Jay couldn't help but feel a little insecure.

That wasn't the most important thing right then, though. Angel's health and well-being was.

"Honestly, only time will tell how long it's going to last," Dr. Lee said in response to his question. "I hope it will only be temporary, but the human brain is a very complex organism." She tilted her head. "I don't suppose Mr. Shields grew up nearby, did he?"

"He lived in Pine Cove until he was eighteen," said Jay excitedly. "We were best friends at school together."

Dr. Lee gave him a real, bright smile. "Childhood sweethearts. That's lovely." Her words were a small kick to Jay's gut, but he kept his smile in place so she didn't doubt his charade. "That also works tremendously in our favor. Long-term memory is generally stronger than short-term in almost every instance of head trauma. With you, he has both. When he's feeling better physically, I'd recommend that you take him to visit some familiar places around town, as well as talking to him about past shared experiences you've had. It will help start rebuilding those neural pathways."

Jay took a deep breath, trying to listen to everything the doctor was saying purely from the perspective of aiding in Angel's recovery. Of course Jay could play nurse and take his best friend for a walk down memory lane.

Luckily they could drop the fiancé charade soon, but Jay had a feeling that this was more intimacy than his poor, pining heart would be able to stand. But the most important thing was that Angel got better.

Jay could worry about his unrequited love later.

"I'll do anything," Jay promised. "Can I see him now?"

41

Dr. Lee shook her head. "Not yet, but soon. A nurse will come and get you. Or we can call you if you need to go home. If you leave your number with—"

"I'll wait," Jay interrupted.

Angel had protected Jay his whole life, even when they hadn't seen each other for years. Now Angel needed Jay to take care of him.

Jay wasn't going anywhere.

4

ANGEL

HE WAS FLYING.

No. He was falling.

He tried to scream, but his mouth was so dry. He screwed his already closed eyes up, feeling like there were needles in his head. Why were the lights so bright?

Shapes danced through his mind, like smoke drifting through his hand as he tried to reach for something, anything.

Then there he was.

The boy was beautiful, with big brown eyes and soft dark curls. "Don't leave me," the boy said, reaching for his hand.

No. Not a boy. A young man.

His heart sped up. He had to get to the dark-haired man. That was all that mattered, but his feet felt like they were in molasses, no matter how hard he tried to run. He would never leave the dark-haired man, but he couldn't reach him, and the man started turning away from him…

"Angel?"

"No," he whimpered as the young man vanished into the ether. The shapes swirled as he tried to move his limbs, not sure which way was up, but everything ached so badly, and he couldn't seem to breathe properly.

"Mr. Shields? It's Dr. Lee. Can you hear me?"

Painfully, he pried his eyes open, blinking against the bright light.

"Angel?" the same voice asked as before – not Dr. Lee, who was presumably the woman above him.

He – Angel – he was *Angel* – searched for the owner of the voice who had called his name, but it hurt to even move his eyes. Everything was muddled. Where was he? He just wanted the young man to come back. He knew everything would be all right. He needed...

"Jay?"

The name surprised him as it fell off his dry lips. But that was him, the young man he'd been reaching for. If only-

"I'm here, Angel."

A warm hand slipped against his, and Angel blinked his eyes back open. He hadn't even realized he'd closed them again. He felt like he was drowning, like he couldn't swallow, couldn't breathe...

"Take a sip of water for me, Mr. Shields," another woman's voice said. "You're dehydrated."

He felt flimsy plastic press against his lower lip, then blessed water trickled into his mouth, and he gulped it down eagerly. The woman – a nurse, judging from her uniform – only let him have a little, though.

"Not so fast. Slowly does it."

He took a few minutes to clumsily swallow half the cup with the help of the nurse. As he did, a few details came back to him. He was in the hospital, but he didn't know why or which hospital. He traveled around so much...at least he remembered that...

He scrunched his dry eyes again in frustration. His

thoughts felt just as fleeting as they had when he'd been waking up.

"Mr. Shields, do you remember where you are?" Dr. Lee asked him. She was an Asian woman peering over glasses at him as she did something or other with the IV bag attached to his arm.

"Hospital?" he croaked.

"Yes, which hospital?" she asked, moving to take his pulse. "Do you remember us discussing where you are?"

He closed his eyes and took a few deep breaths. He ached all over, but he was also very floaty, like he wasn't really in his own body.

Painkillers, his muddled brain suggested. Yes. Painkillers. Because he'd been in an accident. Had Dr. Lee said it was a car accident? Surely he'd remember if he'd crashed his car...

"Your fiancé is here, Mr. Shields. Can you open your eyes for me?"

Fiancé?

Angel's eyes flew open, blinking at the nurse with the short pixie hair. She gave him a kind smile but shook her head. It wasn't her, obviously. Then she jutted her chin and indicated the other side of the bed.

Angel turned his head, feeling like he was rolling a melon, not sure who to expect. As he moved, an image of a stunning blonde flashed through his mind, but he knew that wasn't right. Whoever that woman was, she wasn't his fiancé. In fact, the wave of revulsion that flashed through him suggested that Angel didn't even like that woman.

He managed to turn to the right, eager to see who she was. But...whoever his fiancé was, he wasn't a woman.

Angel stared for a second at the pale-as-milk face and beautiful brown eyes brimming with tears. "Angel?" he said, gently squeezing the hand he was still holding. "How are you feeling?"

His fiancé was a man? He was gay? That didn't seem right...

But...*oh, hang on!* Those dark curls! This was the boy – the young man! Except he wasn't young like he'd been in Angel's dream. He was a grown man, Angel's fiancé...

It was Jay.

Holy fuck, I'm engaged to Jay Coal?

Angel could feel himself frowning at Jay, who was definitely his best friend. Yes, his best friend from school, since kindergarten. Jay was gay. This was all starting to make sense!

But was he, Angel, gay?

"Do you remember the car crash?" Jay asked. His thumb was rubbing the sweetest circles against the back of Angel's hand, calming him. "On the film set?"

Filming. That sounded right. Yes, he worked on film sets all the time, driving cars and jumping off buildings and faking punches. But an accident?

He shook his head, then wished he hadn't. "I don't remember," he said when the pain eased and the urge to vomit subsided. *Slow* moves. "Jay? Am I back in Pine Cove?" That had been Angel's childhood home, right? That was where Jay lived, Angel thought.

When he thought of the word 'home,' several images flashed through his mind. A porch swing in his mother's arms as a child. A flashy apartment by the ocean. A cramped trailer.

But when he looked at Jay, he *felt* like he was home. That deep sense of comfort that only came from shutting your front door and knowing it stood between you and the rest of the world, and you were safe. He squeezed Jay's hand.

It seemed strange for them to be holding hands. Nothing about it felt familiar. But it felt so *right*. Why was his mind so scrambled? He pushed through the fog. It had been enough to form words and open his eyes until now, but he was starting to realize that something was *seriously* wrong.

"What's going on? Why can't I remember?" he asked, fear and panic rising in him. "What happened?"

"You were in a single-vehicle car accident, Mr. Shields," said Dr. Lee. Apparently, she'd finished doing whatever it was with the IV bag. "You suffered some head trauma, and as a result, are experiencing some memory loss. We're still assessing to what extent, but luckily your fiancé is here to help us fill in some blanks. You'll be staying with us overnight so we can keep a close eye on the brain swelling."

The nurse handed Jay the refilled plastic cup of water, then offered Angel a sympathetic smile before checking the chart that was hanging at the end of his bed.

Angel closed his eyes and groaned. Head trauma? Memory loss? He felt sick. That sounded pretty damn serious. But then he felt Jay's comforting grip on his hand, and he opened his eyes again, taking a deep breath.

If he'd been in such a bad crash, then he was lucky to be alive. And he had Jay by his side…

"Side-by-side," he mumbled, blinking at Jay.

"What's that?" Dr. Lee asked, but Jay's face split into a beaming smile.

"That's what we used to say when we were kids," Jay explained, his words thick with emotion. "Side-by-side. It's how we do most things." He laughed and wiped a stray tear away from his cheek. "I'm so relieved you obviously haven't forgotten everything," he said weakly.

Was it really that surprising to Angel that they were engaged? Jay was *breathtakingly* beautiful, even when he was all blotchy from crying. It terrified Angel that he couldn't remember how or when they'd gone from being friends to more. But although the idea kind of shocked him, it didn't feel exactly *wrong*. If he wasn't gay...oh! Maybe he was bisexual?

Bisexuals are dirty cheats.

Angel snatched his hand back from Jay so fast it made *everything* hurt. He didn't even know why he did it. It was as if those words – wherever the *hell* they had come from – had scalded him.

"Sorry, sorry," he rasped, reaching for Jay's hand again. But Jay's expression was wary, and he seemed reluctant to take it. "I just...I don't know what happened," he said truthfully.

Poor Jay. Angel was probably freaking him the fuck out. And why had such an awful thought popped into his mind, seemingly of its own volition? Angel didn't think that about bisexuals. Hell, he was pretty sure he *was* one, and the idea of ever cheating on Jay – of hurting him in any way – was totally abhorrent. He'd do *anything* to protect Jay. He might have forgotten a lot of things, but he knew that as sure as he knew his own name.

The panic threatened to rise again. How could he not trust his own mind? How could he forget something so important as being with Jay? What year was it? Who was president?

"Mr. Shields," said Dr. Lee, pulling him from his spiraling thoughts. "I've just given you your next dose of painkillers, okay? They're going to make you drowsy, and I don't want you to fight that. Your body needs rest to heal, and sleep is the best medicine there is for that." She quirked a smile. "As well as all the hard-core drugs we've pumped through you."

"Can Jay stay?" Angel asked.

He was pretty sure he was a fully grown man, nearly in his thirties – or maybe already in his thirties? Either way, he wasn't afraid of a lot of things. He was as sure of that as he could be. But in that moment, the thought of Jay leaving made his heart skip a beat. He didn't want to be alone. He wanted Jay by his side.

Dr. Lee offered him a sympathetic smile. "He can stay until you fall asleep. If he can get you to drink that cup of water before you do, he'll get a cookie from me."

She winked at them before leaving Angel's room.

Angel blew out his cheeks, already feeling the drugs sink through him, dragging him toward sleep. But he wanted a few minutes with Jay, so he fought it.

"Here," said Jay, offering Angel the water. It was different than when the nurse had helped him drink. More intimate. His heart thumped loudly in his chest, and he tried not to stare at Jay as he swallowed. Although he wasn't sure why. Surely he and Jay had done more intimate things than this if they were engaged.

Holy fuck!

He choked on the last of the water.

"Sorry, sorry!" Jay cried, grabbing some tissues from the box by the bed and mopping Angel's hospital gown up.

But Angel shook his head and coughed up the last of the water. "No, I'm fine, just clumsy," he lied.

He wasn't clumsy.

He just had the sudden, visceral realization that he and Jay *must* have had sex.

Right? There was no way they'd be engaged without getting down to business first. So why the hell couldn't Angel remember that, for crying out loud? That seemed like a *very* important memory. Sex with his best friend. That was kind of a wild thought.

"Jay..." he began, but he honestly didn't know where to start, and he was getting more drowsy by the minute.

Jay placed the now empty plastic cup down on the nightstand and brushed Angel's hair back. The simple gesture made Angel's heart flip.

He'd always known he loved Jay Coal, but he'd thought it was in a brotherly kind of way. So many memories flashed through his mind, all in a jumble, of their childhood years together. Running around playing superheroes, eating ice cream, camping out in the back yard. He hated that more recent memories seemed to dance away from him like the smoke in his dream, but they'd come back. He knew it.

He couldn't forget Jay.

They locked eyes, and Jay gave him a searching look. "I'm so sorry about that," he whispered, his gaze darting to the window out into the corridor beyond. "They wouldn't have let me in here otherwise, or even told me anything."

Angel frowned. He wasn't following. "Sorry 'bout what?" he slurred.

Jay bit his lip, and even though Angel was banged up and all muddled, a kind of *electricity* still flew through him. If he'd been in any fit state at all, he was pretty sure that seeing Jay bite his lip like that would have started getting him hard. Jay was so *pretty* and *kind* and *sweet* and *preeeetty*...okay, yeah, the painkillers were definitely kicking in. But that didn't mean that stuff wasn't true.

"That whole thing about being your fiancé," Jay said, rolling his eyes. "I'd be impressed you played along so well if I wasn't worried to death about how scrambled your memories really are." He tried to laugh, but it came out as half a sob, and he blinked back tears.

"Oh, hey, no, don't cry," said Angel, reaching for his hand. *Damn it.* Was Jay upset because Angel hadn't proposed yet? "We can be engaged if you want, baby."

Jay really did laugh at that. He squeezed Angel's hand and gently ran his fingers through Angel's hair again. "Yeah, okay. You must be pretty high."

"Am not," said Angel grumpily as the room span and his eyelids threatened to close.

But – *no!* Open eyes! Jay was sad, and Angel had to fix it. "If we're not engaged yet, then I'll propose now, 'kay?"

Jay sighed sadly, his humor fading. "Hon? I only said that so the doctor would treat me like next-of-kin. It's okay. Don't fret. You need to heal. Rest now."

"But..." Angel protested. His stupid eyelids weren't listening to him.

"When you wake up and remember you're straight, I'm going to tease the crap out of you," Jay said with a bright smile that – even in his sleepy state – Angel didn't think reached his eyes. "But well done for playing along. We just need to keep it up until you leave the hospital, okay? You rest now. Heal."

Angel groaned. In fact, he might have whimpered. He couldn't really tell as darkness clouded his vision and his bones felt like lead.

He was straight? He and Jay weren't really engaged?

That didn't seem fair.

5

JAY

JAY DIDN'T NEED SLEEP. OR A CHANGE OF CLOTHES. OR deodorant. But his mean friends seemed to insist that he did, and eventually, they dragged him from Pine Cove General.

He would have happily dozed in the chair by Angel's bed all night, but Dr. Lee had shooed him off, insisting that Angel wasn't going to wake up again anytime soon. Until he did, Jay was just in the way, so begrudgingly he'd allowed Robin to pull him from the room, Emery to insist he take all the rest of the energy bars, and Kamran to drive him home.

As he left the car, he agreed that Kamran could pick him up tomorrow so he could rescue his own car that was still at the film set lot. Then he waved his friend goodbye and trudged toward his apartment block, the weight of the cold January night settling over him like a heavy coat.

What a day.

He stumbled from exhaustion and shredded nerves as he got to the building's front door. He grabbed the wall for support, taking in deep breaths of frigid air into his lungs, hoping that would clear his head.

"Angel is *okay*," he hissed to himself. If he said it enough, maybe he'd start believing it.

He wiped his sore eyes and fumbled in his bag with cold hands to find his key fob. Once the door was open, he hurried inside and up the flights of stairs to his apartment on the top floor. He was cold and bone-tired, and his brain was fried, but apparently it was still trying to process a million thoughts. Jay would have liked to shut it up, but it had too many questions it kept demanding answers too.

Dangerous questions.

Luckily, where his willpower to ignore himself failed, he had a back-up distraction that never let him down.

"Shush! Shush!" Jay said urgently as his two-year-old corgi, Button, threatened to bark the whole place down at his return. If he had to translate (as he hastily shut the door, then dropped to his knees to fuss over her), he would guess she was telling him off for being ridiculously late coming home to dish up her dinner. "I know, I know, I'm a terrible daddy," he cooed into her thick tan-and-white fur as she wriggled and whined in his arms, her tail almost wagging her whole butt off. "I'll get your nom noms now."

Like magic, Button stopped grumbling immediately and ran straight to the kitchen to the spot where her 'nom noms' were about to be put down. She was a real drill sergeant when it came to following the rules, and a late dinner definitely meant the world had already fallen into chaos.

Jay sighed as he dropped his bag to the floor and shrugged his coat off so he could hang it on the hooks on the wall. Routine was good. Routine stopped him from spiraling. So he opened a packet of Button's wet food, tipped it into her special bowl, then set it down for her. Obediently, she looked up at him, waiting until he spoke. "Good girl," he said after a few seconds, and she attacked the chunks of meaty goodness with the fervor of a shark in blood-infested waters. But much cuter, though.

In the few seconds it took for Jay to pull a microwave dinner from his freezer, she was already finished and licking her button nose for which she'd been named after. He chuckled weakly to himself as he stabbed the plastic covering the creamy chicken pasta with a fork before shoving it into the microwave and twisting the dial to the necessary amount of time.

"Oh, Button," he said heavily, dragging himself to the sofa and pulling a blanket over himself. She trotted over to join him and only took three attempts to jump up with her stubby little legs. "What am I going to do?"

He rubbed his chest over his heart as if that might help with the pain. How could this whole mess have gotten even *more* complicated?

He'd hoped Angel wouldn't blow his cover by blurting out that, of course, Jay wasn't his fiancé. But Jay had absolutely not expected the opposite. Angel had appeared totally into the ruse, even confused when Jay had reminded him that it was obviously not true.

Just how scrambled were his memories?

All of a sudden, Jay burst into such noisy tears he startled Button to the other end of the couch. In that moment, all of his many, many worries of the evening and night came tumbling out, and apparently, there was nothing he could do to stem the tide.

"It's okay, baby girl," he sniffled, reaching for his box of tissues and blowing his nose loudly. "Daddy's fine. He's just very, very tired."

She rotated her ears like satellite dishes trying to catch a frequency. But when she seemed sure her daddy wasn't going to explode again, she came creeping back, slowly wagging her tail. Jay petted her and concentrated on taking deep breaths. His microwave pinged to indicate his pasta was ready, but he left it for a minute.

"Angel is going to be okay," he said out loud.

Physically, that was true. Dr. Lee had explained that he was going to have a lot of bruising, and his knee seemed to be pretty banged up, but the rest of the injuries should heal fully within six weeks.

But mentally? Jay had done some internet searching on memory loss and head trauma while he'd been languishing in the waiting room, and basically, it came in all shapes and sizes. Dr. Lee was right. They had to wait for the swelling to go down. But she'd told Jay that her educated guess was that Angel would never remember the accident, as his brain wouldn't have had time to 'save that information to its hard drive,' as she'd put it.

However, she'd said that most research indicated Angel's long-term memories would be much stronger, so Jay was already making a list on his phone of places to take him when he felt able. They could spend a whole day at the high school, not to mention the boardwalk and the main street, and even though Angel's folks had moved long ago, they could still drive past the house. Jay smiled weakly, pondering all the stories he could tell to prompt Angel's memory.

The fact that he'd remembered 'side-by-side' warmed Jay's heart. Everything would be okay if they stayed side-by-side, as they'd always said.

But that had been their phrase since middle school. What did Angel remember since graduation?

Did he remember Lisa?

Jay bit his thumbnail without Kamran there to stop him. Jay had absolutely no right to be bitter if Angel did remember Lisa soon. They'd been together on and off for six years. Angel was bound to recall her before long, and that was *fine.*

55

Mostly because he remembered me first, Jay thought triumphantly.

Jay didn't know Lisa all that well, but she hadn't struck him as a particularly nurturing person. He was glad Angel wasn't going home to her care.

But he *was* going to be coming here, to Jay's apartment, because the hospital thought they were engaged, and honestly, where else was he going to go? Certainly not back to that small trailer out in the woods.

Jay sighed and rubbed his eyes before forcing himself up and over to the microwave. He wasn't really that hungry. His stomach was in knots. But he figured he should try and get something down him to get his strength up. Tomorrow was already going to be hell, trying to get to school in and around picking up his car and visiting Angel as much as he was allowed. He'd already contacted HR about possibly getting one of his colleagues to sub, but he never missed classes unless he absolutely had to, so he was going to do his best to make it in for the whole day.

He rolled his eyes at himself as he tipped the steaming pasta into a bowl and grabbed a fork from the drawer. He was worrying about school because he didn't want to think about pretending to be engaged to Angel, even if it was just for another day or so.

Because the real problem was that Angel was going to be with him twenty-four seven soon enough, and Jay was seriously worried about controlling not just his heart but other organs too. Dr. Lee had mentioned that Jay might need to help Angel bathe, and even though he *knew* that would be in a medical setting, Jay was only human.

Seeing Angel's body – his *naked* body – might be too much for him to handle.

He'd never want to perv on Angel, but Angel wasn't exactly making things easy, either. He'd proposed to Jay *twice* that night when he'd found out they weren't really engaged. Really, though, that wasn't all that surprising. When Jay had a problem, Angel wanted to find a solution. With the amnesia and the painkillers, that had probably seemed quite a logical solution to Angel.

But god fucking *damnit*, it hurt. What Jay wouldn't give for a real proposal from Angel. Hell, just a kiss was a wild fantasy. He dropped his fork into the bowl with a clatter, making Button lift her head.

This was what he'd been afraid of. His crush burned like a star, and he'd been working so hard to keep a supernova in a box for all these years. Under close scrutiny, how easy would it be for other people to realize just how in love with Angel he was?

What if Angel found out?

Jay groaned as he put his half-eaten dinner on the coffee table. He massaged his temples as Button crawled into his lap. He refused to let himself dwell on why it hadn't seemed preposterous to Angel that they might be engaged. Not just to Jay, to any man. Why hadn't Angel laughed in his face at the mere prospect? Jay was glad because it hadn't blown his cover, but surely in his unfiltered state, Angel would have found the idea of dating a man ridiculous.

So why hadn't he?

Why had he clung to Jay and looked at him with puppy dog eyes?

"Because you're his best friend, and he was shocked, scared, and in pain," Jay said out loud to himself. "And the fact that you're even wishing he meant it is sick and twisted. What kind of friend are you?"

A pitiful one, he decided as he pulled the blanket over himself and curled up on the sofa with Button's warm body pressed up against him. He sniffed back more tears as he closed his eyes and tried to find some inner peace. His heartache paled in comparison to Angel's very real medical issues. Jay would see that after a good night's sleep. It had been a long and crazy day, after all.

His last thought was that he should really move to his bed, but he was so comfortable. He'd move in a minute...

6

JAY

OF COURSE HE'D FALLEN ASLEEP AND WOKEN WITH A CRICK IN his neck. Luckily, he had his alarm set for every school day. Otherwise he could have easily passed out until lunchtime. As it was, he dragged himself through the shower, bribing himself with the promise of a fancy coffee from the Rise and Shine bakery in town. Ben Turner would sort him out good with one of his famous spiced apple muffins.

Until there was a buzz through the intercom, and Jay suddenly remembered that Kamran was there to give him a lift to pick up his car.

He groaned. That meant staff room coffee for him, then. Gross.

The day passed in a blur. He managed to make it to school just before first period started, and he threw himself into each class with as much gusto as he could muster. But then, at lunch, he had a gay-straight alliance meeting to preside over, and he felt shaky at the prospect of no breakfast or lunch all day. Teachers could go to the cafeteria, of course, but Jay always felt like he was stepping into the kids' space when he did that.

Luckily for him, one of his many siblings came to the rescue.

His baby sister Kestrel was a senior and normally spent her time pretending that the slightly dorky drama teacher was not in fact one of her older brothers. The GSA was one of the few places he was permitted to talk to her, but only if she talked to him first. Today, however, she came bounding up to him with a Tupperware box that she proudly shoved in front of him.

"Robin told me everything that happened, so I got Mom to make your favorite lunch because I knew you'd run out of time for unimportant things like food."

She grinned and waggled the box at him, and Jay resisted the urge to burst into tears and throw his arms around her. "Thank you," he mumbled earnestly instead, taking the box and opening it eagerly. "Oh *god*," he moaned as he inhaled the scent that wafted out. His mom's homemade beef on rye with pickles and three kinds of cheese was sure to cure all ills, and he gratefully took a huge bite as the GSA meeting got going in the classroom.

Jay felt a sense of calm wash over him as he watched the twenty or so students pull chairs together so they could talk excitedly about the upcoming film shoot they'd been invited to audition for. Libby had told Jay that all the kids who wanted to be involved would be, but some of them could try out for more prominent shots if they wanted. He got the feeling there was a great deal of interest in that, and just a touch of healthy competition.

That was if Kenny and his idiot group of petitioners didn't get in the way.

Jay sighed as the sandwich worked its magic in making him feel a little more human again. He observed the kids with a sense of pride as they led their own discussion. They didn't really need him there, but Jay didn't so much run the meetings as protect them from any unwanted types from causing trouble. Now more than ever, this was a safe space for all of them, and Jay would be damned if the likes of Kenny endangered that.

Worries about his kids and Kenny's group rolled around Jay's head all afternoon, along with his fears about Angel. He'd called the hospital a couple of times to get updates on Angel, but he'd been mostly sleeping since the night before. However, the nurse who he'd spoken to last had said that Dr. Lee had managed to speak to him once more before her shift ended, and he'd remembered more of his situation that time.

That gave Jay hope.

Hope that the swelling was going down and he was already getting better, but also hope that there would be no more confusion between them.

Angel knew he was straight. He was probably going to be embarrassed when he realized how into the fiancé charade he'd gotten. Jay would tease him about it because laughing was the best way to get through all this and save face.

Finally, the last bell rang, and Jay was able to escape. Luckily, he didn't have any after-school activities today, and he'd do his class prep work later. Right now, he absolutely had to get back to the hospital.

As soon as he walked back into Angel's room and saw him sitting up in bed with some color in his cheeks, Jay had to swallow a sob of relief. Otherwise he would have burst into tears on the spot. Angel still had the IV attached to his hand, and several bruises were already blossoming on his face and arms. But the bandage covering his head wound was about half the size and didn't look nearly as scary today. When Angel looked up from his phone after Jay walked in, Angel broke into that smile that Jay had loved for sixteen years, and everything felt like it was going to be okay.

"Hey," Jay said with a sniff. He rallied his cheeriness and moved to sit in the chair by the bed. "How are you feeling?"

Angel beamed. His eyes were tired, but they still sparkled. "Okay, yeah. I remembered where I was this morning when I spoke to the doc. I called my mom, and we talked about a bunch of stuff. She was kind of freaking out but all right. Thanks for calling them."

"Of course," said Jay, filled with pride that he could help Angel in any way.

Was this how Angel usually felt when he took care of Jay? Jay had to admit he kind of saw the appeal of being the protector for once. It filled his chest with a warm glow to know that he'd taken care of his best friend. But he wouldn't be sad when things went back to normal and it was Angel fussing over him again. That was the way their relationship worked best.

Angel gingerly moved the leg Jay was pretty sure was the one with the busted knee. It must be sore. "They think my memory is doing okay," Angel said. "Especially when people ask me questions and get me to use it." He chuckled, then sighed, reaching out his hand. "I'm so glad you're back."

Jay's heart flipped. He realized Angel was holding out his hand because he wanted Jay to take it. Jay would do whatever Angel wanted, but he and Angel didn't usually hold hands, or they hadn't before he'd moved away, at least. There weren't any members of staff around to convince they were engaged.

But Jay supposed anyone could walk in at any time, so if Angel wanted to keep up the ruse, that was what Jay would do.

He slipped his hand into Angel's, feeling how warm it was against his skin. Tingles flurried over his body from the touch. He knew it was just pretend, but he allowed himself to privately enjoy them a moment anyway. No one would ever know.

"Of course I'm back," said Jay with an eye roll, like it was no big deal. Then, what he meant to do was say 'It's not like I have anywhere important to be' and laugh. But what happened was that sob threatened to escape his throat again, and he rasped, "There's nowhere else I'd rather be."

Their gazes locked, and Angel's thumb brushed over Jay's hand as if he was the one doing the comforting.

"Jay…?"

A knock on the door made Jay jump so hard he dropped Angel's hand guiltily. Until he remembered that he was *supposed* to be Angel's fiancé, and holding hands was actually encouraged in that scenario.

As he fumbled to take Angel's hand again, he looked around to see a slim woman in her late thirties or early forties standing at the threshold to the room. She wore a gray pantsuit with her chestnut-brown hair in a high ponytail, and an enormous takeout cup of coffee clutched in the hand that hadn't knocked against the door. That hand held a shiny badge.

"Angel Shields?" she asked. "I'm Detective Padilla with the Pine Cove Police. Mind if I come in and ask you a few questions?"

Angel cleared his throat and glanced at Jay. "Uh, yeah, sure. I might not be able to answer them, but I can try. Is it about the accident?"

Padilla nodded and made her way into the room, standing at the foot of the bed. "Yep. No biggie, though," she said as she pocketed her badge. "Your boss wants to rule out any foul play. Can you tell me what you remember?"

Angel hung his head and looked ashamed.

"Hey," said Jay firmly. He stood to carefully rub Angel's shoulder. "It's okay. It's not your fault."

But Angel shrugged. "We don't actually know if it's my fault or not, do we?" He turned to Padilla and cleared his throat. "I can't remember a thing. Certainly not from last night, but so far not much from last *year*, even."

Oh. That was news to Jay. His heart dropped.

Did he still think he was with Lisa?

"Ah," said Padilla and nodded as she frowned. "They mentioned the amnesia. That's rough. I'm sorry."

"It's getting better," said Angel with a hopeful note to his words. "But I'm sorry I can't be of more help. I can barely remember what the film was, and that's after one of the other stunt guys talked me through it in detail."

That would have been Kamran, Jay guessed fondly.

Angel suddenly looked to him and then back to Padilla. "My fiancé might be able to help, though?"

"That's you, I take it?" Padilla asked Jay.

Nerves fluttered through him at the prospect of lying about their relationship to a police officer. But really, who would it hurt?

"Uh, yeah," he said, forcing a smile. "I don't know anything about cars, though, and I can't say I saw anything unusual."

Padilla didn't look disappointed, however. She just shrugged. "We're trying to cover all the bases. In all likelihood, it was just an accident. Humans have them in cars all the time. Your boss, Ms. Jones, just needs us to do our thing so the insurance company can do their thing."

Angel groaned and looked guilty again. "Kamran said the Chevy was toast. They have to get a new one with the same custom build to match the rest of the footage."

Jay scowled. "Damn the car. I just care that you're okay," he said fiercely.

Angel gave him a sympathetic look and squeezed his hand. "I think the insurance company might care a *little*."

Padilla scoffed. "I'm with Mr. Fiancé. They'll get over it." She lightly patted Angel's foot through the blankets. "You feel better, Mr. Shields. If either of you remember anything or need me, here's my card."

She passed it to Jay on her way out, then Jay pocketed it and turned back to Angel. "Do you think it was just an accident?" he asked anxiously. "Or technical malfunction?"

Angel blew a raspberry. "I couldn't remember how old I was earlier until the doc looked at my chart and told me. I have no idea about the car, I'm afraid."

"Of course. That was stupid of me—" Jay began in distress at his thoughtlessness, but Angel shook his head and cut him off.

"Hey, no. The doc also said that asking questions is the best way to kickstart the old gourd again." He grinned and tapped his temple with his finger. "No question is bad. And you're probably the best person to ask them."

Okay, then. Jay took a breath and let Angel go as he sat back down. Time to ask a tough one.

"Do you remember Lisa?"

Angel's mouth popped open as he took a breath, and his eyes widened. "Um…" He chewed his lip and averted his eyes from Jay's. "Is that the blonde woman I remember, um, being with?"

Jay tried not to substitute 'being with' for 'having sex with.'

"Uh, yep. You broke up almost exactly a year ago. I mean, she broke up with you."

He winced internally, waiting for Angel to be sad. What he did not expect was for Angel to bark out a loud laugh and sag with relief.

"Thank *god*," he cried. "I kept thinking I should call her or something, but I really, really didn't want to. Phew! Dilemma solved." He tilted his head and considered Jay. "And we're just friends? Nothing's, uh, changed about that?"

Jay laughed a little too loudly, then cleared his throat to

try and cover it up. "Yes. Just friends. Best friends. Sorry, I probably confused you with all that fiancé talk last night."

Angel dropped his head and looked at his fingers as he pulled at a hangnail. "Oh, cool," he said, looking back up with a smile. Jay thought for a second he might have been disappointed by that answer, but he knew that was ludicrous and didn't give the speculation another thought.

He was just hugely relieved that Angel hadn't woken up desperate to get back with someone who was no good for him. Honestly, Jay had been silently hoping he and Lisa would break up for years, and he didn't want to go through that again.

Angel deserved to be with someone who cherished him, not someone incredibly hot and successful but with the heart of an icicle. If Jay had to see Angel with someone else, at the very least she could be a nice person.

In the meantime, Jay was going to be the very *best* best friend and nurse Angel back to health.

And if he indulged in a little more make-believe over the next day or two that he was Angel's fiancé for real, who would that really harm?

Him, in the long run, and he knew it. But it seemed he was incapable of stopping himself.

7

ANGEL

"This is your place, huh?"

"Yep," said Jay as he helped Angel and his new crutches through the front door of his apartment. "Home sweet home. Here we go."

It was a small building away from the town center, only four stories high. But Jay was on the top floor, and there wasn't an elevator, so Jay had insisted that Angel sling his arm around Jay's shoulders so he could assist Angel in hobbling up all the stairs. Of all his injuries, his knee was hurting the most. He had a couple of pulled ligaments that would need PT and a lot of rest, not to mention all the other cuts and bruises over the rest of his body. Thank fuck the stunt car had been reinforced (according to Kamran), or Dr. Lee had said it could have been even worse.

Angel felt like crap, but he kind of enjoyed Jay bossing him around and being his nurse for a little while. It made his insides squirm a little in a good way. It was probably just relief mixed with pain meds combined with the fact that Angel was going to get to stay with his best buddy for a few days. That was an unexpected bonus in an otherwise shitty time.

Angel liked having Jay's hands on him. It felt comfortable. Right. But then he'd catch himself and worry that he shouldn't feel like that. Jay was very clear that the two of them were just friends and Angel was totally straight.

It made Angel feel even more keenly that he couldn't trust his own mind, and that was as scary as it was frustrating. But at least he had Jay there to look out for him. There probably wasn't a person in the world who knew him better, and he'd already helped Angel recall a lot of things from their childhood and teenage years. He was lucky to have Jay.

Occasionally, his thoughts drifted to Lisa. He'd had a couple of days to pull together some more memories of her as well as look back through his Instagram. They had a *lot* of photos together. But it was confusing because studying those images had helped him remember a lot of stuff, but he hadn't felt much sadness or loss for her. When he remembered the sex had been spectacular, that helped. But he honestly wondered why they'd stayed together so long.

Perhaps it would come back to him. Dr. Lee had pressed upon him that stressing over things wouldn't help his memories return faster. He had to let his body heal and allow his mind to hopefully keep filling in the blanks. Besides, no one had perfect memory. So long as Angel remembered the big stuff, then he hoped he'd be okay.

It was easier to be positive with his best friend by his side. Jay had explained how they'd hoped they would be able to spend some time together in and around the shoot, but now Angel was going to be staying in Jay's home, like one long sleepover. Health worries aside, it was kind of awesome.

"I like it," said Angel, looking around the place as Jay let him go to close the door behind them.

It was a light and airy space, open plan in a way Angel

appreciated. Having talked a few times with his folks over the phone, he had a reasonably good recollection of the well-kept but pretty cramped shoebox his parents had owned before retirement. He wasn't sure what his apartment in LA was like, but he hoped it was open too. He'd found the address on his phone and looked up the street view, but that hadn't told him anything about the inside.

When he dwelled too long on the fact that he couldn't remember what his *home* looked like, he felt a bit sick. But he trusted that when he went back there, it would be familiar enough once he'd seen it.

Until then, there wasn't much he could do except enjoy his time staying with his best friend. Jay's place was covered in nostalgia and framed art and photos and house plants. There were stacks of homework on one of the counters, probably waiting to be graded, Chinese takeout boxes on the coffee table, and a basket of laundry in the corner by the TV.

"I'm sorry, it's kind of a mess," Jay said as he helped Angel hobble over to the sofa. "We were at the hospital so late, then I had work today before I picked you up—"

"Dude, it's great," Angel insisted as he flopped down onto the couch, taking a couple of breaths. He was used to his body being a well-oiled machine, so to have it all banged up was pretty jarring. "It looks lived in. Cozy. I'm just thankful to be out of that place."

It wasn't that Angel had any special aversion to hospitals, but who really wanted to stay there when they didn't have to? It was all fluorescent lights and nonstop beeping machines. He felt like he'd been through the washer *and* dryer, and he ached down to his bones.

If Angel had to take a few days off to recuperate, he could think of nowhere else he'd rather be than with Jay. But Jay seemed kind of on edge, like he was worried about something. Was it really that his apartment wasn't spotless? Or was it something else?

"Hey, bro," Angel said, snagging Jay's hand before he could run off and start doing dishes or whatever. "Dr. Lee said she was really confident that I'd get most of my memories back. Don't worry."

Jay blinked at him. Huh. Angel had never really noticed how long and dark his eyelashes were before. Or maybe he had, and he didn't remember?

Well, why would he notice something like that? Jay was a guy, and Angel was straight. It would be strange to go around swooning over your best bud's pretty eyelashes. Damn, Angel needed to get a grip. That fiancé stuff had all just been so Jay could visit Angel and get the doctors to talk to him. Why was he thinking like this?

"Oh, I know it should be okay," said Jay, biting his lip. "We just need to give you time. When you're less sore, I'll take you to see some old sights to see what we can jog loose."

"Exactly," said Angel, smiling up at him and rubbing the back of his hand with his thumb. "Thank you, by the way."

"For what?"

"For putting me up," Angel said, indicating the apartment. "Being my tour guide. Being my 'fiancé,'" he added with a wink, and Jay laughed nervously. "You're the best."

Finally, Jay's expression softened, and the anxiety seemed to slip away. "Of course," he said emphatically as he sat beside Angel on the sofa. His hand slipped from Angel's grasp, and he kind of missed the touch. "It's the least I could do," Jay continued. "We'll have you back on your feet in no time. But I want to get you comfortable. So you just rest here and see if you can get some sleep while I go change the sheets on my bed."

"Why?" asked Angel, genuinely confused. "It's not like I'm going to go inspect them."

Jay frowned. "Because you'll take the bed, and I'll take the couch," he said as if that was obvious. But when Angel opened his mouth to protest, Jay raised a finger and shook his head. "Nope. No negotiating. You've got healing to do, and I don't have a spare room. So you'll be sleeping in the bed."

Angel was *absolutely* going to negotiate. This was Jay's place, and he was working a demanding job. Angel wasn't going to inconvenience him more than he already was. But then some keys jangled on the other side of Jay's door, and there was a loud bark that grabbed Angel's interest immediately.

"Oh, shit," said Jay, jumping to his feet. "Brace yourself."

A gangly girl in her late teens burst through the door with a corgi straining on a leash. "Oh, hey, bro," she said as the dog yanked her inside the apartment. She had choppy brown hair with green streaks through it. Grinning, she kicked the door shut behind her. "All right, you terror, off you go. All walked as promised," she said with a salute as she released the furball from their leash.

"Hang on, no!" Jay cried, lunging for the white-and-tan ball of fluff as the little one sprinted on their stumpy legs, making a beeline for Angel like their life depended on it. But Jay swooped down and scooped up the dog just as they launched themselves toward Angel's lap. Jay cried "Oof!" as he hauled the small beast up in his arms.

"Aww, I wanted to say hello," Angel protested with a pout, reaching his arm over to let the dog sniff his fingers. The corgi wagged their whole butt and panted as they tried to squirm closer to Angel. Their tongue dropped out of their mouth, making it look like they were grinning.

Jay shook his head. "She's heavier than she looks, and you're fragile right now. Button, this is Angel. You have to be *gentle* with him." Button looked at Jay and perked up her enormous ears, like she understood what he was saying.

"Button?" Angel repeated. "Oh, fuck. Yeah. *Button.* I remember!"

Jay blinked at him, then broke into a relieved smile. "You do?"

"Hell yeah," said Angel happily. "Who could forget a gorgeous girl like Button?"

Her ears twisted comically at every mention of her name, and Angel's heart overflowed with affection for the small pooch. He'd totally forgotten about Jay's beloved dog until that moment. But now the memories came flooding back. He'd seen loads of photos and videos over the past couple of years and heard even more stories.

He couldn't have met her before, though, because Jay had explained how Angel hadn't been back to Pine Cove since he'd graduated college. Which...Angel was struggling to explain why that was. Jay had said it was because he had been busy with work and his folks had moved to Florida, but Angel found it very strange that he hadn't made time to visit his best friend in all that time.

It was frustrating that his own mind didn't have answers for him like that. But all he could really do was hope someday soon he would again.

"She still can't maul you," Jay said reproachfully. "Hey, missus. Calm down. Then you can say hi."

"Oh, damn, sorry, Jay," the girl said as she dropped the leash onto the small dining table that stood between the sofa and the kitchen. "I didn't think before I released the beast. Hey, Angel. How's your head?"

Angel blinked for a second, confused how this skinny kid knew his name. But then realization dawned on him, and he was pretty sure his not knowing her had nothing to do with his amnesia.

"Kes Coal?" he cried. "Is that you?"

She gave him a lopsided smile and opened the fridge. "It's Kestrel now, but yeah. Hi! Long time no see, you big lug."

He waved as Jay put Button back on the wooden floor, murmuring to her about being *calm* and *gentle*, and did he mention *calm?* It was pretty adorable. Of course Button immediately came running to Angel's feet as soon as Jay let her go, but at least she allowed Angel to pet her on the floor rather than trying to jump up into his lap.

"I think the last time I saw you, you were in kindergarten," Angel said to Jay's baby sister in disbelief.

She snorted as she emerged from the fridge with a tub of some kind of leftovers and grabbed a fork from one of the drawers. "I don't think I was quite that young. But yeah, I'm a senior now. Jay's my *teacher.*" She pulled a face that made Angel laugh.

"Wow, that's kind of nuts." Angel shook his head. "I guess I have been away a long time."

Kestrel shrugged and speared a bit of chicken with her fork. "You left, and Robin left. Poor Jay's been lonely. Why do you think he got himself a dog when he gave up on dating? Not that you're not the most adorablist pooch, isn't that right, Button Butt?"

Jay spluttered in indignation. "That's not...can you not make my life sound *quite* so pathetic, please, Kes?"

"Kestrel," she corrected, then grinned around the fork tines between her teeth.

"Sorry," Jay mumbled, then threw a look at Angel as he rubbed the back of his neck.

Angel scoffed. "Your life is so not pathetic, dude."

Jay gave him a smile that didn't reach his eyes. "To be fair, how would you know?" he asked with a sad laugh. Angel felt like he'd been trying to make a joke and it hadn't landed.

But...Jay had an incredible job, an amazing, happy family,

his own place – hell – he even had a fur baby. His life was great! So what if he didn't have a boyfriend?

Or did he?

"Oh, shit. Do you have a boyfriend right now?" he blurted out to Jay.

For all Angel knew, Jay was in a serious relationship. He hadn't even thought to ask, and if he was honest, the idea made him feel kind of weird. It wasn't like Jay had never had boyfriends. Angel remembered that much. But if Angel had to share him right now when he was staying over, that made him feel kind of growly and possessive.

God, he was an asshole. Jay was *allowed* to have a boyfriend.

The question was, did he? Maybe that was why Jay was acting kind of funny about having Angel stay with him. Was Angel cockblocking him?

"Am I messing up your social life? I should have checked before crashing here!"

Angel told himself that if the answer was yes, he would not begrudge sharing Jay's time with whoever he was. But that didn't stop the strange relief pooling in his stomach when Jay hastily shook his head.

"No, definitely no boyfriend," he said, shooting a glare at his sister. "You're not messing anything up. I'm happy to have you here, seriously. But speaking of which, I really do need to get those bedsheets changed." He looked between Angel and Kestrel, then jabbed a finger at his sister. "Behave."

She drew an imaginary halo around her head, then pressed her hands together in prayer, like an angel. It was somewhat undermined by the wicked grin on her face, but Jay just hummed and stalked off to the bedroom.

Button looked between the half-closed door and Angel, then apparently decided she wanted to stay and be adored by her new bestie. Angel scratched absently between her ears but looked thoughtfully at Kestrel as she munched on more chicken and rice.

"Has he really been...lonely?" he asked in a hushed voice.

Kestrel's eyebrows slowly went up. "Uhh..."

Angel bit his lip. He recalled in that moment that he'd always felt bad that Jay had suddenly found himself without either him or Robin back home in Pine Cove. But Angel was sure that Jay had always been so happy and positive when they spoke on the phone. Of course he had bad days with work and the like. That was only natural. But he had so many friends and the rest of his family close by. Surely he couldn't have been that lonely, could he?

"I think it's good that both you and Robin are back," said Kestrel eventually, putting the lid on the leftovers and shoving the tub back into the fridge. "Even if it's only for a while in your case. I'll let you rest up now. Feel better soon."

Angel was just about to tell her that she didn't need to rush off when there was a knock on the door.

"I'll get it," Kestrel called to Jay, who was presumably still wrestling with his bedding. Angel watched Kestrel skip to the door and swing it open...

...and then jump back in shock, her hands flying to her mouth.

Angel couldn't help but chuckle, not blaming her slightly over-the-top reaction.

Because yes, Kamran was standing there with a bag Angel recognized as his battered high school football one. As soon as Angel laid eyes on it, he remembered that he traveled almost everywhere with it, and he'd even had it repaired at some point.

He also remembered that Lisa had hated it with a passion and tried to buy him new fancy luggage on more than one occasion, which Angel had refused to use.

He smirked to himself. She certainly wasn't here now, and

Angel was glad to see he was still using the same bag. Hopefully, it was full of all the things that Angel had asked Kamran to bring to Jay's apartment. But that wasn't why Kestrel had gasped.

Next to Kamran stood Bella Dalton with a huge bouquet of colorful flowers, looking effortlessly radiant in a slim pair of jeans, pumps, and a crisp white shirt. Angel couldn't fault the youngest Coal sibling for being starstruck. When Kamran had talked Angel through the film, Angel had looked its stars up online and remembered pretty quickly how famous they were. Angel had expected to feel starstruck himself, but he was almost certain that Bella was a very relaxed celebrity, from what his patchy memories were telling him.

"Hey, kiddo," said Kamran brightly as if nothing was amiss. He stepped over the door's threshold and held out his fist to her. She went through the motions of a rather complicated handshake with him, suggesting they knew each other pretty well, but her wide eyes never looked away from Bella.

Bella didn't seem fazed and merely smiled at her young fan. "Hello, darling," she said in her beautiful British accent.

Angel got the feeling he was pretty hooked on her himself, but not in a horndog kind of way. She was just one of the nicest people he'd had the pleasure of meeting as far as he was aware, as well as being gorgeous and a genuinely good actress. It was rare to work with a star who hadn't succumbed even a little bit to their own success.

"You're...hi!" said Kestrel, apparently regaining her wits. "Would you like to come in? *Jay, you have company!*" she yelled unnecessarily loudly.

Jay emerged from his bedroom just as Bella stepped inside and closed the front door behind her. "Oh – *wow*," Jay said, sounding shocked. But then he recovered a little faster than his sister had. "This is a nice surprise."

"Kamran said I could come visit the patient," she said happily, waving over at Angel. "Hello, darling! Are you quite finished worrying us all sick now?"

Angel grinned at her, ignoring the ache that was starting to creep back into, well, everywhere, but especially his knee. He was probably due some more meds soon. "Nah," he said with a wink, tapping the crutches that were propped up against the sofa. "If it means I get flowers from you, I think I'll get in car wrecks more often."

"Not funny," snapped Jay, clearly unamused. Angel reminded himself that he really had given them a scare. He should probably stop joking around until Jay could see the funny side of it. Jay smiled at Bella, though, and held out his hands. "Those are beautiful. Shall I put them in water?"

"Please, thank you," said Bella before gasping. "And who is *this* treasure?" Button was apparently fickle with her love, as she threw herself away from Angel and at the latest newcomer, barking as Bella crouched down to pet her. "Oh, aren't you beautiful? Good girl!"

Kamran dropped Angel's duffel bag, and reached out his hand to clasp with Angel's. Kamran wrapped his other hand around the shake, squeezing tightly. "Glad you're okay, bud. Jay said you were doing better today, but it's good to see you with my own eyes."

Angel chuckled, a little overwhelmed with his sincerity. "Please," he said playfully. "You think a little car crash is going to take me out?"

"There were a couple of minutes there, yeah," Kamran scoffed.

"You have caused quite the drama, you know," said Bella. She'd managed to sit so gracefully on the floor, even with Button hopping all over her, with her shoes neatly beside her and her feet tucked under her. "They're going to take the car apart. Meryl is putting on a brave face, but the insurance company is kicking up a fuss, blaming human error." She scoffed and rubbed Button's belly. "I think they just don't want to cough up, do they, puppy?"

Button yapped in agreement.

"I...I don't remember anything," Angel said worriedly. He tried yet again to picture the moments before the crash, but he had nothing specifically to recall from last night. That was scary.

"They're blaming Angel?" Jay asked in horror. "Well, that's bullshit. There had to be a malfunction or a pothole or *something.*"

Even though he was angry, Angel was very pleased when Jay sat back down next to him. It was like the closer Jay was, the easier Angel could breathe. How lucky was he that if he'd had to have an accident, it had been when he was back home with Jay and not in the middle of the desert or something?

Bella nodded earnestly, tucking a lock of blonde hair behind her ear. Kestrel had apparently forgotten that she'd said she was leaving, and was now perched on a dining room chair, her mouth slightly open as she watched Bella's every move.

"Meryl is furious," said Bella gravely. Her dark words were moderately undermined by the way Button was squirming on her back, demanding belly rubs. "With the insurance people and the accident in general," Bella qualified. "Not with you, darling. She actually sends her best wishes."

Angel could sort of remember the director from the film, but the details were hazy. Still, he wasn't going to throw away any well-wishes.

"Tell her thanks. Has production halted?" Angel asked. That was the last thing he wanted. But thankfully, both Bella and Kamran shook their heads.

"We only lost a few hours last night," Bella assured him. "We'll need a replacement car, and Libby is already flying in another stuntman to replace you – sorry," she added with a wince, but Angel waved her off.

"No, no, the show must go on," he said genuinely. "I'll talk to my union rep, but I'm pretty sure I still get a little sick pay, and my worker's comp should cover the main bulk of the hospital bills."

Her face lit up with a dazzling smile. "Oh, good. I was dreadfully worried you'd feel like you'd been disposed of. We're all rooting for your speedy recovery, I promise! And is this your charming nurse for the time being? The infamous best friend?"

"Oh, you know Jay?" Angel asked, feeling proud that Bella had called him both charming and infamous.

"Yes, Kamran filled me in on the way over," said Bella, beaming at Jay. "Thank you for coming to Angel's rescue. We're all very fond of him on set."

Jay blushed, but he nodded at her. "I'm – uh – fond of him, too. But I'm more like moral support than any real medical care. Hopefully Angel can relax here while I'm at work. Then Dr. Lee said I could try and help jog his memories by visiting some of our favorite childhood spots."

Bella declared that was wonderful, and the small group began discussing a few of the places that Jay had in mind to visit. But Angel tuned out for a few moments.

He might have been struggling with amnesia, but he *knew* Jay. And there was something off with him.

Something about having Angel staying with him.

Angel's stomach dropped. Did Jay not want him here? Was he just being polite? Was there actually a boyfriend despite Jay's protests to the contrary? If there was, Kestrel didn't know about him either, from what she'd said.

Or was Jay really upset that Angel hadn't visited him in years? Why *had* Angel stayed away so long?

The idea that Angel had hurt Jay made him feel way worse than the car crash had, which was pretty dumb, but Angel couldn't deny the pain that lanced through his heart. Had he been an idiot thinking everything was fine when they spoke on the phone all those times? Or had Angel missed some signs? Were there signs he couldn't remember he knew? Shit, that was a scary thought.

He bit his lip and took a deep breath. Well, if there was something amiss between him and his best friend, this was the best time to try and fix it. They were together in person for the first time in years, and Angel wasn't going anywhere fast. If something was broken between him and Jay, he'd fix it.

If this brush with death had taught him anything, it was that Jay meant *everything* to him.

8

JAY

"WELL? WHAT DO YOU THINK?"

Jay might have been bone-tired and emotionally wrecked, but he couldn't help but smile as he walked onto the school's football field through the tunnel for the first time. Of course, in Angel's case, he'd done this hundreds of times when he'd been on the varsity team. Jay watched as he beamed and turned in a circle in the bright wintery sunshine of the Saturday morning, breathing deeply and briefly closing his eyes.

"It's like it's Friday nights all over again," Angel said excitedly. "Yeah, yeah, I remember this!"

His eyes danced over the stadium. Suddenly, he shot his gaze to the right and frowned. Jay's heart skipped a beat.

"You always sat there," said Angel with dawning realization. He wagged his finger at the spot that Jay knew all too well. "Didn't you? You always had a terrible sign!"

Jay scoffed, trying not to read too much into the fact that was the first thing Angel had recalled here. Not where he'd scored a particular touchdown or caught an amazing throw. Not even where he'd lost his virginity after one of the best games of the season to his then girlfriend under a different section of the bleachers. No. He'd remembered the spot Jay always used to try and sit in when he'd come and watch every single one of Angel's games.

Maybe it was because he was with Jay, so he'd automatically remembered something that was special to both of them. Or maybe it was because Jay was more important to Angel than all those other things. Jay had no way of knowing.

"My signs were amazing, thank you very much," he said, keeping the tone light like he had the last few days. "I claim credit for at least twenty-five percent of your success with those lovingly hand-crafted posters."

Angel snorted and continued spinning around slowly, swinging his head this way and that as he drank in the stadium where he'd spent so much time training and playing games. "I couldn't have done it without you," he murmured.

Did he mean football? High school? *Life?*

Jay swallowed and tried not to let the moment overwhelm him. He felt like that was all he'd been doing since he'd walked onto that film set four days ago. Had it really been four days already? In some ways, Jay couldn't believe it had *only* been four days. It was like time had ceased to have any meaning.

Angel was now in his apartment when Jay woke up and there when he went to sleep, albeit in a different room. Jay had struggled to sleep the first night Angel had been there, and not just because Button had insisted on worming her way onto the sofa to sleep as well. Jay felt like he was aware of Angel's every heartbeat. He was ashamed to say at one point he'd stuck his head around the bedroom door to make sure Angel was still breathing, like an anxious new parent.

Except Jay was afraid of...what? Yes, he'd been terrified about Angel's physical health to start with, but he said his aches and pains were slightly better already after many hot baths and painkillers. His skin had come out in an array of spectacular bruising that had left them both joking that he looked like some kind of muddy-colored rainbow, all dark blues and purples and greens surrounded by mustardy yellows. But Jay was okay with the discoloration, really. It showed his body was healing.

It was everything else that was driving him to the edge.

He was in this horrible limbo of torment. If he forgot himself, if he let *his* memory slide, then he could believe he was just having a great time reminiscing with his best friend over their awesome childhood together.

But then reality would sneak up on him, reminding him that he could never have Angel. Not the way he wanted. Angel might not have died in that car wreck, but one day he was going to drift away from Jay's life again when he met a lovely woman and settled down somewhere far, far away.

This was why Jay had never pushed for Angel to come visit. Not that he'd ever seemed to particularly want to. But Jay had been pretty sure that seeing Angel again would remind him of all the reasons he loved Angel, the ones he'd been trying so desperately to push down since that day on the railway bridge.

So he had been existing in a kind of superficial limbo where he tried not to dwell too much on any of it, but if anything, that was even more exhausting. Despite Angel's recovery going well, he was still stiff and sore, getting tired very easily. Jay had worn himself out jumping up and doing every little thing for his houseguest, but that was nothing compared to the conflicting rush he got when he had to rub arnica gel over Angel's hard-to-reach bruises. The skin-on-skin contact gave Jay a heady rush each time.

Jay would keep control of it, but it was wearing him down.

"So you remember this place well enough?" Jay prompted, waving his hand around to indicate the stadium before putting it back in his pocket. It might have been bright and sunny, but it was still January, and there was a real nip in the air.

Angel nodded and exhaled, his breath coming out in a cloud. "I think so. Sorry, you must be getting pretty fed up with all this."

Jay frowned. "Not in the slightest," he replied honestly. "It's fun going back and reminiscing over stuff together. I see a lot of these places on a weekly or even daily basis. This is kind of like seeing them through fresh eyes again."

Angel grinned at him. "That's kind of cool in that case," he said warmly.

His black eye was already fading under the bandage where he'd gotten stitches for the bump that had altered his memories. Jay had been helping him change the dressings and keep it clean and dry, but Jay was very much looking forward to getting Angel's usual handsome face back.

Yes, helping Angel recuperate on top of full-time teaching was a lot, but Jay was more than happy to do it for the sake of his best friend's health. So long as Jay ignored his own pining heart.

Angel had done his best to explain how a lot of the time he didn't know what he didn't remember until he tried to recall something specific and found it wasn't there. Like with Button. Angel loved her and had been cooing over her for a couple of years now. It was kind of a shock to hear he'd forgotten her until she'd come back from her walk, but after he'd seen her, Angel had said he remembered all about the feisty corgi.

Unlike the accident, which was apparently still a complete blank.

So was the confrontation with Kenny, which Jay didn't

really mind. He'd hated that their stupid school nemesis had ruined his and Angel's reunion, and he was mortified that Kenny had a band of idiots around him who were still protesting filming. In fact, his group was using the news of Angel's accident to try and claim that not only was the film immoral but its set unsafe.

Jay pushed Kenny from his mind. He was all bark and no bite, as his mom always said. They would all be better off ignoring his stupid little protests.

Jay had to keep reminding himself that his big, tough best friend was still in recovery. He'd been the strong one the entire time they'd known each other, and not just physically. He'd always been the one looking after Jay, and it was taking a little time to get used to the role reversal.

Jay saw tiredness wash over Angel's features. He'd been a stubborn ass and refused to bring his crutches out for the day, saying he was fine. Jay should have fought him harder on it, but it was difficult when all he ever wanted to do was just give Angel what he wanted.

Jay immediately went to his side, slipping his arm around him and propping him up. *Damn.* He smelled like sandalwood and the slightly sagey scent of the arnica gel he'd been rubbing over his bruised body. It reminded Jay of their high school days, when Angel would use the stuff nonstop to help with his football aches. He was so solid in Jay's embrace it almost broke his heart to be so close yet so far away from what he wanted.

"Hey, let's get you back to the car, okay?" he said, patting Angel's back. Jay could feel his back muscles even through the coat and sweater he was wearing. He *refused* to think how good they'd be to drag his nails over. "We can drive to the next spot, and you don't even have to get out. If you feel able, that is," Jay added. "If you're wiped, we can call it a day."

Angel blinked, like he was coming out of a trance from

looking around the stadium, then grinned at Jay. "No, I'm okay," he said. "I'm fine to drive somewhere else if there's not much walking. Especially if we can open the boxes from Rise and Shine."

Jay scoffed. "I think you bought half the bakery," he teased, but he didn't really mean it. Angel kept fretting about needing to get back to the gym soon, and Jay did understand that it took a lot of work to get a body as impressive as Angel's. But as far as Jay was concerned, he owed himself at least a couple of weeks' rest, and that meant eating whatever he liked.

"Because it all looked so delicious," Angel protested as they started making their way back through the tunnel. It was a few minutes' walk back to Jay's car, so he kept Angel distracted by reminding him of all the scrumptious pastries they'd bought from Pine Cove's bakery. It wasn't that Angel couldn't make the walk, it was more that he got frustrated at being slow.

Sure, Angel had been knocked down plenty of times playing football, and he'd had a couple of incidences with work over the years. But he'd voiced his frustration several times over the past couple of days at being so tired all the time from so many little ailments that added up to one big problem. He usually worked out every day, but right now, he got exhausted from a little walking.

So it was Jay's job to make things as easy for him as possible as they continued their quest to prompt Angel's memory with as many old sights as Jay could think of around town.

They'd started their Saturday morning on the boardwalk, visiting the pier by the lake. Angel had missed their ten-year high school reunion because of work, so Jay had taken him to the dock by the country club where they'd had their big party. He'd recounted the story of how Robin's crazy ex,

Mac, had created quite a scene until Dair had come to the rescue. Jay had told Angel the story at the time, but he repeated it for the sake of Angel's memory.

"I remember Mac," Angel had said as he nodded, frowning in concentration. "He was the reason Robin was never around as much in high school, right? You were pretty hurt by that, I think?"

Jay had smiled at him. He was glad when Angel remembered anything new, but that was a bittersweet memory. "Yeah, but it's okay now he's moved back home, and he's with Dair. And lucky for me, I had you at school."

"Hell yeah, you did!" Angel cried. He'd ruffled Jay's hair like he always used to do. "Man, I'm sorry I missed the reunion. It sounded eventful. But...then I might not even remember it now if I went."

Jay nudged Angel's thigh on his good leg. "Hey, now. None of that. You're doing amazing remembering so much. Just cut yourself some slack, okay? You just need time." He grinned and looked out over the expansive lake, then back at his friend. "Besides, you've got me to remember a bunch of stuff for you. We'll get through it."

Angel smiled at him. "Side-by-side."

"Side-by-side," Jay had promised.

The breeze off the lake had been cold, but it was heavy with the scent of the pine trees that surrounded the lake. The mountains rose in the distance, and for a while, they'd just sat in comfortable silence, watching the waves lap against the dock.

Then they'd had breakfast in the Sunny Side Up diner, where Sunny and his husband Tyee had made quite a fuss over Angel's return, insisting their food was on the house. Their family had become even closer with Jay's recently thanks to their son Micha dating Jay's brother Swift. They'd gotten engaged that summer, so the Coals and Perkinses were going to be officially united in the not-too-distant-future. Jay couldn't help but feel like Tyee, in particular, treated Angel like he was Jay's boyfriend rather than just a friend. He called Angel 'son,' like he did with Dair and said more than once how nice it was to see the two 'boys' back together.

It made Jay's heart pang.

As they'd walked down Main Street, Jay had introduced Angel to Taylan Demir, who ran the Turkish barbershop and had recently started dating one of Sunny and Tyee's other sons, Hudson. "I'm going to need a bubble diagram to keep all these names and relationships straight," Angel had said once they'd left, shaking his head.

"Or not so straight," Jay had joked, bumping playfully into Angel's side. It was moments like that when he forgot himself. After the awkwardness with the fiancé ruse, maybe Jay shouldn't say things like that. But Angel had just laughed at the gay joke, totally unbothered, like always.

After that, they'd wandered around the drugstore and arcade, where Jay was delighted to see Angel remember several stories from their youth totally unprompted. Whatever was going on with his brain, it seemed to be affecting more recent memories over the past couple of years. Jay was pleased he could help with everything until they graduated high school, but that left about twelve years' worth of memories from college and the years since that Jay couldn't do much about here in Pine Cove.

He'd briefly considered calling Lisa, Angel's ex, to see if she might have wanted to help. But she'd dumped Angel quite cruelly in the end. Via text. After six years together. Jay knew he had a vested interest in Angel's love life, but he felt absolutely vindicated in his hate of her for that. No. Either of them talking to her would almost certainly do more harm than good.

So instead, Jay had taken them to visit his friend Ben at the bakery and they chatted happily while buying half the pastry display. That wasn't so much for Angel's memory as it was to make sure that Angel had plenty of sugary goodies to munch through over the next few days.

Ben knew Jay through Emery and was a few years younger than them, so he didn't know Angel from school. But he was pleased to introduce himself and talk about his recent surprise proposal by his lawyer fiancé in an English stately home, modestly leaving out the part where he *owned* the mansion in question. But that was a story for another day. Angel was trying to remember as many forgotten memories as possible, not get overloaded with new ones.

As they paid for their numerous goodies, Jay had remembered an obvious place to take Angel to test out more of his memories. That was how they'd ended up on the high school's playing field, reliving Angel's glory days on the football team. While they made their way back to Jay's car, they began reminiscing over his most memorable games, and for a while, Jay just lost himself in the past.

He drove on autopilot to their last stop, the one Jay had been most nervous about, so he almost surprised himself when they were nearing the railway bridge. Pine Cove had several, but he and Angel only had one.

The one where Angel had saved Jay's life.

The one where Jay had fallen in love with Angel.

"Oh, shit!" said Angel excitedly when he realized where they were. He leaned forward to peer out the front window of Jay's car. "Now this is a blast from the past!"

They hadn't really ever come back here after that day with Kenny. It had shaken them quite badly, for one thing. But they'd grown up and found other places to hang, like the arcade, and then farther out of town when they'd gotten their driver's licenses.

"A good blast?" Jay asked.

He'd been of two minds about coming here because of his own personal significance. But he'd figured it was pretty important for Angel too, and it was worth a shot. All memories he recovered were a step in the right direction. This had been a significant place for them long before Jay had fallen off the bridge and in love with Angel. So in the end he'd decided to make the time to visit.

"Yeah, man," said Angel, craning his neck to look in all directions. Jay felt a little relieved that his gamble had paid off. Angel was obviously thrilled to be here. "Can we get out?"

Jay had been driving slowly, but now he stopped altogether and put the car in park. It was still a very quiet road, so they shouldn't have any issues while they were there.

Angel rolled his shoulders and cracked his neck as he got out. Jay was going to bully him into at least another hot shower, if not a bath, when they got back. They definitely weren't leaving the crutches at home next time. He checked his watch, but Angel wasn't due for his pain meds for another couple of hours.

He realized he'd thought of his apartment as both his and Angel's home. He supposed it was while Angel was here, like a vacation rental. But still, Jay couldn't help but wish they *did* both live there.

Angel whistled and looked over the rusty railings. When they'd been teenagers, they'd only been able to look through. But they were tall enough now that they reached the top, especially Angel. As fate would have it, a train horn rang faintly in the distance, signaling its approach.

"Hey, you remember the time Kenny Brooker jumped out of nowhere and scared us so badly you almost fell off the bridge?"

Jay laughed ruefully. As if he could forget. "He scared *me,* not you. I was the small one who got freaked out easily. And I definitely did fall, nothing 'almost' about it. You just caught me."

Angel frowned. "No, you caught yourself, thank god. That still scared me plenty, even if Kenny didn't exactly. Thank fuck you were so skinny back then. If it had been me who had fallen, I would have hit the ground for sure. Also, I wouldn't have been able to help pull you back up if you'd been any bigger."

"Lucky me," said Jay, rolling his eyes as he came to stand beside Angel, watching the tiny blip of the train approaching from miles away on the straight track through the forest.

Angel nudged him and waggled his eyebrows as Jay looked at him. "You always were a perfect fit," he joked, dropping his arm around Jay's shoulders.

They used to hug all the time growing up, and Jay had certainly given Angel a fair share of gentle hugs since the accident to try and convey how relieved he was that Angel was okay and on the mend. But something shifted in that moment, and Jay found himself staring into Angel's gray-blue eyes. There was something about those eyes that had always given Jay a dangerous thrill, like he was looking at an oncoming storm.

His breath hitched.

It was like there was a sudden tug between them that he had to be imagining. It was just the fact that Angel had chosen to hug him at the exact spot Jay knew he'd fallen in love with him. It was all in his mind. It had to be.

Except Angel was looking at him, a faint smile playing on his plump lips as his eyes flickered over Jay's features. His cold breath made Jay's own lips tingle as it smoked between them, and Jay could just about taste the sweet syrup from Angel's pancakes and the sugar from the pastries.

He tried to say something, but the words died in his throat.

Because at that moment, Angel leaned fractionally closer...

Then he snapped back, letting Jay go as he laughed and rubbed the back of his neck. "Wow, look, here comes the train," he said, pointing awkwardly at the locomotive hurtling toward them. "Do you want to hang on to the railings while it passes for old time's sake? On this side, of course. I think we've had enough accidents for one week."

Jay forced himself to smile and nod, stepping up to the edge of the bridge, wrapping his hands around the metal that seeped cold into his skin, even through his gloves. He then forced himself to believe that he'd imagined Angel had leaned in. There could be no *way* he'd thought about kissing Jay. If anything, it must have been *Jay* who had subconsciously leaned in and made Angel feel awkward, hence his spluttering about the train.

It had to be.

Right?

9

ANGEL

IT WAS AS IF ANGEL HAD BEEN LOST IN A MEMORY. BUT FOR A few seconds, he hadn't realized which one.

One moment, he'd been hugging Jay to his side, marveling at how perfectly he still fit under his arm. The next, he'd felt the overwhelming urge to get closer to Jay, to lean in…

And then it hit him in the face. Kind of literally.

He had done this before.

But not with Jay.

He remembered like it was yesterday. The guy's name had been Michael. They'd worked together on a film a couple of years ago. Angel had thought they were great buddies. It was around the time that Jay had been dating his last boyfriend, and Angel had been trying to give him space. It was also one of the times when Lisa had gotten mad over something and informed Angel they were on a break, the way she often did. So Angel and Michael had hung out all the time. Michael had been a good laugh but kind of sensitive too, with sparkling hazel eyes.

One night after filming, they'd had a couple of beers out on the pier, watching the moon over the waves of the Pacific

Ocean. Something about that moment had just felt so right. Angel remembered the way he'd looked at Michael, feeling that tug, like an almost physical pull between them.

Kind of like he'd just felt with Jay.

So he'd done something he'd never done in his entire life. He'd leaned in and thought maybe he might kiss another guy.

Except in that moment, Michael's expression had dropped, and he'd pulled his fist back and sucker-punched Angel so hard that he'd almost broken his eye socket. He'd run away from the pier, shouting about fucking queers, and hadn't spoken to Angel again the entire shoot.

Angel winced in the here and now, moving away from the railings as the train finished passing underneath them, the pain as fresh in his mind as the moment it had happened.

"What's wrong?" Jay asked. Had he noticed what Angel had almost done? *Shit.*

Angel shook his head, shocked by his own revelation, completely blindsided and unsure what the hell to think. He couldn't believe that deeply relevant information had been hiding somewhere in his own mind.

He was maybe perhaps possibly bi. Or at least not totally straight.

So why was his instinct to hide that from his gay best friend? Not share it? Jay obviously didn't know that about him, because he'd insisted several times that Angel was straight when he'd gotten confused about that whole fake fiancé thing.

And oh, god – what did that mean about Angel's reaction to thinking they *were* engaged? Was that why it hadn't seemed so strange to him? Because he'd forgotten that he was maybe a little bit bisexual?

Rediscovering his memories had been a bit of a messy task so far, but this felt like he'd just ripped the top off a huge can of writhing worms. He didn't know how to explain it or if he even should. Why had he tried to kiss Jay? Had he confused him for Michael in that moment?

Or did Angel have feelings for Jay that he'd forgotten he even had?

"Sorry...nothing," he managed to say before things got too weird.

It was like he didn't even know himself. There was this part of him that had been lurking deep within, and it had taken losing his memory to discover it.

A few years ago, he'd almost kissed a guy.

And he'd got punched for his troubles.

But that wasn't really the point. The point was, he'd kind of wanted to kiss *Jay*. Was he remembering more than he knew? Was he secretly in love with his best friend?

Wow. That was a leap. No matter what his toxic ex used to say, two guys could be close friends without it being sexual. Urgh, she'd always been so awful, making excuses about why they couldn't visit Pine Cove. She'd made it sound like...

Cheating.

Because 'bisexuals cheat.' That was what she always used to say. That was the voice Angel had heard in his mind not long after waking up from the accident. When he'd thought he and Jay were engaged for real. It had been Lisa hissing those disdainful words from the past to him.

Nausea rushed through Angel as the memories jumbled on top of each other. It seemed so clear to him now he was seeing the past few years all at once in a fresh light.

Lisa had been convinced that Angel was cheating on her with Jay, no matter what he'd said, and had always found ways to stop Angel from visiting him while they'd been dating.

And Angel had let her.

But had she been right? Angel adored Jay. He had since

they were five-years-old, for crying out loud. That didn't make him bi. Did it?

Shame and confusion washed through him, and he wasn't sure how he was really feeling. Maybe he'd just...he'd been lost in the moment. Jay was his best friend, his most awesome bud! He'd never felt like that about him before. Surely he'd remember *that* if he had, no matter what awful things Lisa used to say.

Angel realized that Jay's expression had become pained, and Angel worried again that he was being a burden. But Jay rubbed his arm and smiled kindly at him.

"I think we should go home," Jay said affectionately.

Angel's heart warmed at the word. He liked calling Jay's place 'home,' even if it was only temporarily. But there was the worry back in his eyes that Angel kept catching ever since his accident.

"That's probably more than enough excitement for one day, yeah?" Jay said.

"Yeah, you're probably right," Angel agreed gratefully.

He had enough to think about for a whole *week*.

Or maybe at least a couple of days before he cracked.

The rest of the weekend had been perfectly fine in a painfully polite way as Angel had tried to keep his spirits up and his actions proper. He wasn't sure how he felt about Jay anymore and what he might have forgotten he felt. All he knew was that for a split second, he'd leaned in close to his best friend, and his heart had raced.

But every time he recalled the moment, he winced like he'd been punched by Michael all over again. It was as if his muddled-up brain had now gotten the two moments confused and blended them together, and now Angel didn't know *what* he was feeling. On top of the shame he'd been taught to feel by Lisa about the word 'bisexual,' he was in a bit of a mess.

The worst thing was, the person he wanted to talk it all through with was the one he was worrying about, and now he didn't know who to turn to.

Ironically, he was having an identity crisis over his sexuality, and there were literally dozens of people in town he could probably talk to. But they were all Jay's friends and family. Angel needed to find his own people to hash it over with. Otherwise he was going to go out of his mind if he kept bottling it up.

He didn't want to blurt out to Jay or one of his friends that he might have a crush on Jay or something if it was just old memories getting confused with the present. The very last thing he wanted to do was risk making things weird with Jay.

So come Monday morning, when Jay went back to school, Angel ordered himself an Uber and took himself back to his world to see what people he could find.

He missed driving like a limb. It had been years since he'd gone this long without being behind the wheel. Even with the huge gaps in his memory, he knew that much. But as much as he was craving his favorite adrenaline rush, he felt wobbly even considering driving just yet, and his banged-up knee certainly didn't like the idea. He hoped it wouldn't take too long until he could drive again, though.

He stared out of the Uber car window as they drove through his hometown. He remembered most of it with deep fondness. His older memories were much stronger than his more recent ones, after all. But Dr. Lee had warned him that he might never remember the accident itself, and he could have trouble retaining new memories down the line. He'd learned to drive as a teenager, though, and he was confident that his muscle memory would still be there when he recovered.

But it was hard being patient. Angel wanted his life back.

He wanted to feel like he was on stable ground again so he could work out how he was really feeling about Jay. Luckily, he'd been ordered to take several days off from work, and for once, he could just stand still. Soon enough, he'd be onto the next leg of this film shoot and then a different project altogether. He never seemed to pause for breath anymore, especially since he and Lisa had broken up and he'd thrown himself into a crazy busy work schedule. Or at least, that was what his gut was telling him. The specific memories of Lisa and work over the last year felt hazy if he tried to concentrate on them too long.

Jay was different, though. He felt like a beacon shining through the fog, guiding Angel home. Even if Angel couldn't remember exact details of things right now, Jay was his port in a storm, his safe harbor. Or at least he had been until things had gotten so confusing on Saturday morning.

The thing was, when Angel stopped overanalyzing everything, he'd actually had a lovely weekend with his best friend. Jay had made him feel cared for and important in a way Angel was sure Lisa had never done. She had always been far too busy with her marketing career to take time for what she'd considered to be irrelevant things.

But Jay had cooked spaghetti and meatballs for them, using his mom's recipe that made Angel feel sixteen years old again, staying around Jay's house to do their homework together. It had been their staple shared meal for years, and Angel swore it had just as much healing power as anything Dr. Lee had prescribed. Jay had fussed over how many pillows Angel had propping him up, and sat on the sofa just talking and reminiscing about the good old days. It had felt gentle and sweet.

But then Jay would apparently catch himself, and something about him would change. Angel could see it, even if he didn't understand what had caused it. Then Jay would go busy himself with emptying the trash or lesson planning, urging Angel to get some rest while he was gone.

Angel really did need a shocking amount of rest after the accident, but he wasn't sleeping well for worrying, either. When Jay pulled away like that, it made Angel feel like something was seriously wrong. Was it his fault? First, he'd believed that they were actually engaged. Then, he'd almost kissed Jay. He really hoped Jay hadn't noticed that second one, but Angel couldn't lie to himself. Was he crossing a line and ruining their friendship by making it weird? It was like he had a hole in his heart that was slowly but surely getting bigger.

He couldn't imagine his life without Jay, but he knew his actions over the past several years said otherwise. He'd been so spellbound by Lisa's beauty and success, but more than that, he'd been so desperate not to set off her filthy temper he'd stopped arguing for what was important to him in their relationship.

Like seeing his best friend.

Damnit, she hadn't been worth it in the end. Angel had been a fool to let her manipulate him for so long. But all her friends were always telling him how they were a dream of a power couple, sure to get married and be together forever. He'd allowed himself to believe everything was okay.

And yet he'd never once thought about proposing. Even with his patchy memory, he was sure that was true.

Yet he'd believed he and Jay could have been engaged in a heartbeat.

And he was here now, about to drag himself through a cold forest in January, just so he could try and talk through things with someone so he could fix whatever had gone wrong with Jay. Didn't that tell him something?

Only that I'm thoroughly confused, he thought ruefully. He pulled his coat tighter as he braced for the elements, wondering if he should have brought his crutches, but he hated using them. He had to laugh at himself. This was kind of a ridiculous situation he'd found himself in. But he couldn't say he was regretting it.

Unless it pushed Jay away.

Was Angel changing his and Jay's friendship by being weird in ways he wasn't even aware of? Was Jay sensing something was amiss with Angel? Or was Angel making everything up and Jay was just acting normal? After all, Angel hadn't seen Jay in person in years. How was he to know what was out of character in his day-to-day life? Especially with his memory loss.

He rubbed his temple and thanked the driver as he dropped him off at the closest point to where the film set was operating. They had a detour on local traffic, so Angel would have to walk the rest of the way, and his body was already protesting the thought. He should have brought the damn crutches, but he didn't want people to pity him, and anyway, it was too late now. He'd just have to limp his way to the set.

Because Angel needed help. He owed it to Jay to sort his shit out, so that was what he was going to do.

10

ANGEL

Being back at work was...weird. Angel had found the location by looking through his phone, but his memory of this particular set was almost nonexistent. Kamran had explained that they'd only been operating for a couple of days before Angel had been in the accident, so that made sense that his recollection of it would be lost with all his other most recent memories.

But everyone else remembered *him*. He said hello to so many people who approached him and asked if he was okay. The first few he admitted he had no idea who they were, and they happily introduced themselves again. But the looks of pity and sympathy he got became exhausting very quickly, and not just because his knee was protesting already. After the first half a dozen, he stopped asking and just nodded and pretended he knew who everyone was.

Pretty much all the places he'd been to with Jay had prompted some kind of memory flash. He'd thought the same thing would happen when he'd decided to come back to work, but his job wasn't at an office with a desk that he'd sat at for the last eight years since college. It was an ever-rotating set of different people and places.

He hadn't come here to jog his memory, though, so he tried his best to ignore the sense of disorientation he was experiencing. He'd come here to find Kamran.

The strange thing was, Angel didn't really remember Kamran from the couple of days they'd spent filming. But Kamran certainly remembered him, and he was fiercely loyal to Jay as a friend. Which meant in the past week or so, Angel had been talking with Kamran almost as much as his own parents.

Kamran had taken it upon himself to keep Angel up-to-date with everything happening on set and asking Angel for daily reports so he could let everyone here know how his recovery was going. He'd sent Angel a *lot* of memes and links to funny tweets. As well as bringing Angel his bag of stuff from his trailer, Kamran had even gone and done a grocery shop for Angel and Jay the other day. So it might have felt fast, but this was a crazy time, and Angel was confident in calling Kamran *his* friend, not just Jay's.

The other thing Angel had learned about Kamran in this short time was that he was a *massive* ho, and very proud of it. In this past week alone, Angel had been informed by the man himself that he'd hooked up with two guys, a chick, and then a married man and woman couple. Angel had been privy to details that would raise anyone's eyebrows. But he had a kind of mad respect for someone who was so comfortable in their own sexuality like that, which was why Angel was hoping to talk to him.

He wasn't sure he wanted to bring up the confusing, uncertain thoughts he was experiencing about Jay. He didn't know if he could trust the feelings that had seemed so strong when he'd first come round from the accident, when he'd found it perfectly plausible that he could not only be in a relationship with his best friend but ready to marry him.

Instead, Angel was hoping to simply keep the discussion vague and hypothetical. Just a general chat about whether or not he could consider himself bisexual when he'd only been attracted to a couple of men that he was really good friends with. He knew he didn't experience lust the same way Kamran did. From his short list of long-term girlfriends, Angel was pretty certain he was a serial monogamist. Was what he was feeling – had felt – enough to be bi?

Unfortunately, after asking around, he found out that Kamran's schedule must have changed. He'd said he wasn't going to be filming until tonight, but apparently, he was already driving and would be for another couple of hours at least.

Which left Angel in sort of a dilemma. Now he was here he didn't want to waste the visit. It had taken a lot of effort to haul his busted ass up here, and he wasn't convinced he'd be able to face it again anytime soon. The walk from the Uber drop-off point and then all the interacting with people had already sapped his energy. Besides, he was getting himself wound up overthinking his situation, and every time he tried to assess whether he could really be bi, the sneering voice of his ex, Lisa, echoed around his skull.

Bisexuals are just attention seekers. Bisexuals are cheats. Who would ever want to date someone like that?

Angel gritted his teeth and shook his head, hoping to expel the thoughts. Maybe he was hoping someone would hear his story and just tell him he was bi so he didn't have to make the assessment himself. Because every time he tried, Lisa just laughed in his mind's eye and told him to stop being *so* ridiculous.

Besides, Angel had been around Jay most of his life, so he was well aware of LGBT issues, not to mention he'd had almost three decades to develop an attraction to his best friend if it was going to happen. Surely if he was attracted to him, he would have figured that out by now, right?

So why did he absolutely know that he'd leaned in with the intention of kissing Jay on Saturday, just like he had done with Michael a couple of years back? Why couldn't he let go of just how good – how *right* – it had felt to think they were engaged? He really needed to talk this through with someone.

He decided he would just wait. The next person who recognized him, he asked where the food truck was. He could at least grab himself some lunch and find a place to sit until Kamran was done. Yes, that sounded like a good plan. So he followed the directions, looking forward to some hot food and getting off his protesting knee.

His luck changed, however, when he ran into someone else on the way there. Two someones, actually.

"Darling!" Bella cried, getting Angel's attention.

He'd been lost in thought, focusing on the forest floor as he walked. The last thing he needed on top of everything else was to trip and hurt himself again. But he looked up to see two of the movie's stars walking together, carrying several tinfoil pouches that they'd probably gotten from the food truck for lunch.

"What are you doing here? How are you feeling?" Bella asked.

He waved as he approached her and her co-star, Sabina Max. It kind of felt like he and Bella were friends already, but Angel couldn't help but wave awkwardly at Sabina, one of the other 'fallen angels' in the spy film. The one with the fictional girlfriend who Kenny and other bigots were getting ridiculously upset about.

"Hey, Bella," Angel said. "I'm okay, thanks. I was looking

for Kamran, but apparently he's working." He then nodded at Sabina. "Hi, I'm Angel."

Sabina gave him a teasing smile. She was effortlessly cool, all black eyeliner and black leather, picking at her tinfoil with chipped black nails. She was dressed as her character, but it wasn't far off her real-life persona from what Angel knew from the internet. In their discussions about the film, Kamran had seemed pretty certain that he hadn't met her before now.

"I know who you are," she said with a quirk of an eyebrow. Her voice was rich and husky. "You're the guy who totaled his car for attention. Grats on not busting up your pretty face too much."

Angel blinked and touched the fresh bandage Jay had put on his forehead last night. Was she serious about him having the accident for attention? Or flirting by calling him pretty? It showed what kind of a state he was in that the idea of Sabina-fucking-Max giving him a come-on sparked absolutely no reaction in the pants region.

He knew he'd worked with countless talent over the years and was almost certain that he'd never gotten intimidated before, but suddenly he felt kind of shy. He usually didn't care if someone was famous, because he had a job to do. He saw himself as an equal on set.

But Sabina was openly bisexual, playing a queer woman in the film they were all working on and, reportedly, gave zero shits that people were protesting it. Apparently, she'd become an executive producer for the franchise specifically so she could push for her character to get a girlfriend. She was a loud voice for the LGBT community, according to Angel's online reading. And Bella was one of the only openly asexual celebrities in Hollywood.

Could he talk to *them* about his hesitations in trusting himself and his sexuality? Surely not. They were A-list stars, and he was just the dumb stunt guy who'd gone and totaled his car right on film. He wrestled with himself for half a second before deciding that if his accident had hammered anything home to him, it was that life was short. He was doing this for Jay as much as himself, and Jay was worth the possibility of embarrassing himself. *Fuck it.*

"Hey, you guys don't have a second, do you?" he asked. "I could really use someone to talk to about stuff."

Bella raised her eyebrows. "Film stuff? Or personal?" Her eyes lit up. "Ohhh my goodness, is it about that lovely friend you're staying with?"

Angel took a moment to be impressed by her intuition skills, but mostly what he felt was relief. "Actually, yeah. It is kind of about Jay."

Bella nodded happily and looked at Sabina. "We were just going to have lunch in my trailer and run lines. Why don't you join us? There's nothing that can't be fixed over a nice hot cup of tea. We even have spare burritos!"

Sabina chuckled. "Well, *she* has spares. These babies are all mine."

Angel waved his hands. "Oh, no, I don't want to intrude—"

Sabina pushed his chest gently with a grin. "Come on, daredevil. Now I'm intrigued."

Angel rubbed his neck and felt kind of awkward, but ultimately allowed himself to be turned around and walked in the direction of Bella's large trailer, which wasn't that far away. On the door, it read 'Ms. Dalton – Fallen Angels Club 2: Fall Harder.'

"You're going to think I'm a terrible Brit," said Bella as Angel followed her into her trailer, which was all cream leather, wooden flooring, and chrome finishes, "but I only have decaffeinated tea and unsweetened soy milk. No breakfast tea and certainly no coffee. I do have sugar if you want to—"

Angel waved his hands and shook his head. "It's fine. I'll take it however you have it."

"You're sure?" Bella said anxiously. "I can send someone to the truck for a proper tea or coffee if you'd prefer? It's no trouble at all. Sebby already has a coffee." Angel realized that nestled behind the numerous burritos, Sabina did indeed have a takeout cup.

Angel laughed. "I think I've had more than enough sugar over the last couple of days," he promised, thinking of their haul from Rise and Shine. He usually drank black coffee, so didn't have much of a tea preference as far as he was aware.

Bella insisted that he get himself comfortable on the sofa and start eating one of her 'just in case I needed a snack later' burritos while she began making tea. Sabina perched sideways on one of the two chairs by the tiny dining table that was attached to the wall. She was kind of intimidating with her black leather, rings on every finger, and damp curls that look like she'd just stepped out of the shower. She pressed Angel's 'awesome' button, though, not 'hot.'

Angel bit his lip and unwrapped his burrito. Wasn't that the whole problem? Didn't he think Jay was awesome, not hot? Could awesome become hot? Or was his awesomeness a kind of hotness in itself?

Angel knew he'd lost a lot of his memories, but everything he remembered about Jay made his heart clench with such affection. Like how much he loved teaching and the pride he took in helping countless kids become better versions of themselves. Or even silly things like how he loved nature documentaries but he cried whenever any animals died or were eaten. Or how he never got embarrassed, aside from that one time Angel had played him at his own game and brought a huge, glittery sign to watch him in The Importance of Being Earnest. The way he'd turned beet red during the curtain call while Angel had hollered "I'm so proud of you, snookums!" was one of his favorite memories he'd recalled so far.

But was that just how you were supposed to feel about your best friend? Or was this really attraction? Why couldn't he tell the difference? At what point did that love stop becoming platonic and turn into desire?

"Right! Tea!" Bella said as she placed mismatching mugs in front of him and herself. Angel's said 'Game! Set! Match!' with a cartoon of a kissing couple wearing tennis clothes, surrounded by love hearts. He was pretty sure Bella's husband played tennis or coached it or something. Before that, she'd dated some guy from a boy band, but he'd come out as gay since then.

"So, who's Jay?" Sabina asked around a mouthful of food, waggling her eyebrows at Angel.

He sighed, not sure if he was hungry anymore. He swallowed and wiped his mouth. The last thing he wanted to do was pour his heart out while he had guacamole on his lips.

"Jay's my best friend. We grew up here in Pine Cove together. I hadn't seen him for years, but now I'm staying at his place while I recuperate."

"*Just* your best friend?" Sabina asked slyly. Bella nodded pointedly as she chewed, looking at Angel for his answer.

He bit his lip and fiddled with a bit of tinfoil. He was scared to voice his feelings, but he couldn't go on like this. "I thought so."

Bella swallowed. "But…" she prompted excitedly.

"But he's gay, and I always thought I was straight," said Angel, running his finger around the rim of the mug, focusing on the steaming toffee-colored liquid inside. "When I was in the hospital, he pretended to be my fiancé so the staff would treat him like my next-of-kin, but when I first woke up and couldn't remember anything, I thought that was the truth, and that made me *happy*. I was kind of disappointed it wasn't the case, but that's nuts – we've never been more than friends. Then the other day I thought I wanted to kiss him, and now I don't know what to think."

"That you might be bisexual?" Sabina offered with a happy smirk.

"Does the word really matter so much?" Angel asked, rubbing the back of his neck in confusion. He felt so overwhelmed. There was a part of him that knew there was *nothing* shameful about that word. But it was like Lisa had trained him to flinch at it, like a dog and a rolled-up newspaper.

Sabina shook her head and gave him a small, sympathetic smile. "It doesn't have to," she said. "It does to me. I'm pretty damn proud of having a reputation as being a disaster bisexual." She laughed deeply. "But for other people, I guess it might make them feel, I don't know, claustrophobic or something. Does it really matter? To you, I mean."

Angel chewed his lip. "Well, it should, shouldn't it? Isn't that why there are so many flags now, so everyone can be proud of who they are?"

Sabina and Bella shared a look. "Well, not necessarily," said Sabina. "There's a reason they say 'love is love.' If you love someone, you don't have to stick a label on it like a jar of pickles if you don't want to."

Angel frowned. He'd always just been attracted to women as far as he was aware. Well, except for Michael, he was now appreciating, but that was different. That could have just been a moment of madness or curiosity with a guy he hardly knew. But this was *Jay*.

He chewed his lip. He'd always supported Jay and his brother being gay. He'd even gone to a couple of Pride parades in Seattle with them in junior and senior year. So he'd been around the LGBT community during those years. It wasn't completely alien to him.

And then he'd met Lisa, and he'd stopped having anything to do with Pride or the community at all. She'd taken that away from him, and he'd let her because he'd wanted an easy life. She'd convinced him that it was kind of creepy for a straight guy to go to those things. God, she'd had him wrapped around her finger.

But had she had a point? Angel had just always thought he was an ally. He didn't think he belonged to it. Was that right? Could he call himself bisexual? Was he bisexual *enough?*

Bella laughed kindly. "I can see the cogs turning in your head," she said.

Angel sighed and took a sip of his tea, getting used to the taste. "It just feels wrong in some way," he tried to explain. "Like I don't have the right to call myself anything. It feels like I haven't had to go through what Jay or his brother did. Like I'd just be jumping on the bandwagon based on a couple of confusing feelings."

Sabina shrugged. "You don't have to play by anybody else's rules," she said. "You certainly don't have to feel guilty over being a late bloomer or finding what label is best for you or not picking one at all. Queer is a nice catch-all without being specific."

Angel rubbed his chin. "Jay's tried telling me that word is okay now, but guys used to yell it at him, Robin, and Emery when we were all at school." *Michael yelled it at me as he ran away from our near kiss.* "Would it really be cool to use?"

"Q can also stand for questioning," said Bella gently, daintily sipping her tea. "And I see where you're coming from. It might not feel like your word to reclaim. I'm ace but attracted to men. So while I absolutely see myself as part of the LGBTQA plus community, I wouldn't necessarily call myself queer."

"Whereas I am queer as all fuck," said Sabina with a wink.

Angel bit his lip, figuring he better ask the question that was burning within him.

"So…queer is okay to say if it feels right to you personally," he began, choosing his words carefully. "Then…" He sighed, done tiptoeing around. Lisa might have been beautiful, but she was a bitch, and Angel was so over letting her run his life. "Bisexual isn't a bad word, right? It's not something…other people look down on. They don't think we're just all going to cheat?"

Sabina raised her eyebrows. "Well, uh, yeah. I'm sorry to say, but gay and straight people absolutely look down on us beautiful bi unicorns and call us filthy cheats."

"But they can go fuck themselves," Bella said fiercely. In her fancy British accent, the profanity sounded even better, and Angel couldn't help the small relieved laugh that escaped his throat. "If anyone's made you feel like that, Angel, you need to cut them out of your life right now."

He sighed and took another sip of tea. It certainly wasn't coffee, but there was something fortifying about it all the same. "Don't worry. She's already gone." He shook his head. "My ex used to rant about bi people being dirty cheats any chance she got. I think she was threatened by my relationship with Jay and was trying to turn me off him."

Sabina scoffed. "Bitch."

"Look," said Bella firmly. "It's absolutely not a bad word, and no one should look down on you if that's the label you feel suits you best."

Sabina made a 'rock on' devil's horns fist and took a big bite of her second burrito. "And we have the best flag. Fight me," she mumbled around her food.

Bella patted her knee, then beamed at Angel. "I wouldn't

get your knickers in a twist over the terminology, honestly. If you felt a spark between you and Jay, that's wonderful. He seems lovely, in case you needed any approval," she added warmly with a wink.

Sabina tucked her foot under her thigh, her arm draped over the back of the chair. It was amazing she was still sitting on the thing in Angel's opinion. She looked like a pretzel.

"It's about how you feel and how he feels," she said earnestly. "Do you think he's on the same wavelength as you?"

That made Angel's stomach drop. If he was confused about how he felt, he had no idea what was going on in Jay's mind, despite the fact that he knew him better than anyone else on the planet. They'd been best friends for so long. What was Angel thinking messing with that? Was he going to ruin the best relationship he had ever had in his life?

He blew out a long breath. "No clue. It feels kind of fragile. I think I feel better about the word bisexual now at least, and I can see how that sits with me. But I stayed away from Jay for so long because I let my psycho ex talk shit. She always double-booked things for us on the weekends I tried to come here to see him. I've really let him down."

"You haven't, I promise," said Bella. "I've only met him once, but I'm certain he cares deeply for you still."

"True," said Angel somberly. "But I still let my ex control my life. What the hell was wrong with me?"

Sabina grinned. "Let me guess. She was insanely hot?"

Angel managed a small, guilty smile. "Like...*smoking.*"

Sabina nodded, still grinning. "Been there."

Bella waved her elegant hand. "You can't change the past, trust me. Don't beat yourself up for what you did or didn't do, and *definitely* don't allow it to ruin your future. Allow yourself to feel these feelings, good and deep. If you really are attracted to the lovely Jay, I'm sure he would want to know."

"But he can't possibly be interested in me," Angel scoffed, a different kind of fear creeping in. What if he was developing a crush on Jay, but Jay only saw him as a friend? There had been nothing in their entire shared history to suggest that Jay felt anything more than brotherly affection for him.

Right?

"Men." Sabina snorted.

Bella frowned at her, then smiled kindly at him. "It helps if you talk these kinds of things through and don't make assumptions," she said. "Trust me. Nothing good comes from bottling it all up."

Sabina winked at him. "Hey. I haven't met this guy, but I've got a good feeling, okay? Just give it a shot."

Angel exhaled. "I don't even know how to start having that conversation," he admitted.

Bella looked thoughtful for a second. "Have you had feelings for any other guy before?"

Angel swallowed, trying not to let that sensation of Michael's sucker punch overwhelm him. "Sort of," he said. "Different from Jay, though."

"Well, maybe that's where you start?" suggested Bella earnestly. "Say you've been wondering about your sexuality in general and ask how might he react if you told him you thought you might have feelings for him?"

Biting his lip, Angel rubbed his knee, which throbbing less thanks to sitting down for a while. That didn't sound so terrifying, did it?

Actually, it sounded pretty shit scary, but Angel lived for adrenaline. If he could jump out of a plane, he could have a conversation with his best friend.

"Okay," he said with a small smile. "I could try that."

"Good boy," said Sabina, sounding genuinely proud.

Bella glanced at the clock on the wall. "Oh, shit. Right. I'm absolutely not going to kick you out, my darling. But Sebby and I need to run lines."

Angel shook his head. "No worries," he said. "You've both been a huge help, trust me. Can I test you on your lines to pay you back?"

"Aww, he's fucking adorable," said Sabina, sounding like she was talking about a puppy but somehow making it sound like a compliment. "You can absolutely do that, daredevil."

"And eat the rest of your lunch," Bella fretted as she flicked to the right page on the script and handed it over. "You need to keep your strength up."

They began working, and Angel did as he was told, eating his burrito as he watched in awe at the skill both women had firing their lines back and forth. He was so enraptured, he practically jumped from the sofa when the *'ding!'* of his text message alert went off.

"Sorry, sorry," he apologized. "I should have put that on silent."

"It's cool," said Sabina with a big stretch of her arms. "I need to use the little bisexuals' room, anyway. Let's take five."

Angel agreed gratefully, then opened the text.

KAMRAN: Hey! Heard you were here asking for me. Sorry, dude, I was working. You still around? I was going to head into town later for a drink, if you wanted to hang?

Angel wasn't sure if he needed to talk to Kamran as well, having hashed it through with Bella and Sabina, but Angel kind of liked the idea of spending time with him as a friend regardless. He could see why Jay liked him. Kamran had a knack for making other people feel better, even if his tact was as blunt as a baseball bat at times.

A thrill ran down his spine as he realized something.

He could go hang out with another bisexual guy.

Even thinking the word 'another' made him slightly giddy. It was like he'd just found out he was part of a secret club that he had no idea he already belonged to. And that nasty voice of Lisa's was quietening down when Angel discovered that he was very much not alone.

He definitely didn't want to drink anything alcoholic with how crappy he still felt, but after a good, hot lunch and resting for a while, he found he was up for a little socializing.

ANGEL: Sounds like a plan! I'm running lines with Bella and Sabina (yes, really, haha). Lemme know when you finish for the day.

For the next couple of hours, Angel worked with the actresses, drank tea, ate another burrito, and generally mulled over his pretty profound personal development. The notion that he could really be bi was settling comfortably within him, and he wanted to wrap his arms around it and keep it safe.

Because even though he felt good and powerful with the support from Bella and Sabina, one conversation wasn't going to undo the years of prejudice Lisa had instilled in him. Nor was it going to convince him that he shouldn't have felt these feelings for Jay earlier if they were really real.

But he couldn't deny the facts of how he'd felt when he thought he was engaged to his best friend. It was as if a switch had flipped, and that confusion had allowed him to explore something that had perhaps been buried so deep he'd needed a little head trauma to shake it loose.

For the first time since he'd learned the truth of that lie, Angel dared to allow himself permission to follow an equally scary but amazing thought. What if he did want a relationship with Jay that was more than just friends? And what if Jay felt the same way?

As Angel finally said goodnight to Bella and Sabina, hope blossomed in his chest. Whatever happened between him and Jay, he felt like he'd discovered a very important part of himself today. He was starting to believe that he didn't have to be afraid or ashamed of this part of himself that he'd unlocked.

In fact, he might even be allowed to be excited.

11

JAY

"He hates me."

"What?" spluttered Robin, looking at him over the table that they and their friends had managed to get at Aquarium that night. It was a Monday, and Jay was going to seriously regret this in the morning. But right now, Emery's brightly colored shots were the only thing taking Jay's pain away.

"It's been weird all weekend," Jay said, shaking his head. "I never should have taken him to that bridge."

"What bridge?" Robin's mechanic boyfriend, Dair, asked. He had one of his muscled arms around Robin, the many tattoos from his time in the Marines visible in the low lighting.

Robin shook his head. "Best not to ask, I think."

Jay bit his lip. It wasn't like things were *bad* since the bridge. But it was as if this awkwardness was building up inside him since the almost-kiss that couldn't possibly have been a kiss, and now all those bottled-up feelings were spilling out into a tipsy melancholy.

"More shots!" Emery declared, arriving back at the table

with his fiancé, Scout, and a tray covered in little glass tumblers filled with liquids in all colors of the rainbow.

Aquarium was the only gay bar in Pine Cove, but it was so good it drew people in from all the neighboring towns, too. Even on a Monday night, it was relatively busy with people drinking and grinding in the swirling lights. Jay looked around at the chrome bar and light-up dance floor and wondered how many people here were also trying to cover up their misery.

He hadn't been able to face going home after work, so he'd caved to Emery's suggestion of one – just *one* – drink. Now here they were and Robin surreptitiously slid Jay a glass of water to drink before imbibing any more of the colorful concoctions.

"Okay," Emery said as he and Scout squeezed into the booth. Well, Emery bounced across the leather seat. Scout, a former bodyguard turned boxing instructor, slid in a little more gracefully. Emery grinned at Jay and held up one of the shots in a kind of salute before knocking it back. "Why are we so sad, poppin? I thought you said that Angel was on the mend?"

Jay sighed and downed half the water, then picked up his rum and Coke to sip for a while before risking another shot. "He is," he said. "But I'm starting to think that there was a reason he didn't visit for all those years. Things have just gotten kind of odd between us. It's not like it was before."

Emery scoffed. "Well, of course it's not. A lot of time has passed. Weird how?"

Jay bit his lip. "Nothing. I'm being silly," he mumbled.

Robin slid his hand over Jay's, startling him. Their gazes locked. "C'mon, Jay," said Robin so softly that Jay barely heard him over the thumping pop music. "It's bad enough we've got one dummy in this family. I think it's time you admitted the truth."

Jay's heart started slamming in his chest and his mouth went dry despite all the drinks he'd had. "W-what?" he asked.

Emery huffed. "He means that we all know that my best friend, your sister – Ava – is madly in love with Robin's best friend – Peyton – and one impossible Coal is more than enough to deal with."

"It's okay," Robin said, nodding with wide eyes. "You can tell us why things got weird."

All of a sudden, the last twenty-five years just seemed to catch up with Jay at once, and he choked back a sob, then downed the nearest shot. "Okay!" he cried, coughing and spluttering as the drink went down. "Fine! I'm in love with Angel and have been since high school! And there was this moment on the bridge when I thought he was going to kiss me, but I must have imagined it because he's fucking straight, duh. Then he got super awkward, so *I* must have done something to give myself away, and now it's like we're dancing around each other, being polite, and instead of going home to see him, I'm hiding out in a bar, and it's all fucked *up!*"

He sniffed, then knocked back another shot. This one was green and appley and didn't burn his throat quite so badly. He blew his cheeks out, shaking slightly. There. He'd said it out loud.

"Oh, honey-boo," Emery said with a sigh, clasping his hands in front of his chest. "I bet it's not as bad as all that…"

But he trailed off. Because when the three of them had been growing up gay together, they'd all lamented many times that one of the worst fates they could endure was to fall for a straight guy. It was just masochistic. And yet Jay had gone and done it. Hard.

But then…Robin had thought Dair was straight. So had Dair. And Scout had been so private about his personal life he might as well have been in the closet when Emery met him.

No, no, no! That line of thinking was far too dangerous. Jay's heart couldn't take it. There was no way Angel was secretly bi or anything. Jay had known him almost his whole life. He needed to drown his sorrows with more booze, then tomorrow start a new chapter in his life where he let this nonsense go, once and for all.

Besides, Angel was going to be leaving soon. The movie would head to its next location and take Angel out of Jay's life again. But this time, now that things were weird, would he ever come back?

He wiped his face with the heels of his hands and shook himself with a guttural huff. "No, it's fine. I'm being silly. Things will go back to the way they were, and I'll forget all about this. Out of sight, out of mind. Angel will probably be in Singapore or somewhere else a million miles away by this time next month. I'm making a late New Year's resolution right now to start dating again, and all this will fade. I'm just...it's the accident. Seeing him pulled from that wreck made me completely irrational, but I'll be fine. There's nothing between me and him except friendship, and that's amazing. We all need friends, right? He never tried to kiss me because he's straight. And...well, that's that."

Emery squirmed in his seat, grinning around the paper straw between his lips. "Are you, like, really *really* sure about that?"

Jay narrowed his eyes at him. "Yes," he said with as much conviction as he could muster. "Why?"

"Because he's just walked into a gay bar."

Jay swiveled so fast in his seat that he almost broke his neck. But sure enough, there was Angel ambling into Aquarium with Kamran by his side.

Angel had his mouth open and was looking all around at

the disco balls and glittery blue wallpaper, so he didn't see Jay gawking at him. But Kamran spied their group and waved, so Jay spun back around and slunk down in the booth, like if he tried hard enough, he might be able to make his drunk ass disappear.

"He's just here with Kamran," he hissed to Emery, his gaze flicking around everyone at the table currently staring at him. "They're friends from work. That doesn't mean anything." He moaned and dragged his hand down his face. "Please, *please* don't say anything. I'm begging you."

"Hey, Jay, hey," said Robin urgently, hugging him to his side. "Of course we won't say anything. But he's here, and he's smiling, so maybe there's nothing to worry about, okay?"

Jay opened his mouth to protest, but then Kamran and Angel were upon them.

"My dudes!" Kamran said, slapping his hands together. "Angel came to visit us on set today, and I convinced him to come for a drink with me. Fancy seeing you beauties here."

Jay narrowed his eyes at Emery, who only flinched slightly. But Jay would bet anything that he and Scout had let Kamran know where they were, and this wasn't as much of a coincidence as it appeared to be.

"Hey, Jay," said Angel with a big grin and raised eyebrows. He looked like he was almost quivering with excitement. "I'm really glad you're here. How was your day?"

That was...unexpected. Where had Mr. Awkwardly Polite gone?

"Oh, h-hey," Jay managed to stammer, aware that everyone else was looking at them both.

Fuck. Him and his big mouth. He should never have spilled his guts like that! He'd managed twenty-five years without telling anyone how he felt about Angel. Why had he gone and ruined it now?

"H-how are you feeling? You look tired. Not in a bad way! Just, uh…"

Angel laughed and shook his head. "No, it's fair. I am pretty tired. It's crazy how a little walking around is still knocking me out."

"Well, you need to sit," said Emery, flapping his hands and shooing Scout back out of the booth. "Ben and Elias are on their way, anyway, just to say hi, so we'll just go here, and Angel, you can go there…"

"No, I…" Jay tried to protest, but everyone was already moving.

So that was how he found himself sandwiched between Dair and, more importantly, Angel. "Sorry about the meddling, dude," Dair muttered in his ear. Apparently, he was as aware that Emery was matchmaking as Jay was. "I think it's best to just go with it. Relax." He winked and bumped his elbow against Jay's.

"Right, more drinks – not shots," said Emery, like he was being responsible for a change. He stood at the head of the table and began checking what everyone wanted.

But Jay looked to Angel. "We don't have to stay here if you don't want to," he said quietly and apologetically. "You're tired. We can go home. Or go get dinner. Or grab takeout on the way home. Or go to a straight bar—"

"Whoa, Jay. Slow down, dude," said Angel warmly.

Then – oh dear *god* – he squeezed Jay's thigh, and Jay thought he might combust. It wasn't unusual for them to be quite physical with each other, but Jay was pretty sure that Angel's hand had never been so close to his cock, and it practically jumped out of his pants of its own volition.

"This is great," Angel continued. "You've talked about this place so much. It's nice to see it in person."

Jay blinked at him. "You remembered me talking about a

gay bar?" Jay asked, uncertain. "You forgot my dog, but you remembered Aquarium?"

"Uh, not exactly," said Angel sheepishly. "Kamran had to talk at me for a good ten minutes before anything sparked. But I remember you had a birthday here once, I think? I might have seen pictures, but I feel like I'm looking at it for the first time. It's cool." He shook his head. "God, this is exhausting. I'm not sure if I forgot the bar because it's normal not to remember a place you've never been, or if it's due to the accident."

"Yeah," said Jay, lost in Angel's gray-blue eyes. "Memory is so crazy, even without bumping your head. But, uh, I did have my birthday here last year."

Angel beamed and clicked his fingers happily, even though there was a definite air of tiredness hanging around him. "I knew it!" he proclaimed in triumph.

Jay closed his mouth, torn again. Did it mean anything that Angel remembered where he'd had his birthday last year? Jay had celebrated his birthday here several times, so maybe it wasn't special that Angel had recalled that. Perhaps it had been more of a lucky guess.

"Uh, yeah. I had my party here. It's our favorite place and pretty much the only gay bar around, so we've all celebrated a birthday or promotion or some other thing here."

Angel nodded at him, then looked around. He really did seem fascinated by Aquarium. For all they'd gone to Pride parades in high school, Jay wondered if this was his first time in a gay bar. Jay hoped he didn't feel too uncomfortable or out of place.

"Awesome," said Angel, looking back at Jay. "Maybe next time I'll actually be able to make your birthday." He bumped his shoulder against Jay's. "In fact, I'll make sure I make an effort to keep my schedule clear."

Jay swallowed, not sure what to make of that. Angel had

gone from friendly but distanced to making promises to work his schedule around Jay's birthday plans.

What was he going to do? He didn't want to cut his best friend out of his life for good just because his crush was out of control. But was it going to be like this every time they saw each other?

No. Angel wouldn't get into a life-threatening accident next time. He wouldn't bang his brain around and scramble his memory, meaning Jay wouldn't have to pretend to be his fiancé, then take care of him in his home and visit loads of nostalgic places together. This was just an especially testing time, but he would get through it.

Maybe the next time he visited, Angel would have a new girlfriend. A nice one. The thought caused Jay physical pain, but that would probably be for the best. Maybe that would make Jay move on with his life.

"Hey," said Angel with a frown. "Is everything all right? I'm sorry I missed so many birthdays, but I'll make it up to you from now on, I promise."

A nervous giggle escaped from Jay's throat. *No*, he wanted to say, *everything is really not all right. I'm completely in love with you, and you make it even harder to ignore when you make such sweet promises like that.*

Instead, he managed a deep breath and patted Angel's arm gently, wary of his bruising. "I'm just a little drunk," he whispered loudly in a conspiratorial manner, even though he felt pretty sober now.

"Oh," said Angel, immediately scanning the table. "Then drink some water!"

He picked up the glass in front of them and pressed it into Jay's hands, rubbing his back. Suddenly, a huge sense of rightness washed over Jay. Angel was the one who was supposed to look after Jay, not the other way around. Jay hadn't appreciated that the universe had gone so topsy-turvy until that moment, but he sighed and gulped down the water gratefully.

However, that didn't change the fact that Angel was exhausted. His skin was wan, and his eyelids kept drooping despite his valiant efforts to smile and enjoy himself. As his best friend, Jay was more than happy to continue to be the caregiver, the protector, a little longer.

He kept telling himself that things would go back to the way they had been soon enough, with Angel being the one to look after Jay. But in that moment, Jay realized there was no 'going back to normal.' Things would never be like they had been when they were kids or teenagers. Maybe it was time to accept that his and Angel's relationship was bound to change and evolve.

Perhaps he should stop fighting that.

"Let's go," said Jay after he'd downed all his water. "You look dead on your feet."

But Angel shook his head. "No, no, I want to stay. I feel kind of at home here."

Jay blinked, not sure why he would. As a football fan, surely he'd appreciate a sports bar way more than this glitter explosion. But Jay liked that Angel was being supportive of Jay and his queerness, like he always had been.

"Well," said Jay, trying a different tactic. "I have to deal with several hours of teaching teenagers tomorrow, not to mention the auditions with Libby and the GSA after school. So I'd actually kind of like to get out of here and head home. You can stay if you want, but I think you've had a busy enough day already, and we can totally come back another time before you leave."

Angel looked like he might want to protest. But then he gave a tired smile and nodded. "It is a bit loud for me right now," he confessed. "But I *do* like it, and I definitely want to come hang with your friends another day."

Jay wasn't sure why Angel had taken such an interest in Aquarium all of a sudden, but it was nice. Jay couldn't help but want to share things about his life with his best friend. He held up his little finger. "Pinky promise."

Angel hooked his little finger around Jay's. "Pinky promise."

"Okay, guys," he said to the table. "I'm going to take Angel to grab some food, then we're going to head back to my place. We'll catch you another time. Say hi to Ben and Elias for us."

He expected them to complain or try and dissuade him, but they all just waved and told them to get home safe. Jay felt bad about the drinks Emery had just bought them, but he winked and assured Jay they would find homes for them.

As Jay stepped out onto the sidewalk of Main Street, he inhaled a deep, cold breath and felt better already. All this upset about his feelings would blow over. Meanwhile, he needed to make the most of the time they had until he left Pine Cove again.

"How do gyros sound?" he asked as Angel stopped beside him.

"Oh hell yeah," said Angel, nodding. His breath came out in a cloud. He shoved his hands into his jacket pockets and looked up and down the street like he was reacquainting himself with it. His bandage glowed in the moonlight, and Jay was glad he'd been able to convince him to head home. He needed rest. "Is that place opposite the park still there?"

"It certainly is," said Jay. And then an idea sparked in him. Another trip down memory lane for Angel. "Why don't we grab a couple and go sit on our bench for a while?" They both had coats and hats on, so it shouldn't be too cold if they only sat for a minute.

"Our bench?" Angel repeated.

"You'll see," said Jay with a wink, confident Angel would remember it when he saw it.

"Sounds great," said Angel with a warm smile. Jay's heart flipped, but he tried to ignore it for now. "Lead the way."

They walked in amicable silence down the street to the gyro place, where they each got a big fat pita stuffed with hot tangy meat, crunchy salad, and cool tzatziki. They had them wrapped up thoroughly so the food would stay warm until they got home, then headed out into the park.

It wasn't that late, so there were plenty of people still out and about in town. But sitting on their bench in the quiet park, looking up at the starry night, Jay felt like it was just him and Angel in the whole world.

"I remember this now," said Angel, patting the wood beneath him. "We came here to eat gyros a *lot* when we were studying for finals."

Jay laughed. "That we did." He paused for a second. "Do you remember what we said the last time we sat here?" he asked in a softer voice. "The summer before college?"

Angel puffed his cheeks out and frowned slightly as he looked down at the old wooden bench that overlooked the green space. The pine forest that the town was named after rustled in the distance, and the shadow of the mountain beyond the lake was just visible in the moonlight. It was incredibly peaceful.

Angel turned to Jay, his face lit up with excitement. "This was where we promised each other that no matter what we did in life, we'd do our best to bring joy into the world."

Jay smiled back at him, ridiculously happy that he'd remembered. "Hell yeah we did. And that's what we achieved. You help make exciting movies that people love, and I help kids to find their confidence and be the best they can be. I think we should be proud of ourselves."

Angel bit his lip and looked up at the sky. "I'm sorry I

haven't been around more, though, dude. That was lame of me."

Jay waved his hand and tried not to let his heart clench. "We've both been busy."

But Angel shook his head. "No," he insisted. There was an earnest look on his face that surprised Jay. "I let Lisa bully me into not seeing you, and then I just threw myself into work. That'll change now, I promise."

Jay patted his arm. His heart couldn't take Angel making well-intended promises that he wouldn't be able to keep. "Let's just focus on you feeling better for now, okay? Starting with getting you out of the cold and filling your belly up with dinner."

Angel gave him a lopsided smile and seemed like he was thinking about what to say. He bit his lip and looked out over the park. "You know you're the best, Jay, right?" he said eventually, his voice gruff and sending dangerous shivers down Jay's spine. "I promise I'll be there more for you from now on."

Jay's heart threatened to summersault again, but he smiled and swallowed down his emotions. "Home," he said gently but firmly. "Sleep. We can talk more about the future after the school's auditions for the film."

Angel's face lit up as they stood. "Oh! Could I come join you for that? I think I could manage to get to the school. Otherwise, I'll just be at home all day."

There he was again, calling Jay's apartment 'home.' How Jay wished that were true.

"You know you're *supposed* to be resting, right?" Jay said as they began walking. His apartment was a little out of town. Normally, he'd be fine to walk, especially to get rid of his alcohol buzz, but Angel was in no condition for that. So he was already opening his Uber app to get them a car. "You snuck off to visit your buddies on the film set today, even though I told you to sleep."

Angel winked at him but did look a little sheepish. "Sorry. I promise I'll stay home all day until the auditions. But I'd like to meet the kids. We never had a club like that when we were young. I think it's awesome."

Jay had to agree with that. Besides, he and Angel were walking proof of one of the best gay-straight alliances the school had probably ever seen.

"Okay, but you can sit quietly in a chair the whole time," Jay told him. "No excitement."

Angel crossed his heart. "I'll be a model student, Mr. Coal."

Jay laughed, then saw their Uber was only about a minute away. Soon, they'd be home, and Jay would have to navigate another night of torment, knowing that Angel was only sleeping down the hall. But he could get through this. It had been kind of cathartic telling his friends his secret, even if his outlook was bleak.

Angel was never going to feel the same way as Jay did, but there was a reason they'd been best friends for all these years. They loved each other in a special kind of way. Even if it was a childish love that was going to fade as Angel moved farther away from Jay, it was still precious.

Jay looked back at their bench before getting in the car. No matter what happened, Jay would always have his memories of Angel, and nothing could take those away from him.

Not even a car crash. Jay dared the universe to even try.

ANGEL

IN THE END, ANGEL COULDN'T FIND THE ENERGY OR THE GUTS to talk to Jay that night. They put the TV on to eat their dinner, then both turned in early for the night. Angel thought after all his exertion getting to the set, talking with Bella and Sabina, then going with Kamran to the bar would have meant he'd have fallen asleep immediately.

But he found himself staring at the ceiling for who knew how long, trying to rehearse the best words to open up his conversation with Jay. At one point, he reached over and spread his hand out on the empty side of the bed, wondering if he really wanted Jay to be there with him.

He'd thought a lot about whether or not this love was really different from friendship, until he'd realized the obvious question he needed to ask himself.

Did he want to kiss Jay? To run his hands over his skin and see him naked? Angel liked to think he was pretty good in bed despite his and Lisa's dwindling intimate relationship toward the end. But until then, he'd been pretty confident. He pictured trailing his lips along Jay's neck, wondering if that would make Jay shudder.

Thinking about it certainly made *him* shudder deliciously.

Angel had always been comfortable being close to Jay when it came to hugging him. Surely, making out and having sex would just be the next logical steps? If that was something Jay would be into.

It was kind of weird thinking about his best friend like that when he wasn't sure how Jay felt, so Angel decided to focus on his own feelings. If he'd tried to kiss Jay (and Michael before him) that must mean he had some interest in guys. So he did something he should have done years ago.

He simply typed 'gay porn' into the search bar on his phone and clicked the image results.

It wasn't like he'd never come across any dude-on-dude action when he'd been browsing porn sites before. But he'd always felt unsure and never clicked on anything. He'd told himself that stuff was totally fine, but it just wasn't for him.

What if it was?

He was suddenly presented with an assortment of naked guys and a lot of hard cocks going into asses and mouths. He gasped a little, his eyes flicking guiltily to the closed bedroom door, but he was alone, and there was no question that his dick had twitched in his underwear. Biting his lip, Angel muted the volume on his phone and began scrolling through the images, looking for a link to click on to find some videos.

The title 'My next-door neighbor turned me gay!' caught his eye, so he tapped on the free site. It was only a montage, not the full video, but Angel didn't need to pay to see the rest. The snippets were good enough.

He swallowed as the clothed guys began kissing on a sofa, laughing as they pawed at each other playfully. That was fucking *hot*. Immediately, Angel couldn't help but picture Jay. If Angel kissed him, that was how he wanted it to be. Fun and loving, just like the rest of their relationship was.

Then the guy on top pulled their gym shorts down,

freeing their cocks, and Angel started aching between his legs. Not overthinking what he was doing too much, he licked his palm, pushed his briefs down, and took himself in hand. He began stroking himself leisurely as the montage showed the guys getting naked, then sucking each other off and fingering their assholes. But Angel liked the shot the most where they were kissing and jerking each other off. They kept grinning and laughing at each other, clearly having a blast.

Even when they moved on to fucking, Angel kept that image in his mind. Although watching the slippery dicks sliding in and out of their asses as they took turns banging each other was fucking sweet, Angel loved the idea that they were friends. That they were having fun and not just getting off.

He was already leaking precum, so his hand was flying over his hard length as the slightly bigger guy bent the smaller one over the couch and rode his ass hard. Without the volume on, he could only imagine their cries of pleasure and the way their skin was slapping together, but it wasn't much of a stretch of the imagination.

This was hot as fuck, and Angel was definitely going to come watching it.

As his climax built, he didn't try to fight it. In the end, he didn't need the video. He dropped his phone onto the mattress and screwed his eyes shut as he let the sensations overcome him. In the throws of his passion, he didn't stop himself from imagining it was Jay's hand on his cock. Angel grunted, his eyes screwed up as he pictured a lot more than just kissing his best friend.

He threw the covers back just in time, coming all over his bare chest rather than making a mess of the bedsheets. He gasped and jerked as his balls emptied, shaking all over from the force of the climax.

He flopped back against the bed, rubbing his dry hand over his forehead, careful to avoid his bandage. He felt every single ache and pain through his body that the car crash had given him, but he didn't care. That had been the best orgasm he'd had in forever, and he was confident that was something he remembered correctly.

"Wow," he whispered to himself, blinking in the dark.

Luckily, Jay had a box of tissues by the bed, so Angel didn't have to dash across the hallway to clean himself up. He mopped up his cum, thankful he'd managed to splatter his chest and not the sheets, then wadded up the tissues into a ball and dropped it on the floor so he could flush it away in the morning.

As much as he wanted to be stealthy and private, he wasn't ashamed of what he'd done. In fact, as his breathing calmed down, he grinned to himself, letting the realization wash through him.

"I think I might be bi," he whispered in the smallest voice, trying the thought out loud for the first time. "I think I'm bisexual. And that's okay."

It wasn't long before he fell into a deep sleep after that, a contentment in his bones that he hadn't felt in a very long time.

"ALL RIGHT, ALL RIGHT," Jay called out, waving his hands at the two dozen students excitedly gathered in the school's auditorium. "Everybody settle down."

They were in a gaggle in the seats while he stood on the stage. Angel and Libby were sitting in chairs next to where Jay was standing. Angel was feeling significantly better for the first time since the crash after spending most of the morning asleep. His venture into gay porn had left him sated and boneless, and his healing body had craved the rest he'd given it.

After a shower, coffee, and some more of the Rise and Shine pastries, Angel had made his way to the school with more of a spring in his step. It was the first day he hadn't put a bandage over the cut on his head, and even though the stitches made him look a little like Frankenstein's monster, not having the bulky material taped to his head was definitely an improvement.

He was still extremely nervous at the thought of talking to Jay about how he was feeling, butterflies swarming his stomach every time he thought about the conversation that needed to happen. But it was being countered by a kind of euphoria that had settled over him. He wasn't sure how long he'd been subconsciously suppressing these kinds of feelings, but he was holding on to the notion that he wasn't straight, and that was okay. In fact, it was kind of awesome.

As Angel looked over the gay-straight alliance club, he bit his lip. These kids would all be so much better educated than he had been, and some of them were only twelve years younger than him and Jay. How different would Angel's life have been if he'd explored these feelings as a teenager instead of at thirty?

He was tempted to feel a little bitter about that, but then he stopped himself. How many people in the generations before him had *never* been able to acknowledge a queer side to themselves? Instead of lamenting the last ten years, Angel decided he was just going to be excited for this new self-discovery moving forward.

One of the students stuck their hand up in the air. "Mr. Coal! Will we get to meet Sabina Max?"

"Mr. Coal! Will we get to take time off school?" shouted another.

"Are all of us going to be in the film, J...I mean, Mr. Coal?" Kestrel asked.

"Okay, so," Jay said, clearing his throat and gesturing toward Libby. "This is Libby Meskin, the casting director for Fallen Angels Club 2. She'll be working with you today and telling you what she needs."

Libby jumped up and grinned at him before waving at the kids. "That's right. Now, I know Mr. Coal has gone over some of this before, but basically we're looking for kids about your age to be on a school bus in stationary traffic when the Angels swoop in and save the day. So I'll be separating you into groups, and we'll be going over some surprised and scared faces, that sort of thing." She beamed at the eager kids before her. "I'm sure we'll be able to have you all involved, but I will be looking for a couple of you to maybe feature in some close-up reaction shots. If that's something you'd be interested in, we can make a note of that and take a few extra photos."

"Oh my goddess, this is so exciting," Kestrel hissed, balling up her fists and bumping shoulders with the girl next to her.

But one of the boys rolled his eyes and raised his hand. Angel wouldn't call himself an expert in queer culture by any means, but from his prissy, pinched expression, this kid looked like a queen bitch. Sure enough, he gave his fellow classmates a scornful look before addressing Libby. "I think the actual gay students should get preference over the allies. Otherwise, that's just homophobic."

"Now, Blair," Jay said, waving his hands in a calming motion as several kids started to protest. "Everyone here will get a fair shot. You're all a part of the alliance, and Libby is excited to meet everyone."

"Yeah, Blair," Kestrel said with a scowl. "Who gets to decide who's queer enough? You?"

Blair scoffed and inspected his perfectly manicured nails.

"Well, certainly not you, Kes Coal. You *say* you're pansexual, but have you ever even kissed a girl?"

Kestrel spluttered, and her face went red, and Angel's heart went out to her.

"That's not..." she managed to stammer.

"Hey now, none of that," said Jay sternly, glowering at Blair. "No one has to prove their sexual or gender identity to anyone here to be valid. We've been over this *many* times. We're an LGBT plus community, and if you want to be in this club, that's enough of a membership requirement for me."

"Yeah," Angel piped up, getting excited. "You don't have to kiss anyone or date anyone to know you're bi or...whatever."

Blair blinked at him, and Kestrel raised an eyebrow, looking amused.

"And I'm sorry, but you are?" Blair asked in disdain.

Angel felt his mouth hanging open. Embarrassment threatened to envelop him. He was just here to observe, not take part, and he was nowhere near ready to tell anyone that he might be bi yet. But he was saved from answering as the doors at the back of the auditorium suddenly burst open, and a group of people started walking in.

On second thought, Angel would have rather answered Blair's question.

As soon as the doors flung inward, a collective chant of *"Protect our kids!"* began. About half the crowd had signs on sticks like they were at a political rally, the slogans all about 'family values.' Angel stood up, immediately on alert as more and more people poured in. There had to be at least fifty adults and several students storming down the middle aisle of the auditorium.

"On the stage, now!" Jay barked, motioning for the kids to come climb up with him, Angel, and Libby. Angel jumped forward and began helping the panicked students up, but some of them were several rows back in the seats, in the middle, not near the aisle.

Including Kestrel and her friend.

Angel didn't think. He lowered himself down off the raised platform, careful of his bad knee, and marched down the aisle, ignoring his protesting knee. He put himself between the mob and everyone else, hoping to give Kestrel and her friend enough time to clamber out of their seats and get up onto the stage.

"Hey, assholes!" Angel yelled at the top of his lungs. "What the fuck do you think you're doing?"

Of course it was Kenny Brooker leading the charge, and he folded his arms over his crumpled beige shirt as he came to face Angel. "We're stopping this immorality," he boasted proudly. "I told you the town wouldn't stand for this."

Angel smirked and looked over the sorry bunch of bigots who had at least stopped chanting. "This doesn't look like the whole town, Kenny," he said in an amused tone. "It looks like a few people with nothing better to do than terrorize a group of teenagers."

"We disapprove of this club and this film!" one of the women yelled. She had a young teen by her side who looked like she would rather be literally anywhere else than there.

"Nobody is making your daughter join this club or watch the film when it's released, Mrs. Reed," said Jay in a loud, clear voice. "I will not allow the intimidation of my students on school property. Please leave immediately, or I will be forced to call the police!"

Angel glanced behind him to make sure that Kestrel and all the other kids had made it onto the stage and were behind Jay and Libby, which they were. Angel's battered body was not up to this, but he balled his fists and stepped closer to Kenny, glaring down at him.

"I won't let you bully these kids," he growled.

He was using his body to take up as much of the aisle as he could to make it clear to Kenny that he wasn't getting past without a fight. The crowd had fanned out behind Kenny into the rows, so most of them were inside the auditorium and could see Angel. Thanks to the bolted-down seats, it would vastly slow down their approach toward the stage if they started climbing over, but they still outnumbered the GSA two to one.

"This is crazy, Kenny!" Angel cried. "What are you going to do? Assault a bunch of students?"

Kenny spluttered. "Of course not! We're exercising our freedom of speech by stopping these auditions. We don't want our school associated with this pornographic filth!"

That got a loud chorus of cheers, and the mob started chanting again. *"Protect our kids! Protect our kids!"*

Angel laughed, though, and held his hand out, palm vertical, as Kenny tried to move forward. "You know you're talking shit, right?"

"Watch your language, young man!" Mrs. Reed shrieked. "There are children present!" Her daughter cringed and tried to move away from her.

Angel scoffed. "Lady, you're the one who brought your kid to a hate rally." He fixed his attention back on Kenny. "What's it going to be, Brooker? Are we going to have to call the police?"

"I already called them," said Libby calmly from the stage.

"On what grounds?" spluttered Kenny.

"Disturbing the peace, harassment, hate speech, trespassing," Libby said, counting on her fingers.

"And I called the principal," Jay added, far less calmly. "She's on her way from her office right now. Get out of here, Mr. Brooker. You're scaring my kids. They've done nothing wrong, and I will press charges against every single one of you if you don't leave now."

Kenny just smirked, though. "You can't do that. We have rights."

"Mom," Mrs. Reed's daughter pleaded. "I don't want to go to jail!"

Mrs. Reed laughed hollowly. "He's bluffing, sweetheart."

"Rebecca, are you okay?" asked Jay.

She had to only be around fifteen, probably a freshman. She bit her lip, then vaulted over the chairs, running down the clear row toward Angel.

"Screw this! I'm going to go stay with Dad!" Rebecca yelped as she tore past Angel.

Mrs. Reed squeaked and tried to push her way past the other people in her row, but there was no room to move. She had a pencil skirt on, so she wasn't climbing anywhere. "Rebecca Reed, you get back here this instant!"

But Jay helped her onto the stage with the other kids, and the girl turned around to face her mother. "You're wrong, Mom! These kids are nice, and I won't stand there and watch you be mean to them!"

Kestrel stepped forward and wrapped her arm around the smaller kid's shoulders. "Hell yeah," she shouted.

"You're on the wrong side of history," Angel bellowed. "All you're doing is terrorizing innocent kids. You should be ashamed of yourselves." He jammed his hand back toward the students on the stage. "There are plenty of Black kids up there with the white ones. Are you going to protest the fact they should be segregated, too? How about the Jewish ones? Are they allowed? Or we could go back to basics and protest all the girls getting an education. How about that?"

"Oh," said Blair in a loud whisper. "I take it back. I like him. He can stay."

It had not escaped Angel's notice that several members of the mob were Black or Hispanic, not to mention over half of them were women, and he had no problem with scowling at all of them for their damned hypocrisy.

"That's completely different," Kenny spluttered in horror. "We're not racist! This is about morals! People are born Black. These kids are being corrupted!"

"I was totally born this way!" Kestrel yelled back at him.

"Yas, qween!" Blair chimed in, clicking his fingers either side of his face. "Mama Monster declared it so!"

"It's exactly the same, and you know it," Angel snarled. "This is hate speech and you're all taking part in a hate crime."

"What the hell does it have to do with you anyway, Shields?" Kenny snapped at Angel. "Why are you always getting involved with Coal's perverted business? You're not gay."

It was like Angel didn't even have control of his mouth. He was so angry and so worried about how this attack was going to fuck up these kids' mental health that he just spat out the first thing that came into his head.

"Actually, yes, I am," he barked, feeling his eyes blazing as he glared at Kenny, then swept his gaze over the mob. "I'm bisexual, and I stand with everyone on that stage. And even if I weren't, I'd *still* stand with them because it's the right thing to do!"

Kenny's face was doing something interesting that might have been funny if Angel hadn't been so worked up. "But – but you had *girlfriends* at school!" Kenny spluttered.

Angel managed a rueful laugh. Sabina was right. "Yeah, Brooker, that's literally what bisexual means."

Kenny's expression went from confused to vicious triumph in a flash. "I always knew you were a filthy *faggot*," he hissed in Angel's face.

It felt like Angel had been doused with cold water. He'd heard that word hundreds of times, but it was something else entirely to have it spat in his face. Shame rinsed through him, quickly followed by rage. He felt his fist clench in a distant kind of way, like he wasn't quite in control of his extremities.

Before he could do something monumentally stupid, a commotion from the stage made him look over his shoulder again.

Principal Archer hadn't changed much since his own graduation. Angel felt like the cavalry had arrived as she stomped up on stage from the wings in her old brown leather Mary-Janes, snatching up her glasses from where they'd been hanging from a chain on her frilly blouse, and snapping them on her face to glare out at the crowd.

"I demand an explanation for what is happening *immediately*." Her voice boomed, echoing off the walls of the auditorium like she was using a loudspeaker.

At the same time, the back of the mob that was spilled out into the lobby started fidgeting as shouts came from local law enforcement. "All right, break it up, people!" a familiar voice bellowed.

Angel breathed out a sigh of relief as exhaustion washed through him. As much as he'd been prepared to stand his ground between the mob and the kids (not to mention Jay), he'd rather have Detective Padilla and her uniformed officers lend a hand.

He flicked an eyebrow in triumph at Kenny, then turned and walked back to the stage. It took everything he had not to collapse or to limp too obviously on his bad leg, but somehow, he made it down the aisle and sat on the edge of the raised platform without incident.

It was amazing how quickly the mob could back themselves out of the auditorium now that there were half a dozen police officers present. Principal Archer marched down to where Kenny was arguing with Padilla. She calmly raised an eyebrow and took a sip of her coffee as he yelled in her face about his constitutional rights.

Angel was overcome with tiredness, and everything felt kind of blurry as he breathed deeply, gripping the edge of the stage. His body was still healing, but the emotional toll of the confrontation had wiped him out completely.

"Hey, are you okay?"

He blinked, realizing Jay was crouched down next to him. "Huh? Oh, yeah, great," Angel said. His smile felt a little woozy, but Jay's face was close to his and…yeah…there was that feeling bubbling inside him again like Champagne. He could totally lean over and press his lips to his best friend's. Not now with all this chaos going on. Not for the first time. But…maybe later?

He felt his smile get bigger as he realized what he'd done. He'd *come out* in front of all these people. In front of Jay. Surely, this would make their conversation later much easier. Excitement and nerves danced inside Angel as he watched Jay's face, but at the moment, he just looked worried.

Jay pressed his hand to the unhurt side of Angel's forehead, checking his temperature. "I need to deal with the detective and Kenny, then make sure the kids are all right. But then I'll get you home, okay?"

Angel shook his head. "I'm fine, dude," he assured him. "Hopefully, the badges will get those idiots out, and you can do the auditions as planned."

But even as he suggested it, he looked over to see the kids hugging each other and looking stressed. Some were even crying. Angel bit his lip. Of course they were upset. A mob had just threatened them and told them they were a bunch of amoral perverts. Angel's heart sank. This was the other side of the euphoria he'd been feeling.

He felt slightly sick as the cold sensation washed over him again as he recalled Kenny calling him the F-word. If he was going to be a part of the LGBT community and no longer just an ally, this was the kind of prejudice he was going to have to deal with, too.

That fucking sucked.

Jay shook his head. "Libby is already talking to them about rescheduling or maybe even video auditions so we don't risk this happening again."

He clenched his jaw and looked daggers at where Kenny was now flapping his hands and hissing at both Detective Padilla and Principal Archer. Angel couldn't hear what he was saying, but he certainly seemed to pipe down and back off when Padilla signaled for one of her guys to get out his handcuffs.

"Hey, thanks for that," said Jay, clapping his hand on Angel's shoulder. The contact felt so good, but then he pulled away again.

Angel frowned. "It was the least I could do," he said truthfully. "The state I'm in, I probably wouldn't have made it three seconds if someone had actually started throwing punches. But I've always got your back. You know that."

He winked and grinned, hoping to get a smile from Jay, but he just looked really tired. "I meant saying you were bi. You didn't have to do that. I know you support us, even though you're straight."

Angel's heart dropped.

Jay thought he'd just said that for effect? "No, I—" he started trying to explain.

"Mr. Coal?" one of the kids called out tearfully.

Jay smiled tightly at Angel, squeezed his good knee, then stood up to go back over to the group.

Angel stared after him, then turned back to the auditorium, coldness washing over him.

Jay hadn't believed him. Angel had come out...and the person who mattered most to him hadn't believed it.

He bit his lip and rubbed his arms, hugging himself. Well, it wasn't like he was gay. Maybe Jay didn't think coming out as bi was as important. Not as real. Angel probably didn't have the right to 'come out' in the same way as someone who was gay. Or lesbian. Or trans. Those were proper identities, right? Angel was just a guy who was probably straight and had just had a few confusing thoughts about other guys.

Suddenly he felt like a total fraud. Kenny was right. He'd only ever dated women. He didn't have the right to say he was queer like these kids. He should have just kept his mouth shut.

He wasn't going to be gay enough for Jay.

That was suddenly very clear.

13

JAY

There was something wrong with Angel.

Jay had been run off his feet, making sure every single one of the kids got home okay, insisting their parents come get them if they could. Half of the mob had fled as soon as the police had shown up, but a couple of dozen people had hung around like a bad smell, maintaining that their children were at risk.

Rebecca had refused to go with Mrs. Reed. Thankfully, Mr. Reed had left his work the moment his daughter had called him, and the couple had ended up having a heated argument out in the lobby. But Rebecca had been able to go with her dad, and that was good enough for Jay for now.

He was mortified that Pine Cove had let down the film crew again, despite Libby telling him multiple times that it wasn't an issue and she wasn't going to be deterred. But Jay felt like this was his town and his responsibility, and he was absolutely furious that Kenny was trying to fuck him over again, just like when they'd been at high school.

All in all, by the time he and Angel climbed into his car, he was feeling exhausted, fed up, and slightly trembly from the adrenaline. "What an evening," he said, shaking his head as he started the engine. "Will you hate me if we get takeout again? I swear I'll cook something nutritious tomorrow night. But I feel like I could burn an egg right about now."

Angel stirred like he'd been lost in a reverie. "Hm? Oh, yeah. That's fine. Whatever you want."

Jay swallowed, trying to keep his thoughts on food. He was *not* going to obsess over that little charade Angel had pulled in front of the mob. He'd just done that to try and protect the kids. Jay was absolutely one hundred percent going to ignore the way his heart had swooped like the damn bird he was named after at Angel claiming to be bisexual. Angel had just been supporting Jay, like he always did.

But *fuck*, wouldn't it be amazing if it were true?

No. Jay would only hurt himself by thinking like that. He needed to focus on caring for Angel, who not only looked dead on his feet but was also unusually quiet.

"I'm sorry," Jay said, squeezing Angel's arm. "If I'm tired, you must be exhausted. Do you feel like Chinese? I can just order a whole bunch of dishes and whatever we don't eat tonight, you can have for lunch tomorrow."

Angel mustered a small smile as he looked at Jay. "Yeah. That sounds great. Let's do that."

But there was a strange vibe in the car as Jay drove them back to his apartment. *Goddamn it.* This was exactly what he was hoping they'd moved beyond after their heart-to-heart on their special bench last night. Had he done something wrong again? He chewed his lip and tried to think.

Maybe Angel was sick of defending Jay and his LGBT issues. The thought sunk in him like a stone. But it would make sense. Maybe this was why he hadn't come back to Pine Cove for so long. Jay just ended up involving him in some problem or other. Angel was probably fed up with being Jay's shield when it came to Kenny. Just because his surname was Shields didn't mean he had to be one. It was shameful that Jay even still needed help with a school bully, for crying out loud.

In the moment, Jay had been so immensely proud and touched that Angel had jumped up to stand up for him, even when he was injured. But maybe Jay had gotten too used to that. Like a crutch he didn't fully appreciate.

He bit his lip and parked the car in front of his building. There was an awkward silence as they got out, then climbed the stairs to his apartment on the top floor. It was a lot of steps for Angel, but he managed them by himself. Jay wanted to offer to help him, but he wasn't sure if it would be appreciated. They should have brought his crutches, but Angel was supposed to have been sitting down for the afternoon.

Jay scrambled for something to say as they finally reached his floor, but he was saved when he opened the door and Button was on them immediately, barking and jumping and wagging her fuzzy butt like she'd thought they'd died and were never coming back.

"Aww, hey, girl," Angel cooed, bending down to pet her. "Did you miss us? It's okay. Yes, I love you, too."

Jay couldn't stop his heart from melting as he watched his best friend fuss over his best girl. "Angel—?" he tried as he closed the door behind him.

"Hey, man, I feel like roadkill," Angel interrupted with a wince, rubbing his side. "Do you mind if I jump in the shower while you order food? I'll eat anything, no stress."

Jay swallowed his question and made himself smile. He could check in with Angel when he'd had a shower and they had bellies full of food. Everything would be better after some Kung Pao chicken and moo shu pork.

"Sure, hon," he told him. "Take your time. I'll order right

now so it gets here soon, and then make you a bed on the couch. Do you want to watch a dumb action movie?"

Angel's smile felt like a ghost as he leaned against the bathroom doorframe. "Sure. You pick. Nothing I worked on," he said with a weak laugh, then disappeared behind a closed door.

Jay swallowed and fought the overwhelming urge to cry. Oh yeah. He'd fucked up.

He just had no idea how.

THE EVENING WAS JUST as tense. Every time Jay tried summoning the words to ask what was wrong, they died in his throat. Instead, he just kept flitting around Angel like a hummingbird, trying to make sure he was comfortable and had everything he needed.

What Jay needed was a hug.

Angel headed to bed early, looking like a zombie, even though he'd had a hot shower, taken his meds, used arnica gel, and rested all evening. It was like he was soul weary, which made Jay feel sick.

Jay had struggled to eat much, so he ended up boxing most of the food up to put in the fridge. He figured he should take a shower himself or read or go over his lesson prep for the next day, but his eyes kept drifting toward his bedroom door. He was dying to know what was going on in Angel's mind, but he felt like he couldn't intrude. Angel was probably asleep by now, and after all the exertion today, Jay knew he shouldn't disturb him.

He cuddled with Button and flicked through the TV, but after a while Button yawned and took herself off to her basket, leaving Jay alone. He bit his thumbnail, not paying attention to the film he had on at all. The volume was minimal so as not to disturb Angel anyway, so Jay's thought's drifted.

I'm bisexual, and I stand with everyone on that stage.

Jay growled in frustration and turned the damned TV off. Angel hadn't meant it. He'd just been standing up to Kenny. That mob had been no joke, and typical of Angel, he'd just done whatever it took to keep them distracted until the cavalry had arrived. It would be utterly selfish of Jay to interpret his words any other way.

Just because he desperately wanted it to be true didn't mean it was.

But that still left the problem of what was up with Angel. Maybe he really was just tired and in pain, but that hadn't dampened his spirits much in the past week. No, Jay knew Angel too well. There was something bothering him, maybe even eating away at him. Regardless of his own messed-up feelings, Jay had to go see if his best friend was okay or if he was putting on a brave face and suffering alone.

Taking a deep breath, he stood and smoothed his pants down, running his hand through his curls. Nerves fluttered in his belly as he crossed the living room and went down the short hallway to his room. But if he didn't do this, he'd never sleep a wink tonight, and he'd never make it through another day of school if he didn't get a good night's rest.

He had to try and fix whatever was wrong with Angel.

He raised his closed fist, ready to tap his knuckles lightly on the door. Except in the moment he paused, rallying his courage...the door flew inward.

Angel was on the other side, dressed only in a pair of tight boxer briefs and a thin T-shirt that clung to every sculpted muscle of his chest. Jay could still see plenty of bruising on his arms and legs, but thankfully, the dark purple colors had faded quite a bit over the week. Angel's eyes widened as he took in Jay hovering on the threshold.

"Oh, uh," said Jay. He realized his arm was still raised in the air, so he quickly dropped it, hugging himself, as if that might protect him from the complicated wave of emotions that was washing over him. Lust and anxiety warred within him. "Did you…I mean, I just…"

The poor guy was probably just going to the bathroom, and here Jay was, lurking outside his room like a creep.

"Jay," said Angel, like he was still processing what he was seeing. He might have already fallen asleep and woken up again in the time Jay had been out here fretting. It had been a hell of an afternoon, after all.

"Sorry," Jay mumbled. "I didn't mean to startle you."

What had he been thinking? He knew he was going to be stewing on this all through work tomorrow, but that didn't give him the right to wake Angel up when he was recovering. They could discuss whatever was going on tomorrow evening.

"I just wanted to make sure you were okay," said Jay, backing up. He smiled and shrugged, trying not to make a big deal out of it. "Did you need something or…?"

Angel blinked, his jaw clenching. Jay's heart sank. He was just making everything worse.

"Sorry," he said again, shaking his head and turning away. "I'll let you—"

"I meant it!" Angel blurted out, sounding desperate, making Jay stop in his tracks.

Jay's heart sped up, and he licked his lips before slowly turning back around. Angel was clinging to the doorframe, his eyes wide and his mouth slightly parted as he took shallow breaths that made his chest rise and fall.

"I meant it, but you didn't hear me, and that hurt," Angel carried on in a rush. In the dim light from the living room lamp, Jay could see his cheeks getting flushed.

Jay swallowed, willing his heart not to jump to

conclusions. But it was almost impossible when Angel was looking at him so urgently with every muscle on display and the line of his cock clear in the front of his underwear.

"I never want to hurt you," Jay rasped through dry lips. "I'm sorry." He took a breath and stepped closer to Angel. *This can't be happening,* Jay thought. This was like something out of a fantasy he'd only dared dream in his darkest, most desperate moments. "What did you mean?"

Angel worried at his lower lip, dragging it through his teeth. His mouth was wet and plump, and Jay ached with the desire to kiss him.

"Look, this is all so new to me," Angel said, rubbing his closed eyes, then gripping the side of the door again. Even in his battered state, he made such an impressive figure. "I know it's not the same as what you've been through, and that wasn't how I'd intended to do it at all, but the words just came out, and—"

"Angel, what are you talking about?" Jay interrupted, unable to take his rambling any longer.

Angel puffed out his cheeks, then looked Jay in the eye. "I'm pretty sure I'm bi," he said, and all the blood threatened to rush from Jay's body down to his toes.

This can't be happening, Jay thought again. This couldn't be real.

"R-really?" he stammered, hardly daring to breathe. "You never...you never said anything, not in all these years."

"I didn't know before," said Angel in little more than a whisper. "I didn't think I could be. That I was allowed to be."

"Why would you—?" Jay began, then shook his head, changing train of thought. He couldn't seem to breathe properly. His hands were tingling, and his knees felt like they were made of water. "Of course you're allowed to be," he said emphatically. "How do you know now?"

Angel took a deep breath, but his gaze didn't flinch from Jay's.

"Because I'm pretty sure I want to kiss you."

The moment stretched out between them. Jay couldn't seem to look away, but he wished he had a doorframe to cling to as his vision swirled and he felt faint.

Never, not in his wildest dreams, had he ever thought he'd hear those words from his best friend's lips.

This can't be happening. But how long could Jay keep ignoring the evidence that was right in front of his face?

"Angel," he whispered.

It was like something broke between them. Jay wasn't sure who moved first, but suddenly, he was rushing forward, crashing into Angel, gripping either side of his face as Angel threw his arms around him. Their lips met in a needy, frantic burst, smashing together.

After a lifetime of desperate desire, Jay was finally kissing his best friend.

14

ANGEL

WHEN ANGEL HAD OPENED THAT DOOR, HE HADN'T REALLY been sure what he'd been intending to say to Jay. He'd only known that he was tormented and unable to sleep. He was mad at Jay for not listening to him and hurt that Jay thought he'd lie or joke about something like that, but the truth was, Jay had no reason to suspect that Angel might not be straight. He'd never given him any hint of it, after all. Hell, Angel had pretty much hidden it from his own self.

But Angel had sworn to himself that he wasn't going to hide any longer, even if it was hard. Being bi was as real as any sexuality, and it was nothing to be ashamed of. If he kept telling himself that, then maybe he'd start truly believing it. But he also needed to know that Jay believed it too.

A logical part of Angel's brain argued that of course Jay had to be okay with it. Aside from Robin, all his siblings were bi or pan. But no matter how hard he tried, Angel felt vulnerable when it came to himself. All those nasty jibes from his years with Lisa kept floating around his head, telling him that he was just being an attention seeker, that he was just messing Jay around. As he'd lain in bed, a voice that sounded a lot like Lisa's kept telling Angel that Jay wanted a *boyfriend*, not some inexperienced baby bi guy who didn't know how to be with another man.

Well, that was what he *had* been thinking. Until Jay had launched himself at Angel, flinging his arms around him and crashing their mouths together.

Jay's face was stubbly, but the kiss was hot and desperate, and really not that dissimilar to kissing a woman. His chest was flat as it bumped against Angel's, but the hardness was a different kind of turn-on.

And then there was the bulge between his legs that was rubbing against Angel's thigh. That was a wholly new and fucking erotic feeling. Angel moaned as he plunged his tongue into Jay's mouth and dropped his hands to cup his ass through his jeans. He pulled him closer, making sure Jay could also feel his dick against his hip.

He didn't want the moment to end. He was floating, and he could have quite happily not have had another thought until he'd orgasmed his brains out. But Jay pulled away, panting and cupping the side of Angel's face. They stared into each other's eyes as they gasped, and Angel moved his hands up to cling to Jay's waist. If Jay wanted to talk, it was probably best if Angel wasn't groping him.

"You kissed me," Jay said faintly, his eyes flicking back and forth as he searched Angel's gaze.

"You kissed me, too," Angel pointed out breathlessly. "I... it was nice."

Nice? It was amazing! But it was like the words were dying in Angel's throat as he waited for Jay to keep talking. Did Jay regret it? *Please, please don't be about to say you've made a mistake*, Angel thought desperately.

Jay bit his lip, his cheeks flushed. *Fuck*, he was beautiful. How had Angel never seen him in this way before? How had he never had these surges of lust pulsing through him? Had he really been that scared of his own feelings? Or just blinded by Lisa's steadfast prejudice?

As bizarre as it was to think, thank fuck for that car accident and Jay's fake fiancé scheme.

"What's happening?" Jay asked, fairly enough. His hands felt warm and secure on either side of Angel's neck, his thumbs gently caressing his cheeks. "I've been right here, this whole time, available for kisses. Are you telling me now something's different?"

Angel's breath caught in his throat. "Do you...are you saying you wanted to kiss me before?"

The sound that escaped Jay's chest was a cross between a sob and a laugh as he rolled his eyes and looked away. "Maybe," he said in a small voice, looking down at the floor, like he was afraid to meet Angel's eye now. "But I always thought you were straight. Why didn't you tell me you were bi?"

Angel's heart skipped a beat. Did Jay have feelings for him? Since when?

"I didn't know," he said truthfully. "I might only be a little bit bi. But there was this one guy I maybe thought..." He trailed off and shook his head, not wanting to waste a second thinking about Michael. "I didn't think someone like me could be queer. And Lisa was pretty clear that bisexuals were liars and cheats. It's why she stopped me from seeing you. I think...I think she worked out something before I did."

Jay looked back up at him, his eyes wide. "Which was?"

Angel took a deep breath. No more hiding. Even if this changed things between him and Jay, he couldn't deny this side of him anymore. "That I *do* find some men attractive. I find *you* attractive. When I thought we were engaged, I was so happy. It seemed totally believable to me. And when you told me that wasn't real...well, that made me really sad."

"Oh, Angel," Jay said, his eyes wide and shimmering with unshed tears. "Are you serious?"

Angel nodded, biting his lip and feeling high from the hope that was lifting him up like a hot air balloon. "It was like something inside me woke up. Jay...I think you're amazing. I always have. But I think that might mean something more than just friends to me now." He closed his eyes briefly and swallowed. He had to check. He didn't want to make any assumptions. "But if that's not the way you feel, that's okay. But I do definitely think I'm bi, regardless."

Jay blinked, cupping the side of Angel's face and sending shivers down his spine as he opened his eyes again. "Angel... in case kissing your face off didn't make my intentions clear, I'll say clearly that I feel like that, too. About you, I mean. I have for a long time. But I never thought...oh, god," he choked back a sob and buried his face against Angel's neck. Angel gasped and rubbed his back, hugging him close.

"Oh, Jay," he murmured, nuzzling against his soft curls. His worries melted away like snow on a sunny day.

Jay felt the same as him. Their attraction was mutual, not something Angel had made up because of the fake fiancé ruse. Relief washed through him.

His unique scent filled Angel's lungs. He'd always known that everything was just so much better with Jay close by. But how long had Jay been suffering? How had Angel been so completely oblivious?

"Did I string you along?" Angel asked in a small voice. The idea of causing his best friend harm, even unintentionally, was devastating. Holding on to all those feelings for so long must have been agonizing.

Jay shook his head. "No," he said in a muffled voice against Angel's T-shirt. "Of course not. I made sure no one ever knew how I felt. I was terrified if I told you, you'd leave.

I know your job keeps you busy and you have a life outside of this town. I don't ever want to hold you back—"

"Whoa, hey," said Angel crossly, pulling Jay back so they could look at one another. Jay's eyes were watery, and he sniffed. Angel brushed his thumb over his cheeks, wiping away any dampness. "You never hold me back, *ever*. You lift me up. No one believes in me like you do!" He barked out a laugh and grinned at his best friend, hoping to lighten the mood. "You just gave me my first man kiss. How's that holding me back? That's shooting me into the stratosphere!"

Jay still seemed unsure. He had his hands resting on Angel's chest like a barrier between them. "Angel," he said faintly. "I can't...I've been so scared of my feelings for so long. I don't want to lose you."

"You're not going to," Angel promised. "I know this is all new and a bit of a shock, but in a way, it's not. You've been my favorite person my whole life. Is it really crazy that just means something a bit more now?" He waggled his eyebrows and rubbed Jay's arms. "If we're both feeling a spark between us, isn't that amazing? Don't you want to explore that?"

Jay swallowed and looked resolved. "What if it changes everything and ruins our friendship?"

Angel arched an eyebrow at him in a challenge. "What if it changes everything for the *better*, and then we get to be best friends *and* have sex?"

Jay gasped, his brown eyes wide. Like he wasn't really sure Angel was serious until that moment. "You would want that?" he whispered.

Running his hands up and down Jay's bare arms, Angel groaned. "I've been watching gay porn," he said, feeling devilish. "I think I've been missing out on a whole different kind of fun. You feel like giving me a crash course on dude sexy times?"

Jay opened and closed his mouth, flexing his fingers

against Angel's T-shirt. He blinked and couple of times, then shook his head, like he was struggling to find the words.

"You want to have sex with me," he said breathlessly. It wasn't a question. It sounded like a statement he couldn't quite believe was true.

Angel captured one of his hands and brought it to his lips, kissing the backs of his fingers. "If I weren't so banged up, I'd pick you up and throw you on that bed before ravishing you."

Jay let out a needy little moan that went straight to Angel's balls. Oh, yeah, this was definitely what he wanted.

If Jay was in any doubt of Angel's feelings and intentions, Angel wanted to nip that in the bud right now. He took one of Jay's fingers and sucked the tip into his mouth, licking the soft pad and looking Jay right in the eyes. Jay's breath hitched, and his pupils dilated. That was better.

"You're hurt, though," Jay said, his voice a little strangled. "Tired. You should be resting."

For some reason, Angel's aches and pains didn't seem nearly as bad as before. He grinned at Jay and kissed his fingertip. Even just that simple act had his cock pulsing. He wanted more. He wanted *everything*. It sounded like Jay had been wanting this for a long time, and Angel was done holding them back.

"Well, how about you come lie down and *rest* with me," he suggested, starting to walk backward, tugging on Jay's hand, and encouraging him to follow. "You can make me feel better."

Jay bit his lip as he stumbled forward, allowing Angel to guide him. "I can't believe this is happening," he said, shaking his head.

Angel stopped just by the bed and pulled Jay flush against him again so he could cup his face and kiss him. This time, their mouths were less frantic, but there was something deeper and more sensual about it that got Angel's blood racing.

"If you want it, it's happening," he said firmly. "I'm sorry it took me so long to wake up and smell the coffee. But I don't have any hesitations if this is what you want. I am *all* in. Is it a bit daunting? Maybe. But in a fun way. Like I'm about to jump off a building. And I wouldn't do that for a living if I didn't love the thrill."

Jay breathed out and nodded at Angel, a tentative smile on his lips. "Lie down," he whispered.

Angel would never admit it when Jay seemed so skittish, but he was very grateful to get off his feet. As much as he wanted to ignore the throbbing in his knee and the other dozen twinges he had, his body was still recovering from the accident. So he sighed happily as he dropped down onto the mattress and pillows, holding his arm out as Jay crawled beside him, draping his arm over Angel's chest. Angel thought of all those sleepovers they'd had growing up. All the times they'd gone camping, squished together in their sleeping bags in Angel's old tent. They'd cuddled a thousand times before as kids and roughhoused as teenagers.

But nothing compared to the feeling of Jay pressing his lips gently to Angel's, their hands entwined and their bodies radiating heat. Angel was obviously still half-hard in his briefs, but he could also still feel Jay's bulge in his jeans. Angel didn't want to push him into anything, but he was pretty desperate to get him out of that denim.

Instead, he let go of Jay's hand so he could trail his fingers over the curve of his hip as they kissed leisurely. A strip of Jay's skin was exposed between his T-shirt and his jeans, so Angel let his fingers travel along the warm flesh, loving it when Jay shivered.

"Is this okay?" he mumbled against Jay's lips, stroking the small of Jay's back under his T-shirt.

Jay growled – actually growled – and abruptly leaned up to yank his T-shirt completely off, throwing it onto the ground. "Better," he harrumphed, flopping back down.

Angel threw his head back and laughed. "Oh, hell yeah, now it's a party!" He did the same, pulling his satiny sleep shirt off as Jay began struggling with his jeans zipper. Angel helped tug the pants and his socks off, and then they were both suddenly just in their briefs, their cocks standing to attention underneath.

Angel kept waiting for the moment this would feel weird, but it never came. As Jay rubbed all his hot, delicious skin against Angel, he briefly thought back to the porn he'd watched of the two friends.

This was exactly what he'd been hoping for, but also somehow so much better. He didn't feel like he had to impress Jay, but he did want to make him feel good. That was apparently the great thing about unexpectedly getting naked with someone you'd known your whole life, though. Angel knew Jay so well it was obvious to him what he was enjoying, and Angel's nerves that he didn't know what he was doing were melting away.

So what if Jay was different between the legs from everyone else Angel had slept with? Kissing, touching, hugging, and laughing were all pretty universal concepts. When Angel trailed his hand down Jay's side, it was easy to see he loved it by the way he shuddered and bit Angel's earlobe (which Angel *really* liked). This wasn't rocket science. It was sex. As long as they were both into it – which they *definitely* were – they just needed to try and help each other have a good time.

Preferably with orgasms.

"Oh, *fuck*, Jay," Angel grunted as he rutted his cock through his briefs against his leg. He wanted to come, but he wasn't sure how he wanted that to happen.

Well, if he were with a woman, he'd spend a lot of time on foreplay, so he did what came naturally to him and put his hand between Jay's legs, feeling his hard length practically jump into his hand through his briefs. Jay yelled out and gripped Angel's shoulder. "Angel!" he cried, pushing into the touch.

Angel bit his lip and ignored his protesting body. He didn't want Jay to treat him like a fragile thing and ruin the moment. So Angel would allow Jay to grab him as much as he wanted. A hot shower later would probably ease any pain, and he could sleep all day tomorrow if necessary. It would be totally worth it.

"I want to make you feel so good," Angel moaned, kissing and licking at Jay's neck. Right now, all he cared about was taking care of Jay, just like he always had, and yet in a way that he'd never imagined before this week. Despite the gaps in his memory, of that he was certain.

But Jay shook his head, other ideas apparently in mind. "Can I suck you?" he asked breathlessly. "I need...please, Angel?"

Angel couldn't help but laugh. How could anyone resist someone begging to give them oral, let alone Angel's sexy, needy, gorgeous best friend? He was pawing at Angel's body and rutting his cock into Angel's hand while they kissed messily.

Angel's voice struggled to work beyond uttering a vague "Yeah." But he nodded frantically and ground his erection against Jay's thigh, showing him how much he wanted this. Of course he'd had countless blow jobs over the years, but there was something totally new and thrilling about watching his best friend peel down his underwear and strip him naked. It was almost like they were doing something forbidden, except it wasn't.

It was a miracle.

Hungrily, Angel watched Jay make short work of his briefs as well. Then he was straddling Angel, gloriously naked as he hovered over him. Jay's cock was a little smaller than Angel's and curved a bit to the right. But it looked fascinating and delicious to Angel as it leaked precum. Jay caught him staring and gave Angel a shy smile.

"Not freaking out yet?" he asked.

Angel surged upward and seized Jay's mouth for a kiss, holding his chin between his thumb and finger. "I'm fucking horny, is what I am," he said breathlessly. "You're so hot. I was a fucking idiot not to see what I've been missing for so long."

Jay sighed happily and kissed Angel again. "Okay," he whispered. "You asked me to take care of you. I want you to lie back and relax and let me do everything, okay?"

Angel hummed, glad he seemed to finally be getting through to Jay that this was what he wanted. "Sounds divine," he said, flopping back against the pillows. He wrapped his hand around his cock, pumping it up and down and smearing the precum he was gushing along the shaft. "I'm so ready for you."

Jay groaned and batted Angel's hand away. He hurriedly positioned himself between Angel's legs, kissing Angel's stomach and the inside of his thigh as he squeezed the base of Angel's cock. Angel thrust into his hand, his skin damp and tingling in anticipation. He ran his fingers through Jay's dark curls as he nuzzled against Angel's pubes, inhaling deeply. *Fuck*, that was a hell of a sight.

It was nothing compared to watching and feeling the end of his shaft disappear inside Jay's hot mouth, his lips stretching wide as he gulped Angel down. Angel cried out and arched his back as Jay lavished Angel's cock with his tongue, still gripping the base and fondling his balls with his other hand.

Angel panted and trembled, unable to tear his gaze away from the sight. Jay was so breathtakingly confident in that moment, and Angel always felt a physical ache of pleasure when he knew that Jay was happy and secure in his own skin.

Of course, this was a little different from watching him perform in The Importance of Being Earnest.

He looked fucking glorious as he doted on Angel's every need, especially when he reached between his own legs and took his own cock in hand.

He looked up, locking eyes with Angel, and it was like electricity was shooting between them. Angel felt connected to him like never before, and he kept caressing the side of Jay's face and his damp hair as he bobbed up and down. His hand was a blur over his cock, and Angel could feel his climax building inside him.

He wished he could make this last all night, but he knew he was pushing his luck with his battered body anyway, and he was also just so desperate to share this moment with Jay that he was chasing it with everything he had.

"Gonna come!" he grunted in warning, but Jay didn't slow or falter. He just kept his eyes on Angel's as he worked hard, moaning and thrusting into his own hand.

All of a sudden, Angel crashed over the edge, coming hard down Jay's throat, writhing as Jay sucked him dry, urging more from him as he began creaming over his own hand. It felt like minutes, but it was probably only a few seconds until Angel finally spent his load, quivering and gasping against the mattress.

"Holy fuck," he uttered.

Jay wiped his hand over his mouth, then crawled up the bed. Angel immediately grabbed him and hugged him to his side, kissing the shit out of him despite his bone-deep exhaustion. He pressed his lips to Jay's cheeks, nose, eyelids, mouth, and neck, all while digging his fingers into Jay's back and moaning.

Angel knew this was complicated and they had a lot to think about, but he also knew he had zero regrets about what had just happened. He'd thought he and Jay couldn't be any closer than they already were, and now he felt like they were just looking at the tip of the iceberg.

He couldn't wait to dive in and discover the rest.

15

JAY

That had really happened.

Jay stared at the wall, looking at the spines on his bookcase without really seeing them. He was zoned in on the rise and fall of Angel's chest as Jay laid his head on it, their naked bodies pressed together as the sweat cooled.

He looked up, suddenly anxious to see if Angel was freaking out. Jay could cope with that from a random hookup (something he was sad to say he'd experienced more than once), but it would kill him if Angel was full of post-coital regret.

Except after Jay moved, Angel lifted his head and beamed down at him. Relief rushed through Jay, and he released the breath he hadn't realized he'd been holding.

"Hello, handsome," said Angel with a grin.

Jay smiled and tried to relax. "Hi," he said softly. "How are you feeling?"

Angel puffed out his cheeks and chuckled. "I came like a fucking freight train. That was amazing. Dude sex is officially awesome."

Warm pride and even more relief flowed through Jay. "I actually meant all your bumps and bruises," he said coyly. "But I won't lie, that's really great to hear."

Angel laughed again and kissed Jay's temple with a loud "Mwah!" sound. "Yeah, if I'm being honest, I also feel like I've been *hit* by a fucking freight train. But it was totally worth it." He sighed and squeezed Jay again, apparently not fazed by what they'd just done at all. "I can't believe it, but, like, in the best possible way."

Jay exhaled slowly. He'd spent so much of his life fighting his attraction to Angel and trying to hide it that he didn't really know how to react now he'd found out it was reciprocated. It wasn't the same for Angel. It sounded like he'd had a revelation thanks to his memory loss, whereas Jay had been heartsick for the better part of sixteen years.

But did that matter?

Surely, the only thing that mattered was the fact that they were both clinging to one another post-orgasm, smiling and joking around. And Jay might not know how long it could last – Angel was only supposed to be in town another couple of weeks, after all. But in that moment, Jay felt like he could overcome any obstacle.

"We should clean up," he said, reaching for the box of tissues. He suddenly wasn't sure if Angel wanted him to sleep in here or not, but they could discuss that when they were less naked.

Except it seemed that Angel had other plans.

"We could take a shower?" he suggested, suddenly far more energetic than he had been. "I've remembered that I like to shower together after sex," he said proudly, but then he frowned. "Oh, sorry. That's probably insensitive to talk about that stuff, yeah?"

Jay offered him a kind smile and stroked back his blond hair. "I know you've been with other people."

Angel scoffed and shook his head. "Yeah, including Lisa, who was *awful,* and I'm really sorry I let that go on so long." He looked sadly at Jay. "You must wonder what the hell I ever saw in her."

Jay bit his lip and raised his eyebrows. "I just wanted you to be happy," he said evasively. Because yes, he'd wondered many a time what on Earth Angel ever saw in that woman when he'd dated such nice girls at school and college.

"I thought I was, to start with," Angel said, exhaling. "She just had this way of lighting up a room. She was so successful and beautiful. I ignored a lot of the warning signs because I kept thinking this was what I was supposed to want, and when you've been with someone for so many years and you're living together...I guess it's easier to just keep ticking along. I actually think she did me a favor by dumping my ass."

Jay nodded and tried not to compare himself. But he never lit up a room just by walking into it. He didn't have an impressive career at a big company or a six-figure salary. Teaching was the most important thing he could ever imagine doing with his life, but it wasn't flashy.

Angel shook his head and rubbed Jay's arm. "We always did things her way. It took me a long time to realize how manipulative she was. I didn't see it at the time, but she just *happened* to schedule something every time I tried to come see you, and I was so dense it didn't occur to me to arrange something in secret."

Jay frowned back at him and took his hand between both his own. "I think it's a *good* thing that you didn't think to sneak around on your girlfriend, even if it meant we didn't get to see each other. You're trustworthy, Angel. It's an admirable quality."

Angel grinned, losing his melancholy as fast as it had

arrived. "Is 'admirable quality' teacher talk for 'hot'? *Oooh –* am I teacher's pet now?"

Jay laughed and hit him playfully. "Ew, no! None of that teacher-student stuff, okay? But yes, honesty is sexy. Are you happy, you maniac?"

Angel caught him off guard as his expression softened, and he gently caressed the side of Jay's face. "I *am* happy," he murmured. "That was a million times better than jumping off a building."

"Yeah?" asked Jay, shifting a little and not daring to really believe Angel was as all in as Jay had daydreamed for all these years.

But Angel surprised him again with a slow, tender kiss. "Yeah," he repeated, his voice husky. "Because you were there to catch me."

Jay swallowed, casting his eyes down as his heart raced and his eyes filled with tears. He wasn't sure if he was happy, relieved, excited, or just downright terrified that this was all going to go up in a puff of smoke.

"You've looked after me so many times over the years," Jay managed to whisper, looking at Angel's shoulder rather than into his eyes. He felt vulnerable, and not just because he was naked. "I'm enjoying looking after you for a change."

Angel hummed and tilted Jay's face up by touching his chin. His expression was warm and excitable, like a puppy. "And you're doing an outstanding job so far," he rasped. "But I kind of like it when we look after each *other*. So why don't we go do that some more? Say…in the shower?"

He waggled his eyebrows and made Jay laugh. Jay needed to stop second-guessing what was in front of his face. Angel was here, and he was happy. He really didn't seem like he regretted crossing the line between friendship and something more.

Jay still wasn't quite sure what this was now, but he reminded himself that was normal after sleeping with someone or taking the next step in a relationship. There was always that uncertainty – this just felt heightened because it was Angel, and that always made everything more complicated.

Instead, he leaned across to capture Angel's mouth in a gentle kiss that he hoped conveyed the tender emotions he was feeling, then tugged on his hand.

"Okay, then, bossy," he said with a grin as he pulled him to his feet and led him to the bathroom across the hall. He didn't feel at all shy being naked in front of his best friend as they stumbled through the door. Jay groped behind the curtain to get the water going. He grinned and leaned up to kiss Angel again. "One shower, coming up, complete with plenty of care and affection."

Angel hummed and kissed down Jay's neck as the room began to steam up. He wrapped his arms around Jay, who did the same, careful of Angel's injuries as they embraced in the middle of his bathroom. With Angel's arms around him, Jay felt like nothing in the world could harm him.

Not even Angel himself.

No. He pushed the thought away. Angel would never intentionally hurt him, but it would do Jay no good to dwell on what might happen once the film moved to its next location and took Angel with it. Or where Angel's next project might be. His home was LA, and his job took him all over the world.

What they had in this moment was a nice, isolated couple of weeks for Angel to explore how he was feeling with the safety of his and Jay's friendship to protect him. What happened after that would be anyone's guess, and Jay couldn't get his hopes up.

He'd already been given the gift of one night with Angel, which was more than he had ever really dared to hope for his wildest dreams. And it wasn't over yet, so he needed to stay out of his own head and stop getting in his own way. If he didn't appreciate this moment, it was going to slip through his fingers.

So appreciate it he did.

The water was perfectly hot as they stepped under the stream together, washing away the sweat and sticky cum from their explosive union just now. But their hands still roamed over each other's bodies, fingers trailing through the almost-scalding water as they kissed, and it didn't really feel like anything was disappearing. It felt like they were only just getting started.

Jay had to admit that Angel was on to something with this post-sex shower idea. He was still tingling and floaty from his recent orgasm, so when Angel's palm rubbed over his still sensitive cock, Jay moaned and shuddered, leaning against Angel and clinging to his muscular arms. He couldn't come again so soon, but it felt damn good.

"Angel," he murmured as they swayed in the water, the steam coiling around them like a lover's caress, caring for them both.

"Hey, handsome," Angel murmured, kissing Jay's temple.

Jay hadn't forgotten Angel's injuries, though, or the flashes of exhaustion he'd caught behind Angel's eyes ever since he'd opened the bedroom door. So Jay made sure they were thoroughly rinsed off, then shut off the water and reached out past the curtain to grab a towel from the rail to hand to Angel before getting one of his own.

It was so ridiculously domesticated as they dried off, then brushed their teeth with their towels slung around their hips. Of course they'd brushed their teeth together countless times as kids on sleepovers. But this felt entirely different. Angel kept bumping their hips together and winking at Jay, like they were both in on the best secret.

Jay tried not to get ahead of himself, but he couldn't help but wonder if Angel would want to keep what had happened – what was happening – between them a secret. Jay couldn't say he'd blame him if he did. It was all so new and different. But a big part of Jay wanted to shout from the rooftops that he'd finally kissed the love of his life and so much more.

There was another part of him, though, that wanted to be cautious. What was happening between them felt fragile and delicate. As much as Jay wanted to believe this was the start of something, who was to say it wasn't just a flash in the pan? A fling? Angel probably felt safe exploring his sexuality with Jay, but would that last? Surely Angel wouldn't want to be with a man – any man, not just Jay – long term? He'd want a wife and kids someday, wouldn't he?

Urgh, that was biphobic, and Jay knew it. But it was as if he couldn't get logic to apply to anything when it came to Angel. He'd spent the last decade and a half utterly convinced Angel was straight. This would just take a while to get used to, to trust.

Perhaps, just for now, it was best if no one knew things had changed between them. If Jay's heart broke, he'd rather nurse it in private rather than with an audience. He'd hidden his crush away for most of his life, after all.

He shook himself internally as he rinsed his mouth out. He and Angel had kissed barely an hour ago, and here he was bracing himself for the worst. Could he quit worrying and live in the moment for just a second?

He could at least try.

He was soon preoccupied once more as he retrieved the tube of arnica and began to apply the cooling gel to Angel's back as he sat on the edge of the tub. Button had woken up and had come to investigate what was going on in the bathroom, much to Angel's delight if his chuckling was anything to go by as he fussed over Jay's dog.

"Hello, beautiful," he cooed as Jay applied the gel. "Who's a good girl, hmm? Have you come to check up on us? It's okay. We're doing great. Your daddy's taking care of me."

Jay couldn't help but grin as he gently massaged a patch of Angel's back that was still particularly purple. This must have been tender as they'd made out a little while ago, but Angel hadn't shown any signs that he'd been in pain.

Jay was going to have to watch that if – when? – they had sex again. He was Angel's caretaker first and foremost, his friend second, and…whatever this new thing was between them…third. So Jay was going to enjoy the fact he got to take care of Angel and his many bruises while they were both in towels for a change, not almost fully dressed like usual, and not obsess on when or whether there would be a next time.

As Jay finished up his work, Angel sighed and dropped his shoulders. "Thank you," he said softly.

Jay bit his lip and screwed the cap back on the tube. "Are you okay?"

Angel nodded and looked up at him with tired but warm eyes. "Very ready for bed," he said with a laugh.

Jay nodded, understanding. "Come on," he murmured, taking both Angel's hands in his. "Let's tuck you in."

Once back in the bedroom, Angel pulled his briefs and silky sleep T-shirt back on. As he was doing that, Jay took the opportunity to grab some fresh underwear to put on himself, then took the damp towels to hang back up in the bathroom.

When he returned, Angel had collapsed in the bed with the duvet pulled back, and Button had used her mini-steps at the end of the mattress to hop up onto the foot of the bed where she usually slept. For a second, Jay took in the beautiful sight, feeling torn. Angel looked so peaceful and perfect in his bed beside Jay's dog. But should Jay call Button out so he and she could go and sleep on the couch like they had been the past several nights? Or…?

Angel moaned and turned his head from where it had been pressed into the pillow. He rubbed the empty space on the mattress beside him and pouted with his eyes still closed. "Hurry up," he grumbled.

Jay's heart flipped.

Apparently, it wasn't even a question. Angel wanted him to sleep beside him, to stay the night.

"One second," Jay promised.

His heart in his throat from excitement and disbelief, he turned out the lights in the rest of the apartment, then hurried back to Angel's side, wanting to reach him before he fell asleep. But he needn't have worried.

As soon as his ass hit the bed, Angel flung his heavy arm around Jay's middle and tugged him down until Jay was spooned up against Angel's bigger body. Angel nuzzled his nose and lips against the back of Jay's neck and sighed deeply. "That's better," he mumbled against Jay's skin. He splayed one hand over Jay's stomach, and with the other he rubbed little circles over Jay's thumping heart.

Jay wondered if Angel could feel – if he possibly comprehended – how elated Jay was at how easy it seemed for Angel to cuddle and kiss him.

"Night night," Jay whispered into the darkness, covering Angel's hand over his heart, stilling it.

"Night night," Angel echoed. He gave Jay's neck one last gentle kiss, then snuggled against the pillows. "Night night, Button," he added sleepily. Button snorted and rolled onto her back, her little legs sticking up as she went back to sleep.

Jay's heart squeezed with happiness that Angel had even thought about his dog before this amazing evening was through.

For however long Jay had with Angel, he was going to

make the most of it before he left again. He'd take as many of these moments as he could and bottle them up, just in case it didn't last.

But deep down inside him, a foolish, optimistic part of him prayed that it would never end.

16

ANGEL

"Are you sure you feel up to this?"

Angel blinked and looked at Jay as he brought the car to a halt in front of Jay's parents' house. Angel had been here a million times when they'd been growing up. Even though he hadn't seen the three-story house surrounded by pine trees in years, he felt a pang of nostalgia as he looked through the car window.

"I'm sure," he said with a smile, trying his best to ignore the writhing snakes in his belly.

The past couple of days had been a blur of sleeping, Jay cooking them proper dinners each night, then trading the most spectacular hand and blow jobs before sharing Jay's bed together.

Well, not exactly trading. Angel was still working up the courage to go down on Jay. It wasn't that he didn't want to. In fact, he was almost surprised at how eager he was. But he had no clue what he was doing, and he desperately wanted it to be good for Jay. So while Angel had received countless blow jobs in his life, now he was taking notes on what Jay was doing that felt absolutely *amazing* so Angel could try and copy him.

So, in some ways, it felt like things had progressed over the past couple of days. But in other ways, Angel knew he was waiting for the other shoe to drop.

Or – more precisely – he was waiting for the punch to land.

Not that he thought Jay was going to freak out about his sexuality and hit him. Of course not. But Jay was definitely holding back in some way, and Angel wasn't sure why. Usually, he was so good at reading his best friend's moods, so it was unnerving to feel like he was missing something. He'd asked if everything was okay the night before, but Jay had smiled and said things were totally fine.

Perhaps he was just taking things slow for Angel's sake. Being bi had come as a shock to both of them, after all. And Jay had talked about how he'd thought about kissing Angel before. Angel wasn't sure for how long, but he got the impression it was quite a while. Maybe since Lisa had broken up with him? So maybe Jay was just making sure they weren't rushing into anything.

But Angel wasn't being cautious, or at least he didn't want to be. He was all in. Being with Jay felt *amazing*. Certainly nothing like being with Lisa, making Angel realize how much he'd just gotten used to and put up with in that relationship.

Angel wasn't good at talking about his feelings, but he'd hoped now it was the weekend, he and Jay could have some time to try and work out where they stood or what they expected from each other. Angel knew he should bring up his filming schedule, but the truth was, he didn't want to think about the fact that he'd be moving on again soon.

He knew it was childish, but he kind of liked being in this fantasy bubble with Jay where they walked Button around the small park (because Angel wasn't up to more than that yet), snuggled up watching TV, and kissed each other good morning and goodnight. Angel didn't want reality to get in the way of that, so he hadn't been too disappointed when their opportunity to maybe talk about what would happen when Angel left had been delayed.

Jay's mom had called that morning and invited them both over for lunch, and Angel had insisted they go. Not only had Jay's face lit up at the idea of seeing his folks, but Angel had liked the idea of them going over together.

Like they were a real couple and this was something they could do any weekend they wanted.

Angel had known the Coals his whole life, and he hoped that Jay's folks and siblings would accept him as Jay's... boyfriend? Partner? Whatever...just like they had as his best friend. But he and Jay hadn't talked about labels yet, and as Angel looked at the house, Angel realized he couldn't go in there and lie. Just because they hadn't talked about the future didn't mean reality was going to seep into their little bubble anyway.

"Jay?" he said as their seat-belts whipped back into their holders.

Jay turned to look at him with his eyebrows raised. "We can still head home," Jay said, reaching out to rub Angel's thigh. "You look better, but I know you're still sore and get tired quickly. We could—"

But Angel cut him off with a shake of his head and by squeezing his hand. "I really want to stay for lunch and see your family, I promise," he said truthfully. "But I don't want to be checking myself every minute we're in there. I know there are things we haven't talked about. The fact that I'm going to be leaving after next week, for one thing. As much as I know that we're just living in the moment and taking one day at a time...but do I have to keep my hands off you when we're inside?"

Jay inhaled and met his eyes as he slowly exhaled. "I don't want to lie or for you to feel like you're in the closet," he said. "But I don't want to confuse them. We don't even know what we're doing here, do we?"

Angel tried not to let that sting, but Jay was right. Angel was only supposed to be in town another ten days, then the shoot would be moving to Europe. Even though he was injured and not working right now, he was still on contract with the production and would hopefully be able to start working again soon. What was Angel's plan with Jay after that?

He'd worked so hard to get ahead in a career he loved. He might be injured right now, but he'd recover, and he'd be back to pushing himself in no time.

So why did it thrill him so much to see his toothbrush in the cup by Jay's? Why did it feel so natural to do the dishes together and line their shoes up by the front door? Yesterday, Angel had used a burst of energy to put a load of laundry on, and he'd loved seeing his T-shirts and socks mixed up with Jay's. He was still living out of his suitcase, but he'd started folding some of his clothes on top of the dresser, like they were *supposed* to be there.

Would it be so bad if he never left Pine Cove again? At least not on a permanent basis. Could he stay here, with Jay? Would Jay want that? Angel didn't know.

Jay was right. It wouldn't be fair to his family to act all loved up if he and Jay ever wanted to go back to just being friends after this. The thought lanced through Angel's heart, but they had to be practical here: this might not work out, for whatever reason. Angel could remain calm for a few hours and keep his hands to himself. Then he could take Jay home, and they could go back to the safety of their fantasy bubble.

So he smiled and squeezed Jay's hand back. "I won't be in the closet. If we're reserved for a couple of hours in front of other people and want to keep our business private for now, that's totally fine. We'll know the truth. This is a big change, and I'm happy to take it slowly. That's why I wanted to check how you wanted to play this. We'll just be casual. Best buddies as always."

Jay sighed and leaned over to press his lips to Angel's, making Angel's heart race and his cock jump in his jeans. Jay was like a drug, and anytime he got a whiff of him, Angel's body went into overdrive. He was definitely going to have to stay away from him this afternoon. Otherwise who knew what might happen?

Despite all the uncertainty, Angel couldn't help but feel how lucky he was that he'd fallen for his best friend and that his best friend felt the same way. Maybe someday they could be open about that if what they had didn't fade once Angel left town. But for now, Angel could keep a little secret for the sake of simplicity.

They finally got out of the car and freed Button from the back seat, where she took a flying leap onto the ground and went hurtling toward the front door, barking her head off, no doubt alerting the family of their arrival better than any doorbell. Sure enough, Kestrel opened the door in a flash, crouching down so Button could jump into her arms.

"You made it!" she cried at Jay and Angel as Button squirmed and whimpered, her whole fuzzy butt wagging as she licked Kestrel's face. "Mom was worried you might not feel up to it, Angel. How's it going?"

Angel smiled and managed to walk over the driveway without wincing. His knee was still being a bitch, which was why Jay had driven. Angel *still* hadn't gotten behind the wheel since the accident, but as much as it was driving him nuts, he knew his body wasn't quite ready yet.

If Angel was brutally honest with himself, it wasn't just his knee that was stopping him from driving. Not being able to remember the accident at all meant he had no idea what had caused it or how to make sure it didn't happen again. When he thought of driving, he felt kind of sick, which then stressed him out. He loved his job. The driving element especially. But what if he had a kind of PTSD that was going to stop him from working, from doing what he loved?

Those were also thoughts that he shoved into a box marked 'future problems' for future Angel to deal with. He was living in the moment for now. No worrying allowed. In theory.

At least he'd had a checkup at the hospital yesterday evening, and the doc had given him some new PT exercises to do that seemed like they were helping. But Angel was ready to get back to fully operational as soon as possible.

Preferably before he left town. So he could show Jay what he was *really* capable of in the bedroom. Or in the shower. Or on the kitchen counter...

Angel cleared his throat and shoved away all his smutty thoughts. He was just Jay's best friend, going over to see his family like he'd done hundreds of times when they'd been kids. No biggie.

Except some things *had* changed while Angel had been away. A young girl with glasses appeared by Kestrel's side with a mermaid doll in hand and squealed at the sight of Jay's dog.

"Button!" she yelled as the corgi barked and dived for her, almost knocking her over in her enthusiasm. "I missed you *so* much," the girl cried, pushing her sparkly glasses up her nose after Button's enthusiasm had caused them to down. "Daddy said you'd be coming. Let's go play pirates!"

Button barked and spun in a circle, looking up at the girl like that was the best idea ever. Jay chuckled beside Angel and waved. "No 'hello' for your uncle Jay, Imogen?" he teased.

Oh. This was the surprise kid that Jay's older brother, Swift, hadn't known existed until the summer before last. Angel realized he'd just assumed they'd be having lunch with Jay's parents and Kestrel, who still lived at home, but if Imogen was here, that meant her daddies probably were, too.

Who else was going to be in the house? Suddenly Angel felt a little more nervous about playing things cool between him and Jay. He'd been away so long, this wasn't really like all the times he'd hung out when he and Jay had been teenagers. Guilt washed over Angel, like he owed the Coals an explanation for his absence or his complicated feelings toward their son.

Except...his feelings weren't complicated. He loved Jay like he always had...just a little bit more now. Maybe a lot more. He was being ridiculous. He needed to just be himself and enjoy the afternoon. This wasn't like seeing Lisa's hoity-toity parents in Trousdale or going to one of her stuck-up work parties. The Coals were Angel's kind of people.

"Hello, Uncle Jay," Imogen said dutifully. Then she glanced up and apparently noticed Angel for the first time. "Who are you?" she asked suspiciously, pointing her mermaid doll at him.

Kestrel smirked from where she was leaning against the doorframe. "That's Uncle Jay's *special* friend, Angel."

"Oh, are you boyfriends?" Imogen asked easily. Having two daddies probably meant she wasn't fazed, but Angel waved his hands and shook his head as Jay scowled at his sister.

"Oh, no, we're just—" Angel spluttered, not wanting to break his promise to Jay to keep things simple.

We're just sleeping and living together. We're just maybe madly

in love or totally kidding ourselves. We're just stepping out of our
fantasy bubble and working out what the hell we are in real life.

"We've been best friends since we were about your age," said Jay, coming to the rescue.

"Oh, cool," said Imogen, beaming up at Angel. "Do you want to come play pirates as well, Angel?"

"Oh, no, I'm sure Angel doesn't want—" Jay began.

"I'd love to," Angel interrupted, winking at Jay, then smiling down at Imogen. "I hurt my leg last week, so maybe I could have a wooden one instead?"

Imogen gasped. "Oh, yes, and a parrot on your shoulder to keep you company!" She grabbed Angel's hand and tugged him inside. "Button is *my* loyal companion," she informed him in a conspiratorial whisper, "but a parrot is almost as good. I'll show you where the buried treasure is!"

Angel glanced over his shoulder and laughed at Jay and Kestrel as they watched him go. Jay looked apologetic, but Angel shook his head. "I'll come say hi to your folks in a bit," he promised.

"I'll get you a beer," Jay told him in a tone that suggested he'd need it.

But Angel quite enjoyed being pulled into the living room, where Imogen had littered the floor with several more dolls, an empty shoebox that was apparently her pirate ship, and a bunch of colorful plastic jewelry that made a very convincing bounty.

"You can have Mimi," Imogen said, thrusting another mermaid with a purple tail and matching hair at Angel as he carefully lowered himself to the floor. His knee wasn't happy about it, but he could just ice it later.

"Why, thank you," he said, accepting the doll. Button settled herself between him and Imogen, wagging her tail and looking at the dolls like she was deciding which one to maul first.

"She's my second favorite, but it's okay. I know you'll look after her," said Imogen solemnly as she flopped to the floor as well. Angel felt oddly touched by that.

"Here you go," Jay said, appearing behind Angel and offering him a light beer. Now that Angel was on much less pain medication, he'd had a couple of beers with dinner the past couple of days, but he was glad that Jay had gotten him a light one for now. He was so thoughtful like that.

Their fingers brushed as Angel took the bottle, their eyes meeting. Angel's heart leaped, speeding up as his breath caught in his throat. He wondered when this feeling was going to fade – where he felt like he was really seeing Jay for the first time over and over.

"Thanks," he murmured.

He watched Jay leave the room, then turned back to see Imogen looking at him with a little frown.

"Are you sure Uncle Jay isn't your boyfriend?" she asked, toying with her doll's hair.

Angel coughed and took a swig of beer to cover it up. "He's my best friend," he repeated.

Imogen narrowed her eyes and pushed her glasses up her nose again. "Do you have another boyfriend, then? Or a girlfriend? My mummy and daddy *both* have boyfriends, except Micha is Daddy's fee-ahn-say now, which means they're going to get married soon and I get to be a flower girl and wear a princess dress."

Angel blinked. That was a lot of information in one sentence. "That's awesome," he said with a nod. "I bet you'll make a great flower girl. And, um, no. I don't have a boyfriend or girlfriend." *Just a hot AF best friend with benefits and a whole load of unanswered questions.*

Imogen scrunched up her nose and sat her mermaid in the shoebox that someone had drawn a pretty good skull and crossbones on the side of. "I think you'd make a good boyfriend for Uncle Jay. You're pretty, and you like playing mermaid pirates."

"Admirable qualities for a boyfriend," Angel said, trying to keep a straight face. His heart fluttered at hearing someone say he'd be a good boyfriend for Jay, but he tried to ignore that for now.

"Exactly!" Imogen agreed, although Angel wasn't entirely convinced she understood what 'admirable' really meant. She seemed to take Angel's agreeing with her as a sign to push on. "Have you asked him to be your boyfriend?"

"Uh, no," Angel admitted before he realized what he was admitting to.

Imogen rolled her eyes and tapped Angel's good knee urgently. "Silly! You have to ask him, then. Otherwise he won't know how good a boyfriend you can be. Now, we must set sail if we're going to reach Spain by lunchtime."

Angel blinked and realized she was talking about her pirate ship, so he nodded and let her take charge of the game, babbling sweetly on about sea monsters and walking the plank. But he was stuck on her innocent wisdom.

She was *right.*

If Jay was holding himself back because he wasn't sure Angel was committed to taking things further, then Angel would just have to show him how all in he really was. He should stop overthinking and just jump in with both feet. Maybe the B-word was a step too far, but he could move forward in other ways. Bedroom ways. He wasn't scared of his newly discovered sexuality. He was *excited* by it.

And if he wasn't good with words, then he needed to find a way to *show* Jay that.

Today.

17

JAY

"ANGEL'S LOOKING GOOD."

Jay looked over at his brother Swift across the kitchen table. He was sitting with Micha beside him, holding hands. They both grinned as Swift twisted the engagement ring decorated with roses on Micha's finger.

"Especially for a guy who was pulled out of a car wreck last week and faced an angry mob this week," Kestrel added sagely from where she was perched on the countertop.

"If you're not going to help, then *scoot*," Jay's mom said, shooing her youngest away. "Yes, dear. Where is Angel? I've been dying to see him now that he's back on his feet. How's that thing with his memory?"

"He got kidnapped by pirates," said Jay warily. He should have known that with Angel out of the room, his family would jump on the chance to probe. "He's still got no memory of the accident, but the rest of it is pretty okay, and his bumps and bruises are healing. You'll have plenty of time to fuss over him later, Mom."

She sighed as she chopped up veggies, glancing over her

shoulder at him. "He always was such a *nice* young man. I wondered why you two never dated."

Jay spluttered on his beer. "Uh, we've been over this, Mom. He's straight."

The lie stuck in his throat, but there was no way he was outing Angel to anyone.

Except Kestrel frowned as she dropped into one of the free chairs around the table. "He told that asshat Kenny Brooker he was bi in the auditorium," she said with an arched eyebrow. "It was pretty spectacular," she said with a grin to Swift and Micha.

"Language, Kestrel," said their mom.

"Bi? Really?" Swift asked. "That's new."

Jay blinked. He'd been so quick to deny anything was happening or *could* be happening between him and Angel, he'd forgotten all about Angel's declaration. "Oh, yeah," he said stupidly, sipping his beer as he gathered his thoughts. "It is all pretty new. I think he's still thinking things over."

"Oh, like what?" his mom asked eagerly.

Jay rolled his eyes. "Like how he's feeling about being bi, probably. Please don't hound him, okay? This is kind of a big deal and he's working stuff out."

"Is he now?" said Swift with a sly grin. "You wouldn't be helping him with that, would you?"

Jay scowled at him. "None of your business."

"Oooh, that means yes," said Kestrel, tickling Jay's side.

He batted her hand away and huffed. "Guys, I'm serious. Don't be dicks."

"Language, Jay!" his mom cried and shook her head. "No one is being mean, sweetie. We just really like Angel and always have. Aren't you boys even a little bit interested in each other like that? You're such good friends anyway."

Jay licked his lips and looked down the hall. He could just about hear Angel still playing with Imogen, which was a relief. His family meant well, but things were so up in the air between him and Angel he'd hate for him to overhear their well-intended but totally inappropriate questions.

"We're still good friends, Mom."

"And you don't want to be more?" Swift asked, leaning over the table, his eyes shining. "You're *always* on the phone with him. He's your favorite person in the whole world. He hasn't dated anyone since he dumped that awful Lisa, has he?"

"Actually," said Jay testily, "she did the dumping. Angel had been talking about getting engaged before that."

He didn't know why that was important for him to bring up, especially after they'd talked a little about why Angel had stayed with her for so long when she was so awful. But Jay was stuck on that idea of how impressive Lisa still was on paper. She was already so high up in her marketing career, stunningly gorgeous, and a woman. All things that Jay could never achieve or be. Would Angel really want to be with him when that was what he'd had before?

Kestrel wagged a finger at him. "But they never actually got engaged, did they? And why does that matter, anyway? He's single, you're single…"

Jay sighed and looked between his annoying siblings. *It matters because I'm trying not to get my hopes up*, he thought.

"Just because he's come out as bi doesn't mean he's going to start dating men right away," he said, picking at the label on his beer bottle. "Or at all. Like we said in school the other day, no one has to prove their sexuality by dating certain people." He would have said 'dating or fucking,' but his mom wouldn't have liked that. He and Angel might not be openly dating, but they were definitely having sex. *Amazing* sex.

Swift gave him a kind smile and glanced at Micha. "We just want you to be happy, is all, little bro. You gave me some pretty great advice about not getting in my own way a couple of years ago." He looked at Micha with such warmth it almost took Jay's breath away. "I'm just returning the favor. You and Angel look right together. You always have."

Jay bit his lip and scratched some more at the bottle label. "It's complicated," he said in a small voice. He really didn't want to get into the details, because he wasn't sure of a lot of it himself. But the idea that he and Angel looked good together, that they could maybe be a couple one day, lodged in his heart like a prickly burr clinging to a woolly sweater.

He was mercifully saved from further interrogation by the doorbell ringing, and then they were engulfed by the chaos of Robin and Dair's dog, Smudge, running around after Button, as well as Robin and Dair themselves. Angel eventually came and joined them with Imogen clinging to his hand and demanding they sit next to one another at the table for dinner, and Jay couldn't help but feel warm and fuzzy at the fact that his niece had fallen head over heels for Angel.

He knew the feeling.

The way Angel kept giving him little smiles as the noisy conversation flew around them like a swarm of bees made his stomach swoop. And that was nothing compared to the electricity Jay felt every time his and Angel's knees brushed together. He bit his lip and switched to drinking soda. He was driving, so one beer was enough anyway, but he needed to try and keep his thoughts clear.

Angel was leaving in just over a week, and he might not want to continue this little thing they'd started between them. Jay needed to protect his heart and not imagine what it would be like to have Angel over for every family dinner or marvel at how well Angel fit in with everyone. Angel even high-fived his sister, Ava, when she came back in from tinkering with their dad's car in the garage and talked with Jay's dad about football.

Everything was just better with Angel there. Sometimes

Jay felt like he'd been born with an Angel-shaped hole in his heart, and he could only feel complete with him by his side. But that was ridiculous. Jay was his own person with hopes and dreams of his own. But try as he might, he couldn't fight the feeling of *rightness* that having Angel beside him at the dinner table gave him.

The afternoon passed in something of a blur as Jay relaxed and stopped trying to quantify everything. He made himself just enjoy how well Angel got along with Jay's family and stopped fretting over what the future might hold. As they drove home, Angel reached over and squeezed Jay's thigh at one point. They shared a smile, and Angel lifted his hand away again, but Jay's skin felt warm from the touch all the way home.

"Do you mind if I skip walking Button?" Angel asked as they let themselves back into Jay's apartment. "I had a great day, but I'm wiped."

Jay rubbed Angel's arm and took in his tired features. "Of course," he said earnestly. "I'll just take her for a quick run around the park."

But Angel shook his head. "No, no. She's been having quick walks all week. Why don't you take her on a good run, and I'll have a nap? Then when you come back, maybe we could play a board game or something?"

Jay's heart flipped. "That sounds wonderful," he said truthfully. "Okay. I'll be back in about an hour."

He didn't think as he slid his arms around Angel and pressed a sweet kiss to his stubbly jaw, but Angel hugged him back and kissed his hair, so Jay figured everything was still okay between them after an afternoon of hiding their affections. Better than okay, actually. They'd kept things private at the family lunch, but they'd still had a great time, and now they were back in their own little bubble again where Jay got to kiss his best friend.

It wasn't perfect, but it was pretty close.

Even after a day filled with people and other dogs to tire her out, Button was super excited as Jay got her into the car and drove them to one of his favorite walking routes on the other side of town. The light was just starting to fade, so they didn't meet many other walkers in the woods, but Button had a fine time sniffing all the twigs and pinecones and blades of grass that she liked.

Jay strolled leisurely along, breathing the cold, fresh air deep into his lungs as the sun dipped below the tree line. He let his mind wander to what Swift had said at the kitchen table. The Halloween before last, Jay had absolutely given his big brother a not-so-subtle nudge toward his now-fiancé, Micha. It had been obvious from the moment Jay had seen them together that the chemistry was brewing between them, even though they had both thought the other was straight.

Was that what Swift saw when he looked at Jay and Angel together? Jay couldn't tell. He'd always been far too close to the wall to see anything objectively when it came to Angel. But it felt dangerous to hope that what he'd wanted for so long could possibly come true. Angel wasn't going to change his whole life and move back to Pine Cove to be with Jay, surely? There had to be an insane amount of gorgeous men and women back in LA that he could take his pick from.

But while it was just Jay all alone with his feelings up in the woods, he allowed himself to smile, all warm and tingly at the idea that Angel was currently snuggled up asleep in Jay's bed, waiting for Jay and Button to come home so they could play games, watch TV, and make a little light dinner together. It was so simple, but it was all Jay wanted, so for a second, he just let himself indulge in it.

By the time he and Button got back to the car, his hands and the tip of his nose were pleasantly cold. Jay turned his music up on the drive back, singing loudly and badly, a smile on his face as he hoped that Angel had managed to have himself a good nap. Button joined in, yapping and wagging her tail as she danced around on the back seat.

Before they went inside the apartment block, Jay took a second to calm her down so she wouldn't bark the place down and wake Angel up if he was still asleep. Together, they crept up the stairs, and Jay's tummy tingled with anticipation as he got his key out to unlock the door.

He was still uncertain what would happen when Angel left Pine Cove again, but for now, Jay just enjoyed the fact that Angel was waiting for him to come home. He could enjoy the moment while being realistic about what the future might hold.

However, all sensible thoughts flew out the window as he opened the door and saw the inside of his apartment.

That wasn't the way he'd left it.

He gasped, and Button looked up at him, waiting at the threshold. The floor was strewn with rose petals. The lights were off, but the apartment was illuminated by what looked at first glance to be a hundred flickering tea lights. Soft instrumental music was quietly playing from Jay's sound system, and the air smelled of something spicy and woodsy.

And there, perched on one of the breakfast barstools, was Angel. He was wearing a dark blue shirt instead of his earlier sweater, and a single, long-stem rose dangled from his fingers. He bit his lip and stood up, looking through his eyelashes at Jay, who was still standing in the doorway with his mouth hanging open like a goldfish.

"Hi," said Angel, his voice low and sultry.

Jay blinked and stepped inside, letting the door close behind him. Button trotted inside and then made a sudden beeline for her basket, where she discovered a large meaty chew that hadn't been there before. Jay gulped and looked around the apartment again before settling his gaze on Angel.

"Hi," he said weakly.

Angel approached him, his eyes not deviating as he purposefully walked up to where Jay had frozen. Carefully, he eased the keys from Jay's hand and dropped them in their bowl on the table by the door, then he held out the rose for Jay to take. Carefully, Jay took the stem near the bottom where there weren't any thorns, and let the large head of crimson petals brush his nose.

"I thought you were taking a nap?" he rasped.

Angel grinned and touched Jay's hip. "I ran to the grocery store on the corner instead. I hope this is okay?"

"Okay?" Jay squeaked, looking around again in disbelief. "This is the nicest, loveliest…" He shook his head, unable to get his words out. "Angel?" *What does this mean?*

Angel brushed the back of his fingers against Jay's jaw. "This isn't a phase. I'm not experimenting. My eyes have been opened by you – *for* you – and I don't want to go back to the way things were before. We can go as slow as you want with telling people or labeling anything, but I want everything for us, Jay. I didn't know how to tell you how into this I am, so I thought I'd try and show you."

Jay blinked back tears and looked at all the rose petals on the floor. Angel must have worked like a maniac to buy and then set all this up in just an hour, and yet he was calm and smelling divine, waiting patiently for Jay to take it all in.

"Oh, Angel," he whispered. "I love it." *I love you*, he wanted to add, but he didn't want to overwhelm Angel. He'd been feeling this for years, and Angel was just discovering it. But…

Well, if this was anything to go by, maybe he was catching up to where Jay was faster than he'd thought.

He reached up and cupped the side of Angel's bristly jaw, his heart somersaulting as he leaned up to press their lips together in a gentle, loving kiss. "I think you did a pretty good job of telling me *and* showing me. I'm all in, too," he assured him. "I want to give you everything."

Angel rested their foreheads together and sighed happily. "You already do."

Jay bit his lip and started walking them toward the bedroom, where he couldn't help but notice there were even more rose petals and candles. "Can I show you how much you mean to me?" he asked.

Angel gave him the most delicious growl as he began unzipping Jay's coat. "You can show me *everything.*"

Jay intended to.

18

ANGEL

ANGEL WAS WORKING VERY HARD TO LOOK COOL AND collected on the outside, but inside, his heart was racing like a jackhammer.

As he'd sat there waiting for Jay to come home, he'd kept envisioning Jay walking in and asking what the hell was going on. Or telling Angel that he'd missed the mark and got it all wrong, that this was just sex between them and to clean up the mess immediately. Or just simply laughing at Angel for being ridiculous, then cooking dinner and ignoring that anything was even amiss. Those were all things that Lisa would have been capable of.

But seeing Jay's eyes shine with happy tears as he stared at Angel's hard work with unbridled joy was one of the most beautiful things Angel had ever seen. And now they were stumbling into Jay's bedroom, discarding Jay's coat on the floor and falling on top of the rose petal-covered duvet.

Angel hadn't been sure if the grocery store around the block from Jay's place was going to have everything he'd wanted. In all honesty, he'd just run over there with a general idea of 'romance' and hoped for the best. But he'd gotten incredibly lucky when they'd already been selling bouquets of roses in anticipation of Valentine's Day in a few weeks' time.

Angel didn't want to think about how much money he'd blown on flowers, only to rip their heads off, but the effect of all the petals combined with the cheap pack of a hundred tea lights had been astonishing. Angel had even Instagrammed it with the caption 'Special surprise for a special someone.' Now that Angel knew that Jay loved it, he was going to ask if it would be okay to tag Jay in the post.

Later, though. Now, Angel had plans. Lots of them.

"Oh," said Jay breathlessly. He stopped Angel as they bumped against the bed, and looked at the nightstand. Angel had been living out of his suitcase, but he'd thrown all his crap back in it and shoved the thing in the corner. He didn't want Jay distracted by any clutter, so what he'd spied had been the items Angel had intended him to see.

Angel bit his lip and grinned as Jay's eyes widened. Angel had gotten a box of condoms and a bottle of lubricant, as well as a squeezy bottle of chocolate sauce. As much as he was ready to take the next step with Jay, he didn't want to stop having *fun* first and foremost.

Jay blushed and touched the rose he was still holding to his nose again, peering coyly at Angel through his eyelashes. "All in, huh?"

Angel nodded and rocked them both with his hands on Jay's hips. "I want you to show me exactly what you like. I want tonight to be special."

Jay sighed happily and bopped Angel's nose with the rose head. "It's *already* special. And I'm happy to get more adventurous, but there are lots of ways to do that. I don't want to do anything you're not comfortable with."

"I'm comfortable with *everything*," Angel insisted, nibbling at Jay's neck and skirting his hands under his T-shirt.

But Jay laughed and kissed his temple back. "I mean *literally*. Bottoming can be quite a shock until you get used to it. I like to do both, but maybe today you'd like to top?"

Angel moved to give Jay a warm but slightly firm look. "Do you always have a contract negotiation before you fall into bed?" he asked, not unkindly.

He was normally a 'go with the flow' kind of a guy. But then...Lisa had made it clear from the beginning what she wanted, and Angel was just expected to do some variant on that each time.

It was actually really quite adorable that Jay was asking him what he liked. But Angel wanted passion. So he ignored his aches and pains as he scooped Jay up and spun him around before dropping him on the bed, making the petals flutter around them, and crawling over the top of him. Jay squealed and giggled, and Angel grinned.

His heart raced. It was easy to forget his remaining injuries when his body was flooded with adrenaline and his cock was already as hard as granite. He wanted Jay so badly, and here he was underneath him, looking fucking *delicious.*

"That's better," he growled, plucking the rose from Jay's hand before one of them got pricked in the wrong sort of way and dropping it on the nightstand. "Now, this is *your* fantasy. I don't care what will be most comfortable or polite. I'm not sending any formal invitations here. I'm going to ravish you, and you've got about three seconds to tell me how you'd like that to happen before I just go ahead and start sticking things in holes. Three..."

"Oh, god!" Jay cried, half laughing, half sobbing. He seized Angel's shirt and crushed their mouths together. "Fuck me, please. Hard," he mumbled between kisses. "I want to feel you for days. I want you inside me so badly. I want you to lose your mind because of me."

"Fuuuck," Angel moaned, biting Jay's bottom lip and

palming Jay's stiff cock through his jeans. Those desperate pleas of *'I want...I want...'* were like electricity straight to his balls. "Good plan. I can do that."

He sat up and began undoing his shirt buttons. He'd been aiming for sexy and suave, but now he wished he had a T-shirt that he could just rip off. But Jay immediately reached up to tug the shirt from Angel's jeans and attack it from the bottom, so they soon had it opened all the way as their hands met in the middle.

Angel flung the shirt away, disturbing the air and creating a mini tornado of rose petals swirling through the room. Jay giggled as a couple of the petals landed on Angel's naked torso, sticking to his skin. Angel's heart ached as he watched Jay run his hands over his chest and arms, knocking the petals off him.

"You're gorgeous," Jay whispered.

"So are you," said Angel, kissing Jay's sweet lips again.

Ignoring his body's aches and pains, he helped Jay with his clothes as well until they were both naked and Angel had so much delicious flesh pressed together.

They'd come like this the other night, with Jay holding both their slippery cocks so they could thrust into his hand. But it wasn't the same as being *inside* someone. Angel sucked on his fingers, then hungrily slipped them between Jay's crack, rubbing his most intimate area.

"Oh, fuck, *fuck,*" Jay cried with his eyes screwed up, gasping.

He clung to Angel's shoulders, then bit his collarbone. Angel yelped and grinned. He remembered how expressive Jay was on stage when he was performing, but he was even more playful in bed, and Angel *loved* it.

"With lube?" Jay uttered, meeting Angel's eyes as he pushed his hole against Angel's fingers. He was flushed and panting and oh-so gorgeous. "Stretch me?"

Lisa would never have dreamed of lowering herself to anal or even pegging Angel, and his previous girlfriends had been too inexperienced to suggest anything like that. So this was new territory for Angel. But he'd done some sneaky research, and he trusted Jay would tell him what felt good. As much as Angel would love to try bottoming at some point, tonight was all about what Jay would love.

Besides, Angel had enough new things to try already. He didn't want to rush everything at once. He wanted to take his time exploring this shiny brand-new side of his and Jay's relationship.

As he pushed his dripping wet middle finger inside Jay's impossibly tight, hot hole, Angel watched Jay's face intently as several emotions played over it. Jay gasped at the intrusion, then groaned, his eyes fluttering as he bit his lip. *"Yesss,"* he hissed, rocking his hips as Angel pulsed the digit farther inside him past the knuckle.

Crooking his finger, Angel found the little nub of Jay's prostate. The way Jay jerked and gnashed his teeth was intoxicating, and Angel rushed downward to capture his mouth and taste all his pretty little moans as they escaped.

"Yes, Angel, like that," Jay begged breathlessly, gripping Angel's side and nipping at his lip. Angel nuzzled their noses and cheeks together, inhaling Jay's unique scent of clean soap and musk as he licked and kissed his damp skin.

Jay whimpered as Angel slid his finger out, but Angel chuckled and kissed Jay's pouty mouth. "No need for that, handsome," he soothed, dripping more lube over his hand. "I've got lots more unspeakable things I'm going to do to you yet. Trust me."

"I do," Jay whispered earnestly.

For a heart-stopping moment, Angel looked into his eyes and saw his best friend dangling from a railway bridge, seconds from death.

But Jay had trusted Angel then, and Angel hadn't let him down. He wasn't going to let him down now. Not now, not ever.

In that moment, staring into Jay's wide, vulnerable eyes that were filled with longing and trust, Angel knew he'd do whatever it took to stay with Jay. He'd find a way to get around work and travel. He'd do *anything* to make sure he was the only one in Jay's bed from now on.

Before he could get overcome with emotion, he kissed Jay tenderly and pushed two fingers inside him, making Jay squirm and gasp against Angel's mouth. Then Angel trailed his kisses down Jay's neck and chest until he found one of his nipples to nip and suck while Jay ground down on Angel's fingers. Adding a third finger, Angel continued kissing past Jay's belly button and along his happy trail, nearing closer to his destination.

Angel didn't care about perfect anymore. He'd been holding himself back because he wanted things to be just right for Jay. But there was a difference between perfect and enthusiastic, and Angel knew what he lacked in technique he'd soon make up for with effort. So he sheathed his teeth with his lips and took the plunge, wrapping his mouth over Jay's hot, hard, leaking shaft, absolutely fucking loving the way he jumped and moaned, thrusting up into Angel's mouth.

For about a second, until it hit the back of his throat and gagged him.

"Sorry, sorry!" Jay cried as Angel choked, and his eyes watered, but he wasn't going to be deterred.

"No, it's fine!" he spluttered and cleared his throat before getting right back to it, just this time swallowing a little less.

He loved the salty, musky taste and how it felt rubbing Jay's tip against the inside of his cheek. He loved the pitiful noises Jay was making even more. Angel was undoing him, and he *loved* it. When Jay grabbed Angel's hair and tugged, it sent zings of electricity jolting down his spine. Angel was pretty sure he was in heaven.

He lapped and licked and sucked and nipped as his fingers continued to thrust inside his lover. He stroked Jay's prostate again and licked his taint the way Jay had done to him the other night, and was rewarded with a beautiful sob that echoed from deep within Jay's chest.

That was what he'd been going for. Angel wanted tonight to be *utterly* unforgettable.

He came off Jay's cock with a deep breath, a string of saliva stretching between his mouth and Jay's shiny red cock until it broke. Angel licked his lips and nuzzled his nose against Jay's thatch of dark curls, breathing in deeply again. As much as he wanted to move fast and chase their climaxes, he also wanted to make this last. The whole point of tonight was to show Jay – to *completely* convince him – that it might have taken Angel a while to wake up and smell the coffee, but now that he had, he was all about that dark, glorious caffeine.

He pulled his fingers free and wiped them on the bedsheet. Jay was a quivering mess below him, his skin slick with a sheen of perspiration and his wet, pink lips parted as he breathed heavily. His wide eyes watched as Angel moved to hover above him on all fours. Then Angel reached out for the single stem rose that he'd surprised Jay with when he'd returned from his walk.

"You," he said slowly, draggling the fat head of the rose along Jay's cheek and over his throat, "are beautiful. You're sexy," he continued as he trailed the soft petals down his lover's abdomen, watching the muscles contract and his chest shudder. "You're smart and kind and funny, and now I've got you into bed, I'm not letting you go again. Understood?"

"N-never?" Jay asked before he swallowed. Angel watched his Adam's apple bob and licked his lips.

"Maybe for food," he said, pretending to think about it seriously. "But I absolutely insist that we remain naked if so."

Jay laughed and reached up to caress the side of Angel's jaw, rubbing his thumb over Angel's stubble and looking at him with such adoration it made Angel's heart want to break if he weren't so happy.

"Kiss me," Jay asked sweetly.

So Angel did.

But not on the mouth. Not yet.

He got the bottle of chocolate sauce and flipped the cap open so he could squeeze a swirl of sweet sticky goodness over Jay's chest. He had a dusting of hair over his pecs that got kind of matted with the chocolate, so Angel took his time lapping it up and nibbling on Jay's hard, round nipples until they were shiny and sore looking.

After that, Angel tortured Jay for a while by trailing the rose up and down his body. He tickled the insides of his thighs with it and along his hard, weeping cock. Jay whimpered and tried to thrust his hips up to get more friction, but Angel took the flower away with a chuckle and kissed Jay's mouth forcefully, pushing his tongue inside as he pinned Jay's hands above his head and brushed the rose against his fluttering stomach.

"Angel, *please*," Jay begged, blinking up at him with wet eyelashes. His pupils were blown, and his lips were bitten red. "I *need* you."

"Okay, handsome," Angel said breathlessly, taking pity on him. As much as he wanted to drag this out, he knew he was desperate for release, and by the look of Jay's straining cock, he felt the same. "Give me a second."

He moved to yank open the condom box and pull one out. As he tore at the foil, Jay flipped over onto his elbows and knees, sticking his ass out, ready for Angel in such a primal way that Angel's cock went from half-hard to steel in less than a second.

"You look so gorgeous," he said hoarsely, running his hand along Jay's spine.

Jay turned his head to look at him serenely. "I'm waiting for you," he whispered sweetly.

Angel was not going to disappoint him.

He got the condom on as fast as he could without damaging it, then drizzled lube over his sheathed cock and Jay's crack. There was still resistance as Angel lined up the end of his dick and pressed through the tight ring of muscle, but the way Jay enveloped his tip almost made him come there and then.

"Fuck, Jay," he managed to cry gutturally. "You feel perfect. Is it okay?"

Jay had his cheek resting on his wrist, looking up at Angel over his shoulder as he nodded. Beads of sweat had collected on his brow, and he panted desperately. "Feels good," he rasped. "Need more."

So did Angel.

He tried not to thrust too fast, but Jay *had* said that he wanted Angel to fuck him hard so that he could feel him for days to come. So Angel pushed, trusting that Jay would tell him if it was too much. But as much as Jay whimpered and writhed and grabbed at the bedsheets, he didn't once tell Angel to stop or slow down, so Angel continued to stretch him out until he was fully nestled inside Jay's ass, the end of his cock rubbing Jay's prostate and making him tremble.

"How's that, baby?" Angel asked as he rubbed Jay's back and carded his fingers through his damp hair. He was too busy trying not to lose his shit from how amazing he felt that he only realized the pet name had slipped out well after he'd said it.

But Jay gave him a punch-drunk smile and nodded. "So good," he uttered. "Holy fuck, Angel. Oh my *god*, fuck me, now!"

He pushed back against Angel, and Angel took that as his cue to move. He began to piston his hips, watching his length slide in and out of Jay's perfect hole, which swallowed Angel again and again. The realization struck him that this was *Jay*, and a sense of complete marvel washed over him as he picked up the pace. He felt like he was floating, almost like he was out of his own body, watching this miracle unfolding. Except he'd also never felt so connected to his own body as he joined with Jay's, the two of them becoming one.

This was the most important person in the world to him, and after all these years, something so essential, so fundamental had shifted, and they were now connected in the most intimate way possible. He held Jay's happiness, his pleasure, in his hands, and it was the most precious, overwhelming feeling.

The responsibility was heady. And Angel was proud to bear it.

"Angel!" Jay cried desperately as he fumbled to grab Angel's right hand. "Touch me!"

Angel knew what he wanted, and immediately reached forward to wrap his hand around Jay's slippery length and jerk as fast as he could. Jay threw his head back and howled, starting to come in hot spurts all over the bedsheets and Angel's hand.

Angel had done that. He'd unraveled his best friend at the most base level.

The sight and sounds of Jay's pleasure were too much, and Angel toppled over the edge as well, vibrating as he shot his load deep inside Jay. Even with the condom, it was still spectacular, and Angel clung to Jay as they trembled through the end of their climaxes.

"Jay," Angel whispered as they finally collapsed in a heap on top of the bed. The rose petals clung to their still-connected, sweaty bodies, and Angel brushed Jay's wet hair back to kiss his forehead. "That was…holy fuck."

Jay laughed weakly and leaned over to press his lips to Angel's in the sweetest kiss. "That was everything," he said, his words reverberating with affection.

Angel sighed and smiled, looking into Jay's beautiful brown eyes. "Everything," he agreed.

That was exactly what he intended to give Jay from now on.

19

JAY

"Okay! Two spiced apple muffins, one black coffee, and one cappuccino."

Ben Turner grinned at Jay and handed over their order, a delicious waft of cinnamon coming from the bag. Rise and Shine was pretty busy – unsurprisingly as it was a Sunday morning – but Ben seemed in no hurry to get to his next customer, letting his colleague deal with other patrons. In fact, he beamed as his eyes darted between Jay and Angel like he was looking for gossip.

Jay tried his best not to look like he had any to spill.

"Thanks, hon," he said to Ben, accepting the bags and passing one of the coffees to Angel like it was no big deal they were out in town together. Just because Angel had rocked Jay's entire world last night (and again that morning with a couple of spectacular blow jobs) didn't mean anyone else had to think it was unusual that they were getting coffee and cake together. They'd been inseparable as kids and pretty much joined at the hip since Angel's accident.

No one else needed to know that Jay's entire life had been turned upside down in the best kind of way.

Although it seemed Ben was determined to guess.

"Soooo," said Ben, his hazel eyes twinkling. "Will we see you guys at Aquarium later?"

"Oh, uh, what's the occasion?" Jay asked.

Ben raised his eyebrows. "Emery sent a message to the group, asking if we wanted to go to Aquarium."

"Ah, yes," said Jay, nodding, vaguely recalling such a message now. "Emery is the occasion. Gotcha." His friend didn't need an excuse to summon them for fun times.

Ben looked purposefully at Angel. "You said you wanted to have a proper night out there, right, Angel? Tonight could be a perfect chance! It's really good for Instagramming photos with all the fish tanks and lights and stuff." He winked – actually *winked* – at Angel, and Jay had to wonder what on earth he was going on about. Jay didn't really use Instagram.

Angel cleared his throat and glanced at Jay. Was that a blush that was creeping onto his face? "Uh, yeah, we haven't really discussed what we're doing this evening. But I think I might finally feel like a night out. Jay will let you know, won't you?"

Jay raised his eyebrows, then nodded at Ben. "Yeah, sure. Will Elias be there, too?" He only really asked about Ben's fiancé for politeness' sake, but Ben's face lit up, and he nodded fervently at Angel, even though Jay had asked the question.

"Oh, yes, you haven't met him yet, have you, Angel? We can introduce you later. He's excited to meet Jay's bo…friend. His friend. From school." He grinned at Jay, and Jay did his best to smile back.

As amazing as last night had been, he and Angel hadn't discussed the B-word at all, and he didn't want his well-meaning but overly enthusiastic friends and family jumping to the wrong conclusions.

Except Angel had said something about 'not letting you go' – so Jay did have a *little* hope.

Urgh. Right. They needed to talk without sex to distract them. Jay was trying his best to stop worrying himself into an early grave and also stop bottling things up. Talking would probably smooth everything out. So he needed to go against his nature when it came to Angel and his feelings and have a damn conversation.

"I'll let you know about tonight," he promised, tugging Angel away from the bakery counter. "Have a great day, Ben."

"You too!" he called after them with a wave.

Jay felt like half the room turned their heads to watch them leave, but Jay just focused on gently guiding Angel away as fast as he could with his hand on Angel's arm.

"Wow, people sure are friendly around here," Angel commented with a shake of his head. "I walk around LA, certain in the knowledge that I have total anonymity. It's kind of nice that there are friends of yours everywhere to run into here."

Jay hummed.

Sometimes, he wouldn't mind a *little* space to explore his own thoughts, just every once in a while.

He'd suggested to Angel that they come out for a stroll around town because otherwise there was a very real danger that Jay would have succumbed to Angel's previous wish of never leaving the bed, not even for food. As fabulous and tempting as that had seemed, Jay had decided they needed a little fresh air and perspective, so here they were.

"Shall we head down to the lake?" he suggested as they reached the door. He didn't want to push Angel to walk too far after their sex-a-thon last night and that morning. If Jay had to choose between Angel having the energy to walk or fuck, there really wasn't a decision at all as far as Jay was concerned.

But he had something he needed to ask, and it was time to stop beating around the bush. So if they could find a bench to sit on, that would help his plan a lot.

As soon as they exited the bakery, Button jumped to attention, springing up from where she'd been lying on her belly to dancing on all fours. Jay never worried about tying her leash up and leaving her outside places she couldn't go inside, not in Pine Cove. When he visited Rise and Shine with her, he always secured her to the vintage bicycle that was welded to the sidewalk, its basket overflowing with beautiful flowers. He knew passersby often stopped and took pictures with her, which she was more than happy to pose for.

Speaking of photos…

"What was Ben talking about with Instagram?" he asked Angel curiously as he undid Button's leash, and they began walking down the high street.

"Oh," said Angel sheepishly, rubbing the back of his neck. There was that blush again. "Actually, I was meaning to talk to you about that last night, but then, well…"

It was Jay's turn to blush, but he hoped anyone looking on would just put it down to the brisk January air whipping off the lake down the end of the road. "Yeah," he said shyly, a grin spreading over his face. Damn, that had been some of the best sex of his entire life. Possibly *the* best because it had been with Angel. "We did get a little distracted, didn't we?"

Angel snorted and bumped their shoulders together. "Well, anyway. Maybe it was coincidence and your friend was just making a general comment about the club. Or…"

"Or," Jay prompted.

Angel sighed as they passed by Sunny Side Up. Tyee waved enthusiastically at them through the window, and the two of them waved back. *Just two minutes*, Jay pleaded to the universe. *Can I have two minutes to have a private conversation?*

Luckily, no one came running out of the diner to chase after them, but Jay was grateful when they reached the boardwalk and looked for a free bench to perch on.

"Or," Angel continued, "I've noticed I jumped up about a dozen new Insta followers over the past few days, maybe more. I think your friends found me. I mean, obviously Emery remembers me from school, but it's like he's realized I still exist, and now everyone's just a little…excitable."

Jay swallowed as they took a seat with Button sitting between them. He allowed himself a second to stare out over the choppy dark blue waters of the lake, encircled by the pine forest the town was named for. It was beautiful, even if the strong breeze did make it a little bracing.

"Okay," said Jay, not exactly following, although he wasn't really surprised. It was very like Emery to cyberstalk anyone new and interesting (or rather, someone old who'd just come back), *especially* after Jay's confession of love at Aquarium the other night. "So they know you're active on Instagram, is that it?"

Angel bit his lip, then fished out his phone without saying anything. He sipped his coffee and navigated the screen with his phone until he turned it for Jay to see. "I didn't tag you – yet. I figured I should check before I did. But I guess your friends might have recognized your apartment?"

Jay took the phone, feeling his eyebrows creep up. "'Special surprise for a special someone,'" he said, reading the caption out loud as he looked at the photo of his home so beautifully covered in flowers and candles. He still couldn't quite believe that Angel had done that, but this was the cherry on top. He couldn't help it, his heart soared. "You put that online?" he whispered.

His throat felt thick, and his eyes prickled, but he blinked back any tears. This was possibly a very *good* thing. It meant

Angel was already thinking about going public. He sort of already had. Tagging Jay would just be the last step.

Jay knew he should be cautious. He'd spent so many years working hard to keep his feelings secret he felt like their blossoming relationship was a fragile thing that needed to be protected.

But another, more primal feeling was overwhelming all those doubts. Angel had *claimed* him. *Publicly.* Like a caveman scooping up his woman in front of the rest of the tribe. Jay bit his lip as a tingly sensation flurried all over his body.

"Is that okay?" Angel asked hesitantly.

Jay sniffed and nodded, glancing over at Angel, then handing his phone back with a weak chuckle. "I think it's amazing. You want to tag me in that?"

"If that's what you want?" Angel asked.

Jay exhaled and smiled at him. "Last night, you said you were all in. What does that mean to you exactly?"

For a second, Angel just looked at him, his eyes wide as he bit his lip. Then he reached over and took Jay's hand in his own, rubbing his thumb over the knuckles.

"Honestly?" he said, "I don't know exactly logistics-wise. It's too soon to talk about moving, and my work takes me all over the world. But…but I want to give this a fair chance, Jay. I don't want to be with anyone else. I know some people don't think labels are important, but I think they are for me. I think I want to tell the world I'm bisexual…and I want to tell the world that I'm with you, too. Officially."

Jay's heart leaped into his throat, and the tears threatened to come back. He'd been denying himself even the possibility of having Angel for so long it still felt forbidden, like he didn't deserve it.

"I—" he croaked. "I'd really like that," he managed to say.

Angel blew out a huge breath and laughed, making Button bark at him. "Yeah? Fuck, I was so goddamned nervous, which is seriously strange. You're *Jay*, I shouldn't get nervous around you! But I guess this is kind of a change for us, huh? So…"

Jay took a fortifying breath and brought Angel's hand up in his own to kiss his knuckles, not caring who saw. It was time to be brave and stop trying to manage a potential heartbreak before it even happened.

"It's a change," Jay agreed. "But one that makes me so happy."

Angel swallowed, his Adam's apple bobbing as his eyes danced over Jay's features. Then he leaned over and pressed his lips to Jay's in a sweet, chaste kiss. Electricity flew through Jay, and he didn't care who saw *that* either.

"So I can tag you in the photo?" Angel asked shyly, making Jay think of a schoolboy with a crush. He might have had to wait a decade, but finally, *his* schoolboy crush had noticed him, and it was the most wonderful feeling in the world.

"I'd love that," Jay told him honestly. "And, um, maybe we can take a selfie later?"

"At Aquarium?" Angel suggested, practically bouncing in his seat. "Do you, um, want to tell your friends about us then as well?"

It was as if all the air rushed from his lungs. Angel hadn't been kidding, he really was all in.

Was Jay?

He felt like he was about to fall off the railway bridge that in some ways he'd been hanging on to since he'd been fourteen. There wasn't a parachute. He either needed to let go or give up on a good thing before it even got the chance to fly.

He took the leap.

"I'd love to tell them…" he said firmly, kissing Angel lightly on the lips, "that you're my…boyfriend?"

Angel grinned like the Cheshire cat. "Yes! That's so weird, but in like that craziest best way," he said shaking his head and laughing. "I have a *boyfriend*. Even just saying it makes me want to dance around! If it wasn't for this bum knee." He licked his lips and frowned in concentration. "I have a boyfriend. Wow, it's like I get shivers every time I say it."

Jay laughed at him and slapped his arm playfully. "You dork," he said with deep affection.

"I think you'll find I'm *your* dork, handsome," Angel said with a sudden amount of heat as he leaned in to give Jay a definitely *not* chaste kiss. "You're stuck with me. Sorry."

Jay was about to explain to Angel how very *not* sorry he was, possibly with a demonstration, but that was the moment Button chose to explode back to life.

Jay almost found himself yanked off the bench by her leash as Button sprinted toward the pebbled bank of the lake, chasing after some ducks who had dared to land there. The leash ripped from his hand, and all he could do was scramble to his feet and yell as Button raced into the freezing cold water, barking her head off at the ducks as they smugly flew away.

"Ohh," he groaned, gripping his hair as she groused some more, then began to paddle around, her leash bobbing in the water after her. "Wet dog," he bemoaned. "Wet, *cold* dog."

Angel laughed, but then his phone rang in his pocket, distracting him. While he answered and walked along the shore, Jay steeled himself and jogged toward the water to retrieve his naughty dog.

"Come on, madam," he called out, clapping his hands to get Button's attention as she paddled around. "Out of there, please, before you catch your death."

Button's tongue lolled as she turned and looked at him, like she was being absolutely hilarious and knew it. Then she continued swimming to the right where there were some reeds and other plant life.

"Oh, Button," Jay said, throwing up his hands. "You're going to get all filthy. Come on!" He had towels in the trunk of his car for just this reason, but he was still a little annoyed that his romantic moment with Angel had been interrupted.

However, it was possible it would have been anyway.

"Hey," said Angel as he limped back to Jay's side. "That was my boss. There's a problem on set, and he wondered if I could swing by."

Jay narrowed his eyes, concern flooding through him. "A problem? Is it Kenny? Angel, you're still hurt. You can't—"

"Whoa, whoa, whoa," Angel said, waving Jay down before he could get too distressed. "I think he just wants my input on how to run the stunt. He's been asking me that kind of stuff a lot lately. I'm like the assistant coordinator by this point, just without the pay raise," he added with a chuckle. "It's totally fine. I'll get an Uber there and meet you at the bar later, okay?"

Jay exhaled and nodded. "Sorry, I just worry," he mumbled.

Angel cupped his head and kissed his hair. "And I love that about you. But I'm fine," he insisted. "And this is totally not a clever ploy for me to get out of dog-bathing duties." He wrinkled his nose. "Well...it might be like five percent that."

Jay laughed and shook his head as a drenched and filthy Button came trotting out of the lake, then shook herself vigorously.

"Bad dog," he grumbled affectionately before turning back to Angel. "Okay, if you're sure you feel up to it, I'll see you later."

Angel grinned, already opening the Uber app on his phone. "Oh, our muffins," he said sadly, looking at the bag from Rise and Shine they'd abandoned on the bench. "Could you take them home for us to have later?"

Jay kissed his jaw and nodded. "Of course. See you soon, baby."

"See you soon, baby," Angel repeated, sending the good kind of shivers down Jay's spine.

Grimacing, Jay picked up the soaking wet leash as well as the bag with his and Angel's spiced apple muffins in, then gave Angel one last kiss before walking back to where he'd parked his car. Angel's Uber shouldn't take long to arrive, but Jay still glanced over his shoulder a couple of times, feeling bad for leaving Angel behind after they'd had such an important conversation.

It was okay. They could talk more later. They didn't have a ticking clock hanging over their heads anymore. Sure, Angel would still be leaving at some point, but they'd laid their cards on the table about their feelings and made a commitment.

Angel was now Jay's boyfriend.

Jay's breath caught in his throat, and he bit his lip, grinning with happiness. This was everything he'd ever wanted, but it was better because it was slightly messy and complicated, and that just made it even more real.

As he drove home, he could feel his chest starting to relax, like he could finally trust this good thing that was happening to him. If only his teenage self could see him now. Patience really was a virtue, and sometimes, despite all the odds staring you down, dreams really could come true.

When he wrangled Button into the bathtub, she looked at him like he was nuts as he happily sang off-key to songs playing from his phone. Such was the power of Angel that he was even enjoying the arduous task of rinsing the mud and lake water from his disobedient pooch. She, on the other hand, grumbled and tried to wriggle away the whole time.

But Jay just laughed. Nothing was going to get him down today.

Or so he thought.

He was drying Button's clean fur with his hairdryer when he realized the music had stopped on the phone and his ringtone was striving to be heard over the whooshing air. He quickly turned the appliance off and grabbed his cell, barely registering the caller was unknown before answering.

"Hello?"

"Jay Coal?" a woman's voice asked.

"Yeah, yep, that's me," he said as he gave Button one last towel dry, then abandoned his efforts, letting her run free into the apartment and rub herself all over his sofa. At least he wasn't sleeping on there anymore, but he made a note to Febreze the thing later.

"Hi, you might not remember me. My name is Lisa Young. I'm a friend of Angel Shields?"

The entire world fell away from Jay in less than a second. He clung to the sink for support and took a deep breath. Why the *hell* was Angel's evil ex calling him?

"Uh, yeah," he croaked. "We've met. I didn't know you had my number. How can I help?" That was the politest way he could say 'Why the fuck are you talking to me and what the fuck do you want?'

"Oh, of course we've met. You're right," she said dismissively. "Well, I heard through some friends that Angel was in some kind of accident, and I was terribly worried."

Jay frowned and glanced at the phone, hardly believing what he was hearing. "Uh, yeah," he said, debating whether he should just hang up, but his curiosity got the better of him. "Almost two weeks ago. Why are you calling me and not him?"

"Oh, good heavens, I hope he's all right! I wonder why he didn't tell me," she said with a tut. "You see, Jay, I wanted to make sure I got all the facts straight before I called him. I didn't want him to think I was using a weak excuse to contact him, but then, I probably don't need an excuse, do I?"

She laughed at herself, but Jay stayed quiet, not really finding any of this funny.

"You two were always thick as thieves, Jay," she continued, and Jay got the impression she wasn't paying him a compliment. "I figured you'd know what was going on, especially as he's tagged you on his last few Instagram photos. I didn't realize he was filming near you."

"Yes, I—" Jay began, but Lisa kept right on talking over him.

"The thing is, *Jay*," she said, drawing his name out in a way he didn't like. "I'm confused, and I was hoping you could clear something up. If Angel is injured, when did he have time to get himself a new little girlfriend?"

Jay's heart flipped, and he licked his lips. This woman was several hundred miles away and nothing to Angel anymore. In fact, Jay was pretty sure he hated her. There was nothing for him to get worried about or feel intimidated by.

So why was his heart racing like he had something to feel guilty about?

"Angel doesn't have a new girlfriend," he said truthfully.

Lisa hummed. "You see, the funny thing is, he posted a *very* romantic photo last night, Jay, and he's just tagged you in it. So I'm thinking you helped set that up for whoever she is. So why don't you just tell me the truth, so I'm not blindsided, okay? Angel and I have been talking about getting back together, and I deserve to know if there's someone else in the picture."

Jay opened his mouth to call her a liar, but he stopped himself at the last second. He was almost certain Angel hadn't been talking to Lisa at all, let alone about getting back together, but Jay didn't know *everything* about Angel. Just because it felt like he did sometimes didn't mean that Angel didn't have private things going on.

He took a deep breath. That was just his insecurities raising their ugly heads again. Jay and Angel had literally just agreed to be boyfriends. Lisa was nosing around for gossip, and he wasn't going to give it to her.

"There is no new girlfriend," he said firmly again. "Now, I suggest if you want to find out more about Angel, you call *him* because I—"

"Well, then *why* are you tagged in that photo with all the rose petals?" Lisa demanded, her civil tone slipping away. "I think you owe me an answer, Jay, because you were a big part of why we broke up last year. You know that, right? I think it's the least you can do to show me some respect."

Jay snorted, feeling his temperature rise and his hands tremble with anger. "I don't know why *you* broke up with Angel," he said, doing his best to keep his voice even, "but we're not friends, and I don't owe you anything. If he wants to tag me on Instagram, that's his business. Now, if you'll excuse me—"

"But it's not like all those flowers and candles were for *you*, were they?" Lisa spat with a shrill laugh. "Because, I have to say, Jay, that if they weren't for a new girlfriend, they kind of look like they could be?"

Jay bit his lip. There was no way in hell he was outing Angel to his biphobic ex, but how could he respond to that without lying?

It turned out he didn't need to respond at all.

"Ohh," she said after he paused, followed by a low rumbling laugh. "Oh, you have *got* to be kidding me. Did you finally convince him to have a little ride on you? That's adorable, Jay. You always were sniffing around the scraps from our dinner table."

She laughed harder, and Jay wasn't sure if he was running

hot or cold or both. Shame and fear and anger welled in him, but his throat clamped on him, and he couldn't think of what to say.

"Wow, that's so embarrassing he put that on Insta. He's going to regret that." She hummed happily. "Okay, Jay, thank you for helping me. You've been most enlightening. I was worried I had some actual competition, but fair warning between us *girls*. When I ask him to come back to me, he's going to run so fast you'll disappear in the dust, m'kay? Sorry, but *I* know what Angel needs, and you could never give it to him. My poor baby is hurt and confused, and now I'm here to make it all better."

"N-no!" Jay finally managed to snap, coming back to his senses. "Angel doesn't want to be with you. So if *you* want to embarrass *yourself*, go ahead and call him. See if he'll even pick up when he sees it's your number. This isn't a case of you versus me. This is about Angel knowing who's good for him – who *loves* him – and I don't think that was ever you."

"Oh, Jay, precious," Lisa purred, completely unruffled. "I love him very deeply, and I'm going to get him back – and take him away from *you* – if it's the last thing I do. Enjoy your sad little life. We'll be sure and send you a wedding invite…if we have room left on the guest list, that is."

Jay opened his mouth, but the line went dead. He stared at his phone screen for several seconds before sinking down onto the bathroom floor.

He might have told Lisa this wasn't a fight between them for Angel, but *he* didn't light up a room when he walked in. *He* wasn't drop-dead gorgeous. *His* career wasn't going stratospheric.

Had he just been kidding himself this whole time?

He exhaled and looked at his phone again, tears blurring in his eyes. Even as he tried to remind himself that he and

Angel had just decided to be boyfriends that very afternoon, what they had together felt just as fragile as ever.

It didn't matter that they'd been friends their whole lives. They'd only been *lovers* for a few days, whereas Angel and Lisa had dated for years.

What if Angel had been waiting all this year for her to ask him to come back? Would he forget everything he'd said to Jay today and last night? It was all well and good for Jay to tell himself that people's sexuality evolved and not to be biphobic, but as his heart raced and logic went out the window, a nasty voice in the back of his head told him that Angel had thought he was straight for ninety-nine percent of his life. It was hardly a leap of the imagination to think he'd go back to the life he knew, the easier life.

Jay needed to think. He took a shuddery breath and wiped the tears from his cheeks that he hadn't even realized had fallen, then clamped his thumb down on his phone's power button, turning it off.

He hauled himself to his feet, feeling like he weighed a ton, then grabbed his keys. "Back soon," he promised Button hollowly before locking the apartment door and rushing down the building's stairs to his car.

He needed somewhere private to unscramble all these thoughts, and there was only one place he could think of to go.

ANGEL

IT WASN'T THAT ANGEL HAD MEANT TO LIE TO JAY. HE JUST hadn't wanted him to worry.

Because Angel was worried.

"This is…not good," he said, looking around at the frantic set as the light faded for the day.

"No shit, Sherlock," Meryl growled in frustration. "I've never fallen so badly behind on a shoot before. How can a handful of people cause so much trouble? Where is security?"

There were a *lot* of people shouting in and around the equipment. Mostly crew yelling at the half a dozen protesters who had chained themselves to several trees right in the middle of the scene Meryl had been trying to film.

"They're on their way," someone called out in answer to Meryl's question. In the meantime, Angel stood helplessly with Kamran, Bella, and Sabina, who had been working on the scene in question until several members of the mob that had breached the school the other day had snuck in.

Fuck only knew how they'd managed it. But now they were here, refusing to be moved unless the film packed up and left Pine Cove.

Angel felt incredibly ashamed of the place he'd grown up in, the place he'd been starting to think of as 'home' again.

"This is a progressive, inclusive town," he said in disbelief. "I would never have thought anyone would feel so strongly about a film with a queer storyline shooting here. I would never have thought there'd be so much hate."

"I'm sorry, darling," said Bella, rubbing his arm. She and Sabina were still in costume and makeup from where they'd been filming until the disruption. "We know it's not you or your friend Jay's fault."

"Or mine," Kamran piped up indignantly. "This is my town too, and these *ASSHOLES* don't speak for anyone I know!" He gave the nearest protester the finger, but the woman just waved her sign that read 'Families need a mom AND a dad!' and kept yelling about her rights.

Meryl pinched the bridge of her nose. "Look, at this rate, we might just have to cut our losses. They've been causing trouble on a daily basis, blasting music when we've been trying to film and ruining takes any way they can, but now we have to shut everything down and get the police down here. I don't even know if they can remove peaceful protesters with force. I hate to say it, but we might be better off going to our backup location later in the schedule and re-filming some shots so we can get continuity for the whole scene."

"What!" cried Sabina, throwing her hands out. "No, that's crazy. We got some amazing footage here. I don't want to redo any of our work. Bella and I killed it, not to mention all your hard work, Meryl, and the crew. I refuse to be forced into re-filming because of these bigoted assholes!"

"You think I want that?" snapped Meryl. "I have producers breathing down my neck, not to mention the studio. We're bleeding money here, and then there's our insurance problem."

Angel blinked, coldness rushing through him. "Insurance?"

Meryl rubbed her forehead. "Yes, that's why I asked you to come back to the set, Shields. I'm sorry, but the insurance company can't find what caused the accident, and without you being able to remember the incident or what might have happened at *all*, they're getting twitchy about covering our insurance. I'm not sure we can let you drive again."

Angel tried not to gasp as he composed himself. "For how long?" he asked. He'd had a feeling there'd been another reason he'd been asked to come back here other than just to shake his fist at the homophobic protesters along with the rest of the crew. But they didn't think *he'd* caused the car crash, did they?

"I don't know," said Meryl tiredly. "Maybe not for the rest of the film. And that doesn't do your reputation any good for future work. We'd probably still be able to keep you on for other stunt work, but..." She let out a loud growl of frustration. "Right, here's how it is. If we can't deal with these bigots, we're going to move the film production ASAP. You'd still get paid if you come with us, but honestly, that's just one of about fifty thousand concerns I have right now. I like you, though, Shields, so I didn't want to just kick you off the production without warning. But now I have to go deal with a lot of bullshit." She looked at Bella and Sabina. "I'm calling it a wrap for the night. Go take some time off. Some of us should get a break from this circus."

"Oh, darling, are you sure—?" Bella began to ask, but Meryl had already stormed off and was yelling instructions at other people.

Angel scraped his hand down his chin and wondered how his day could have gone from so great to so bad so fast.

The shoot might leave Pine Cove early, *and* Angel's whole career was in jeopardy. Yet again he cursed the head injury that had wiped all memory of the crash from his mind. He was sure he wouldn't have made such a catastrophic mistake as to total the car and put his colleagues in danger, but how could he know for sure?

Goddamn it. He and Jay were only just sorting things out, and now his whole life was up in the air. All because some basic bitches had a problem with two women kissing in a fictional film. Sabina's love interest wasn't even *in* the part of the film they were shooting here.

"What are we going to do?" Bella asked, looking around at the chaos helplessly.

"Get drunk," said Kamran and Sabina in unison.

Angel looked between them. "That doesn't sound like the worst idea," he admitted. "I was supposed to be going to Aquarium anyway—"

"Me, too," Kamran jumped in. "I'd actually hoped to see you there, buddy. How about we get out of here before I punch one of these fine townspeople? Ladies, would you care to join us in Pine Cove's finest watering hole?"

"Hell yeah," said Sabina, clapping his shoulder. "That sounds much better than drinking in our trailers like the sad losers we are. Bells?"

Bella bit her lip. "Well, if it's a *gay* bar, then I probably shouldn't—"

"Should come, yes, absolutely," interrupted Kamran firmly, wagging a finger at her. "Everyone's welcome at Aquarium, especially our *ace* friends."

Bella smiled, looking strangely honored for someone who could probably walk into any bar on the planet and be more than welcomed. "Well, that's very kind of you. Of course I accept your invitation, then. Angel, will your lovely Jay be joining us?"

It wasn't like all of Angel's problems vanished – far from

it – but hearing Bella say 'your lovely Jay' went a long way to making him feel better.

"Actually, yeah," he said, mustering a smile. "He's going to meet me there with some more friends. We'd love you to join us."

"Splendid!" she cried with a clap.

A particularly loud burst of shouting erupted not too far from them, making them all wince. "Let's get out of here," Sabina said with a sneer. "I can't stand the stench of bigotry any longer. Kam, you good to drive us?"

Kamran's face lit up like he hadn't been driving all day for work, and he didn't drive his precious vintage Ford Mustang every day. "Hell yeah! This way, gang. Your chariot awaits!"

Bella and Sabina decided to get changed so they didn't risk anything spilling on the costumes they would need to wear again tomorrow, so Angel waited with Kamran while they ran to throw something else on. Angel leaned against Kamran's dark blue Mustang with Kamran who happily kept up a more-or-less one-sided conversation about various things while Angel nodded and hummed in agreement. His own thoughts were demanding too much of his attention for anything else.

This wasn't a problem. It was just a bit of an inconvenience. He and Jay had talked about what they wanted, which was to be together. So if he had to leave with the crew to the next location (which he was pretty sure was Bulgaria or some other European country he wasn't convinced he'd be able to find on a map) it would be unfortunate, but he was still committed to making this thing work with Jay. That was all that mattered.

"Evening, ladies," Kamran said appreciatively as Bella and Sabina emerged into the parking lot where the Mustang was parked.

Bella was looking elegant in a little pastel dress with a

jacket and pair of ankle boots, but Sabina looked like she was about to get on a Harley Davidson and fuck some shit up with all the black leather and eyeliner going on. She gave them a rock-on hand and winked as they approached.

"Let's blow this Popsicle stand," she said enthusiastically.

It only took about fifteen minutes to drive from their location in the woods to Main Street, where Aquarium was situated. It was early evening, so although the sidewalks were still pretty busy with shoppers and people going about their business, the bar was relatively quiet. That meant that the four of them were able to grab a large booth and some tables with ease in anticipation of more of their friends arriving.

"Okay, what can I get everyone?" Kamran asked with a clap of his hands as the rest of them sat.

"Beer me," said Sabina, slapping a credit card down on the table. "And start a tab."

"I'd kill for an ice-cold glass of sauvignon blanc," said Bella dreamily.

Angel waved Kamran off. "Just a Diet Coke for me for now. I need to build up to alcohol."

"Wuss," said Sabina with a wink, so he knew she was kidding. Kamran saluted him and spun around to head to the bar, and Bella reached over to rub Angel's hand.

"You look much better," she said kindly. "How are you feeling?"

Angel shrugged. "Okay."

He automatically flexed the knee that was still giving him the most trouble. Even the stitches on his head were looking much better, but that damned knee was still stopping him from driving.

That and the fact that they might not *let* him drive on this movie again. Especially not if he still felt sick at the mere thought of getting behind the wheel. *Goddamn it.*

"I was hoping to come back to work soon, but…"

He trailed off, worry churning in his guts again. But Sabina patted his arm and shook her head. "Hey, don't sweat it. Those assholes aren't going to stop the shoot. Meryl will fix it."

"And in the meantime, we get to have a night off with you and your lovely friends," Bella said cheerfully as Kamran came back with a tray of drinks.

"Cheers to that," he said sincerely, placing everyone's orders in front of them. "This has certainly been one of the most interesting projects I've worked on."

"So you just take whatever work comes through the region?" Bella asked with interest.

Kamran leaned the tray against the side of the booth and sat beside Angel, dropping his keys, wallet, and phone onto the table. His jeans were so tight Angel assumed they'd dig into his leg otherwise.

"Yeah, and the rest of the time I drive for Uber," he said with a nod, clinking his beer bottle with Sabina's, then against Angel's and Bella's glasses. "There are constant film and TV crews coming through here. Not all of them need drivers, especially not for chases like we're doing right now." He whistled happily. "I'll be sad when this shoot is over. But they always need people for all kinds of things. I'm actually looking into some physical training so I can do fights and stuff, like my man Angel here. It's a sweet place to live for a variety of work."

"Hey, guys!"

Angel looked up as Ben from the bakery came bouncing into the bar, which was steadily getting busier. Flanking him was an older guy who was a bit of a silver fox. Probably only in his early forties, but still very handsome. As he had his hand on Ben's back, Angel assumed that was his fiancé, Elias. To his other side was a young woman with a very short pixie cut and a big smile. She waved as they approached.

"We ran into Peyton on the way in," Ben explained.

"I just got off work," said Peyton to Kamran. Then she looked at Angel. "How are you feeling?"

Angel blinked and suddenly realized that she'd been one of his nurses.

"Oh, hello again," he said happily. "Yeah, pretty good. I didn't know you knew these guys."

Peyton laughed and shared a look with Ben. "Everyone knows everyone through Emery eventually. I—" Her words died in her throat and she froze as her gaze swept the rest of the booth, and she spotted Bella Dalton and Sabina Max. "You're…oh…my…" she stammered.

The ladies laughed, and Sabina patted the space next to her on the blue leather. "We're pleased to meet you," she said, finishing Peyton's incomplete sentence. "Do you want to sit or grab some drinks first? We've got a tab open. Order whatever you like."

The three newcomers blinked at each other before shyly smiling. "Okay!" said Peyton a little giddily. Then she grabbed Ben's hand to scamper off to the bar. Elias shook his head and settled where Sabina had patted.

Angel figured Ben already knew what to get his fiancé because they knew each other so intimately. Angel couldn't wait until he and Jay had that. In fact, they probably had a pretty good head start, considering their history, but the thought that they were going to get even closer made him grin all the same.

They were going to tell everyone about them tonight. That made Angel feel much better about all this work bullshit.

"Hey, I'm Elias," the young silver fox said, reaching his hand over toward Angel. "You must be Jay's friend."

"Angel," he confirmed with a nod as they shook. "I sure am. And you're Ben's fiancé. I heard the proposal was *epic*."

"Oh, do tell us!" Bella squealed excitedly.

Sabina laughed at her, but she nodded at Elias all the same. "Oh, we have a Casanova in our midst, do we?"

"You better tell the story before Emery gets here," Kamran urged with a rueful laugh. "He always gets jealous that he was out-proposed," he explained to the rest of the table.

Angel listened as Elias recounted how Ben had inherited an actual English mansion and how Elias had come up with the most romantic way to pop the question when they'd gone to visit over Christmas last month. As much as he enjoyed the story, Angel also just basked at the group of people he was surrounded by.

These were his people. He was hanging out at a gay bar for the first time since acknowledging his own sexuality, and a deep sense of belonging settled over him. These weren't Lisa's prissy friends who judged every single thing one of them said and calculated the worth of every item of clothing, as if that could tell them who was successful or who was a good person.

This was a happy band of misfits squashing into an increasingly crowded booth. They came from all walks of life. The main thing they had in common was that they loved openly and freely, and Angel thought that was beautiful.

Peyton and Ben rejoined them, then Robin and Dair also arrived. Where was Jay? It didn't take that long to bathe a dog, did it? Angel would have thought he'd have been here by now.

Frowning, he pulled out his phone, but he didn't have any missed calls or texts.

Hey, babe! he quickly typed out. *Everything okay? Can't wait for you to get here x*

He sent the text, then joined back in on the conversation, which seemed to be grilling Robin and Dair about when *they* were going to get engaged. But Robin was talking about how they were thinking about kids more than a big wedding, and Angel's heart melted a little for them.

He was distracted by Kamran beside him, though, who suddenly went stiff as he looked at something – or someone – across the bar. Angel flicked his eyes in that direction, but he couldn't see what had spooked the usually unspookable Kamran.

"You all right, buddy?" he asked.

Kamran blinked, then shook himself. "Uh, yeah," he said, not sounding convinced. "I'll, uh, be back in a second, okay? Watch my stuff?"

"Sure," Angel said.

He frowned after Kamran as he extracted himself from the booth (by climbing right over Ben's and Peyton's laps). But then Angel's own phone started ringing where he'd left it on the table, and he was so excited it could be Jay, he forgot about Kamran in his eagerness to answer the call. The number was unknown, but that might just be because Jay was in an area of spotty signal.

"Hey!" he cried happily, sticking his finger in his other ear so he could hear down the line over the music and everyone's conversations.

"Angel, is that you?" a woman's voice asked.

He frowned in confusion. "Uh, yeah. I'm Angel. Who's this?"

The woman laughed, and immediately Angel felt on edge. "Goodness, it is noisy where you are, isn't it? Angel, it's *Lisa.*"

Angel went from feeling on edge to angry snarling in a flash. But he clenched his jaw and tried not to lose his shit. He was wedged between almost a dozen people, people who were *Jay's* friends, and he didn't want them thinking Jay's new boyfriend was a psycho.

"You changed your number," Angel said tensely. But Lisa just laughed.

"This is my new work phone, silly. That doesn't matter. I heard that you were in an accident, and I just had to know if you were all right!"

Angel shifted in his seat uneasily. "How did you hear that?"

They didn't have any mutual acquaintances as far as he knew. Their friends had all really been her friends, and not one of them had reached out to him after the break-up. Had she been stalking his Instagram? He remembered in that moment that was a thing she liked to do.

"Oh, you know, on the grapevine," she said dismissively. "But are you *all right?* I can't believe you didn't tell me you were in a car wreck. I was so upset when I heard."

Angel scowled and noticed that Jay's twin brother, Robin, was watching him. Angel offered him a tight smile, trying to say 'don't worry, I'll hang up soon!' with his eyes.

"Why would I tell you, Lisa? We broke up," Angel said firmly. "And we haven't spoken in a year, which is why you've called from a different number, I'm sure. I probably would have ignored the call otherwise, and you know it. Look, I don't really know what we have to say to each other. So what's this really about?"

Lisa laughed again. "Angel, sweetie, you're really hard to hear. Can you step outside wherever you are?"

"No, I can't," said Angel. Even if he wanted to, he was sandwiched between several people on either side.

He felt a touch on his knee and looked over to see Sabina frowning at him. "Are you okay?" she mouthed. Angel nodded.

He would be as soon as he ended this call.

"Come on. Why are you really calling?" he asked.

The pause at the other end of the phone was positively

icy, but Lisa recovered before Angel could continue. "Oh, precious, I know it's been a while. I just needed some space. But I miss you terribly, and your Instagram looks so fun recently."

Bingo. Damn it. He should have blocked her. But he hadn't remembered that he should have until now.

"Can you blame me for missing you?" she simpered.

Angel rolled his eyes. "I'm sorry if you've missed me, but I honestly think us breaking up was the right thing for us to do."

"Angel," she gasped, scandalized. "I'm sure you don't mean that. We were so good together! We both just needed some time and space to see that. I was thinking, that once your filming is done, maybe you could come see me?" She'd put on her seductive voice, and Angel grimaced, hardly believing that had ever worked on him. He felt so far from turned on he was practically nauseous.

He sighed and rubbed his eyes, suddenly feeling very tired. "I'm not going to come see you, Lisa. Not now, not ever, okay?"

"Why not?" she spat incredulously.

"Because it's over!" said Angel hotly. "Because I'm seeing someone new, and I'm incredibly happy, so I'm going to ask you to please not call me again."

"You're not seeing anyone," she said with a laugh that bordered on sneering. "And even if you were, she couldn't possibly hold a torch to me. You know that."

"Jesus, you are so full of yourself. I can't believe I ever saw anything in you at all." Angel was aware that the whole table was watching him now, most of them with their mouths hanging open, but he didn't care. "And for your information, I very much am seeing someone new, and it's a *guy*. That's right. I'm a filthy bisexual who would only cheat on you anyway, isn't that right, Lisa? So if I were you, I'd run for the hills far, far from my queer ass, which you will never, ever be getting anywhere near ever again."

The open mouths got wider. Sabina punched the air and slapped Angel's arm hard. He winced, but he was also vibrating with adrenaline and pride. *Fuck her.* He wasn't hiding away any longer.

But her audacity ran deep, and she just laughed again. "Oh dear, Angel," she said in a pitying tone. "You don't mean Jay, do you? That sad little friend of yours who was always following you around like a puppy?"

"Don't talk about Jay like that," he snarled. "And yes, I do mean him. He's already a better partner than you ever were, so how about you take a hint?"

"Are you insane?" Lisa cried. "Angel, no. You're straight! I have the receipts! Years of them! A person doesn't just wake up gay one day!"

"Actually, sexuality is fluid," Angel said, looking at Sabina as she gave him a proud grin and two thumbs-up. "And I've probably been bisexual my whole life. I just had people like *you* telling me I couldn't be. Jay's not like that."

"Look, I told him and I'm telling you—" she began, but Angel interrupted her.

"You told him what? When? How?"

There was a pause before another laugh. "He called me, sweetie. That's how I heard about the accident. But we got to discussing you, and I gently suggested that even if something *had* happened with all those rose petals, it was just a phase. You could never *really* love him, not like you could a woman. Like me." She gave a little whine. "You never laid out roses and candles for *me*, you know?"

Angel's blood ran cold. "Jay wouldn't call you," he rasped. "Did you really speak to him, or are you lying?"

"Why are you siding with him?" Lisa wheedled. "Yes, I did

speak to him, actually, and he was *very* mean. I have no idea what you've ever liked about him, honestly—"

"You stay away from Jay!" Angel spat. He'd had enough of this conversation now. "We will both be blocking you, and I suggest you don't embarrass yourself further and leave us alone. You're a pathetic, manipulative narcissist who's more obsessed with what other people think than forming your own opinions. Trust you to come crawling back to me as soon as you thought someone else might be interested. Well, they are, and I wouldn't take you back if you were the last person on this planet. Good*bye*, Lisa."

He finally hung up, dropped the phone on the table, then covered his face with his hands.

Until the sudden raucous burst of applause from the table made him peek between his fingers.

"Fuck yeah, man!" Sabina cried, slapping him repeatedly on the back. "I take it that was the evil ex?"

Angel nodded, looking around at everyone still clapping and wolf-whistling. "Uh, yeah. Thanks, guys."

"I *knew* you and Jay were together," said Ben dreamily, clasping his hands in front of his chest.

"Good for you, standing up to Lisa," said Robin. "Jay never thought she was very good for you." He winked. "My brother is *much* better."

Angel took a breath as they all finally stopped cheering (but didn't stop beaming), and suddenly picked up his phone. *Jay.* If Lisa had pulled her nasty shit on him, there was a strong chance he could be feeling pretty rattled right now.

A quick glance at his messages showed that Jay hadn't even received Angel's previous text. So he left that app and called him instead.

It went straight to voicemail.

Now Jay's absence was worrying him, and from the

falling faces around the table, he wasn't the only one who was concerned.

"What did that bitch say to him?" Sabina asked with steely eyes.

"I don't know, exactly," said Angel. He tried again, but still, the call didn't go through. "But I need to speak to Jay right now and make sure he's okay." He bit his lip and looked around the table. "We were going to tell you that we're together tonight. He was really excited about it."

Now Angel was worried that Lisa had spoiled everything.

No, not everything. He just needed to talk to Jay, and it would all be okay, right?

So why was Jay's phone switched off?

"Damn it," he snapped, hanging up a third time and admitting defeat.

He didn't mind dealing with Lisa. Well, he did, but he'd gotten used to her by the time they'd split. But Jay shouldn't have to have her pouring acid all over their relationship on its first official day. Angel couldn't rest until he knew his boyfriend was all right.

"I need to go find him," he said, looking around the table. Then his eyes fell on Kamran's keys.

He was still off dealing with whatever had spooked him earlier. But Angel reasoned that he wasn't going to be driving home anyway if he was planning on drinking all night. He wouldn't even notice the Mustang was gone.

Angel grabbed the keys and separated the car ones from the others in a flash. "Tell Kamran I'll be careful with his baby!" he cried as he jumped up and climbed over poor Ben and Peyton, ignoring the way his busted knee was protesting.

Jay needed him. Angel didn't have a second to waste.

21

JAY

THE NIGHT AIR WAS COLD, AND JAY CURSED HIMSELF FOR NOT picking up a coat in his haste, but he wasn't moving now. It was as if his feet were rooted to the ground at the spot where this had all began.

Where he'd lost his heart to his best friend.

At least he had a sweater on as he leaned against the rusty old railings of the bridge that crossed over the railway line. This had been the only place he could think of to go as he'd fled the apartment after Lisa's phone call. It was like he needed centering, and the only thing that made sense was to go back to the beginning.

He closed his eyes and focused on the cold air going into his lungs. He was overreacting, he knew. He needed to get off this bridge and go to Aquarium so he and Angel could talk through what had happened. Lisa had no doubt called Angel by now, and Jay had to trust that Angel hadn't already gone running back to LA for her.

He gritted his teeth. She was *not* that attractive. Angel liked Jay for who he was, not how well he took a selfie or what job he had.

Right?

"You're being a fucking idiot, Coal," he muttered, wiping the tears from his eyes. Why was it so hard to believe that Angel would choose him?

Probably because Angel had had sixteen whole years to notice Jay was there, and it had only just happened. Jay had far too much history stacked up against him to be able to trust that this new development was strong enough to last.

He growled in frustration and rubbed the heels of his hands against his eyes. The tears were making his cheeks even colder. He needed to get a grip on himself.

In the distance, a train blared its horn to signal its approach. Jay looked down the long stretch of straight track that vanished into the inky night. His car wasn't running, and the headlights were off, so the only lights he could see in that moment were the train's two tiny pricks of yellow far away.

Or at least, they were the only lights until the flashlight beam swung his way.

Jay frowned and peered into the gloom. Whoever it was, they were coming from the forest, which was kind of the direction of the film set now that he thought about it. Maybe it was a member of the crew?

"Hello?" he called out, moving along the bridge, closer to the trees.

"Oh, there you are," a man's grumpy voice called back as he continued stomping through the undergrowth.

He was a good twenty or thirty feet away still, but even though Jay couldn't see anything, he was pretty sure he recognized that voice.

"I got lost," the man continued. The flashlight beam jumped erratically, swinging all around Jay. "Fucking nightmare getting that done, but I think the distraction worked perfectly. We're all set up. Those sissies won't hang around long after we show them who's boss."

Jay's throat went dry. He reached for his phone to switch on his own light, but then he remembered he'd turned the damn thing *off* off to be alone with his thoughts.

He wished he wasn't alone now.

"Kenny?" he asked, holding his hand up to try and make out anything beyond the beam of light. But Kenny confirmed it for him anyway.

The question was, who did Kenny think Jay was?

"Of course it's me," Kenny snapped as Jay held his power button down, desperately urging the damn thing to come back to life. "Do I sound like Karen Reed? Come on, let's get out of here before we get caught. I wanna do the right thing here, but you know some leftist moron will try and throw us in jail if we get spotted near the blast radius."

Jay backed up, keeping out of the light, edging toward his car. His fucking phone was still thinking about turning back on. "Because you, uh, planted that bomb," he said, making the wildest, most outrageous guess he could think of in an attempt to get Kenny to admit what he'd really done.

"*Yes*, because we planted that bomb, Ricky," Kenny sneered irritably. "Don't get soft on me now. No one's going to get hurt. But it'll sure fuck up that film of theirs, no doubt."

Jay couldn't believe it. He'd been *right*? *There was a bomb?*

Holy fuck. All those people.

Jay's stomach dropped out from under him in panic, and he gave up all pretenses. He broke into a run back to his car, thinking he just needed to get inside. Then he could call the police and Angel so he could alert the people on set…

"Hey!" Kenny cried, maybe finally realizing that Jay wasn't Ricky, whoever that was. "What are you…where are you going?"

While he was busy cursing his slow phone, Jay also cursed himself for locking his car as he skidded to a halt by the door and fumbled to try and get his keys out of his pocket. But his hands were numb from the cold, and when he finally managed to pry the bunch loose from his pocket, they immediately slipped through his fingers to the ground.

"Fuck!" he yelled, fully aware of the heavy footsteps running toward him. He dropped to his knees to look for the keys, but the damn things had bounced under the chassis. He reached to try and grab them, but in a split second, he was being hauled to his feet.

"Coal!" Kenny bellowed, his fists bunched in Jay's sweater as he slammed him against the still locked car door. "What the ever-loving *fuck* are you doing here? Where's Ricky?"

"I don't even know who Ricky is!" Jay cried. He yanked at Kenny's wrists, but his grip was like iron.

So Jay kicked his shins with everything he had.

Kenny howled and leaped back from Jay immediately, letting him go to rub his tender legs. "You *fucker!*" Kenny screamed. "This has nothing to do with you. Why can't you stop meddling?"

Jay scrambled backward while Kenny was temporarily incapacitated. "Meddling? You're the one who's planted a *bomb* on the film set!" His phone was finally awake again, and he jabbed the emergency call button so fast it actually broke through the numbness and hurt his thumb.

"I never said that!" Kenny snarled, limping toward Jay in the dark. The flashlight was still swinging wildly, so it was almost impossible for Jay to see anything behind it. "You can't prove anything! Put that fucking phone *down!*"

He lunged for Jay, slamming him into the bridge railings with the heavy flashlight against his chest and snatching for the phone in Jay's hand. Jay yelled out, twisting and scratching with his free hand at Kenny's face as he clung to the phone for dear life.

"Hello?" he heard the operator say faintly.

"There's a bomb on the film set!" Jay screamed as loud as he could. But Kenny had stopped trying to get the phone from Jay and instead slammed his arm against the railing with such force that Jay gasped in pain and automatically dropped the phone.

It went flying down onto the train tracks. Feeling a bizarre sense of *déjà vu* amid all his fear and panic, Jay heard the train blast its horn, obviously now much closer to the bridge. But Jay couldn't tell how close.

Because he was slightly distracted by the rusty railing behind his back snapping loose and falling away.

"Fuck!" Jay screamed as Kenny's weight on his chest pushed him through the gap. The *déjà vu* was terrifyingly real now as Jay found himself with one foot on the bridge, the other swinging through the air.

Just like when he'd been fourteen.

He grabbed for the railing as Kenny shook him. Jay wasn't sure if he even realized the old metal had broken. His eyes were crazy, and he spat as he bellowed at Jay.

"Why do you have to stick your nose in everything, Coal?" he yelled.

"Get the fuck off me!" Jay yelled back, shoving Kenny with everything he had. Unfortunately, that wasn't much. Jay was pretty fit, but Kenny had more bulk, and he wasn't half hanging off the bridge.

Jay pushed his back against the railing to his right that was still intact. It squealed nauseatingly, though, as Jay fought against Kenny. "You're going to throw us both off the bridge!"

"We're just trying to protect our families!" Kenny howled,

slamming him against the rail. "You can't tell anyone! I won't let you tell anyone!"

The sound of twisting metal sent fear through Jay like a javelin.

Jay tried to force Kenny back, but he didn't have the leverage. "What are you going to do?" Jay demanded, fear making his voice break. "Push me onto the tracks?"

Kenny snarled. "It's not like anyone would miss you, you little *faggot*," Kenny hissed, baring his teeth.

Jay's fury seemed to take on a life of his own that manifested itself in his fist. He'd never hit anyone in his life, but there was a fucking *bomb*, and Kenny was trying to throw him off a *bridge*.

It was as if time slowed down, and Jay was blessed with a moment of clarity.

So many people would miss him.

His family. His friends. His twin brother. But god fucking damn it, Angel Shields *would* miss him because Jay was his best friend, his *everything*. Those were Angel's words, and in that split second, Jay finally heard them.

He had to fight because nothing was going to keep him from being with Angel. Not even himself.

Pain exploded down his arm as he smashed his fist into Kenny's face. Kenny roared, stumbling backward, automatically letting Jay go as well as the flashlight. As it clattered to the ground, the beam swung toward the forest. Jay scrambled away from the gap in the railings, lunging forward in the dark. He'd had the light shone in his eyes so much now he had no night vision and couldn't see Kenny at all. The sound of the train was now so loud Jay couldn't hear anything to tell where he was.

Until Kenny body slammed him to the ground.

Jay coughed and spluttered as he tried to suck in some air. The dark world was pierced with much bigger beams of light as Jay tried to get his bearings. Maybe the train was passing underneath? But why was the light up here?

He didn't have long to process anything more than that as Kenny's foot came swinging into his gut.

Jay sobbed as his whole body spun against the dirty asphalt, his elbow exploding with a sudden burning pain, and he tasted blood in his mouth.

"You're not going to ruin this!" Kenny screamed over the sound of the train thundering past. "We will stand up for our rights! We will—!"

Suddenly, he was gone.

Jay gasped and held his ribs as he pushed himself to sit up, looking around the darkness. The train was still roaring by, but the last carriage suddenly passed under the bridge, and the noise dropped dramatically. The flashlight was just within reach, so he grappled with numb, shaking fingers until he managed to seize it and swing it around until he worked out what was going on.

"You will shut the *fuck* up and go the fuck to *jail*," Angel snarled from where he was sitting on Kenny's back. He had Kenny's arms pinned behind him, and Kenny was whimpering with a bloody nose.

"Fuck you, Shields," Kenny spat out. "Why don't you go crash another car? You almost did our job for us! If you weren't always such a little bitch for Coal—"

"Okay, that's enough out of you," Angel snapped, twisting Kenny's arm and shoving his face into the ground.

"Angel?" Jay whimpered, not daring to believe his own eyes.

"Baby, are you okay?" Angel asked desperately. "What the hell's going on—?"

"He planted a bomb on the set!" Jay cried, unable to stop his tears from falling in horror. "He said something about a distraction. I tried to call the police, but he threw my phone onto the tracks."

Angel reached into his back pocket and threw his phone at Jay without letting Kenny get loose. "The passcode's zero-three-one-seven-nine-one!"

Jay automatically typed it in before he realized something.

"That's my birthday," he whispered.

"Yes, it is," Angel said, looking up at Jay half in exasperation and half in affection. "Because I'm a fucking dumbass who obviously *always* loved you without even knowing it. Please call Meryl first and the cops second so we can save the day, and then I can take you the fuck *home*."

Jay wasted no time in opening Angel's contacts to find the director's number and hit call. As he waited for the line to connect, he stared at Angel, who was staring right back at him.

"I love you," Jay croaked out.

Angel managed a small smile, totally ignoring the wrestling and hissing Kenny beneath him. "I love you, too, handsome."

"It was a good thing you happened to be here, Mr. Coal," said Detective Padilla. She had one hand on her hip and a to-go coffee cup gripped in the other, as usual. She surveyed the busy scene around them on the bridge and in the woods. There had to be two or three dozen police officers combing the area now that Kenny was in custody.

Once he'd appreciated that the jig was up, he'd begrudgingly confessed where he'd planted the bomb. He really had thought about where to put it where it would only damage property and not people. His target had been trees, mostly. The protesters' goal had been to wreck the backdrop to where Meryl had been filming so they'd be forced to go elsewhere and start the scene all over again.

But Jay got a terrible chill thinking about how easily that could have gone wrong. All it would have needed was for one crew member to have gone close to the homemade device at the moment it was set to go off, and the night would have ended in tragedy. As it was, Kenny had also told the police how to defuse the timer, and everybody was safe.

Jay was wrapped in a blanket and sat next to Angel, who hadn't moved his arm from around Jay's back since the moment the cops had come and taken Kenny off his hands (or from under his knees, more accurately). Angel kissed Jay's temple and rubbed his back.

"You're a hero," Angel murmured to Jay in response to Padilla's comment about him being at the right place at the right time. "Who knows what might have happened."

"Why *were* you here?" Padilla asked, sipping from her enormous coffee. "I mean, don't get me wrong, I'm glad as hell you were. But it's kind of an odd place to be hanging out on a Sunday night."

Jay looked at Angel and managed a weak smile. "I was thinking through some stuff. This is the place where I fell in love with my boyfriend."

Angel raised his eyebrows. "That day I almost kissed you?"

Jay shook his head. "The day I almost fell off the bridge. Sixteen years ago."

Angel's eyes got impossibly wider as he cupped the sides of Jay's face. "Oh my god, are you serious?" he asked quietly. "All that time? Fuck, Jay…I had no idea."

"It's okay," Jay said, placing his hand over Angel's heart. "You got there in the end."

Detective Padilla groaned. "I really need to get a cat. This town is infested with happy couples. Okay! You boys sit tight and make goo-goo eyes while I go do police stuff somewhere far away from you. We'll let you know when you can go."

Angel gave her a smile. "Thanks, Detective."

"Thank your boyfriend," she said before she tilted her head. "Wait. I thought he was your fiancé?"

Jay opened his mouth, looking between her and Angel. "I forgot about that," he whispered.

"We can explain," Angel began, but Padilla waved her hand.

"I don't care," she said with a tired smile. "Neither of you are dead despite your best efforts, so all I care about is less paperwork for me." She quirked her eyebrow. "You are a cute couple, though. Like, icky cute. One of you might want to think about proposing if you haven't already." She sighed. "Okay, I'm going now. Try not to get into any more trouble before I get back." She walked off into the madness, sipping her coffee.

Even though they were surrounded by people, it felt like the first time Jay had gotten a moment alone with Angel. He needed to tell him everything.

"I need to explain," Jay began, but Angel shook his head.

"Jay, I'm guessing Lisa called you and that was why you were all the way out here with your phone switched off?"

Jay nodded. "She..." He rubbed his forehead. "She made me doubt myself. Us."

Angel leaned in and kissed him. It took him by surprise for half a second, but then Jay responded eagerly. Angel's lips were cold, but his passion was hot. He claimed Jay's mouth with firm kisses, his tongue seeking Jay's as they calmed each other with the touch of their mouths and hands.

"I'm sorry," Jay mumbled as they broke apart, breathing heavily.

"You have *nothing* to apologize for, baby," said Angel. He

stroked his thumb over Jay's cheek in a soothing motion. *"I'm sorry you had to listen to her garbage. She called me as well, trying to get back together or some shit, and I told her we'd be blocking her and that she should never contact us again."* He bit his lip and ran his hands up and down Jay's arms. "She was lying through her teeth, but I guessed she'd said some pretty terrible things to you. We can talk about it if you want, or not. But please believe me when I tell you that I love you so much and I am one thousand percent never getting back together with her."

Jay took in a shuddery breath, relief coursing through him. "I was so stupid. I should have just gone to the bar to talk to you. But I felt so unsure about everything and I wanted to think." He rubbed away the fresh tears that threatened to fall. "I'm so glad you found me."

"Well," said Angel with a rueful chuckle. "It's a good thing you did come here, right? No one got hurt, but even better, all those awful protesters have been arrested. The film should be able to finish in peace now."

Jay shook his head and snuggled closer to Angel. "Who knew a few bad eggs could rally so many bigots. It makes me sick to think so many people in town secretly hate me. Us."

But Angel hummed in disagreement and kissed Jay's hair. "No, baby. Not 'so many.' A loud but very small minority. This town loves you and all your friends. It's a wonderful place to live, or so I remember."

Jay hummed. "You could live here again if you wanted, you know?" He was too tired and rattled from his encounter with Kenny to worry about tact. He'd held his feelings inside for too many years. From now on, he was going to be honest with Angel all the time.

He'd thought Angel might act surprised at the suggestion of taking such a big step so soon, but instead, he chuckled, the vibrations rumbling through Jay's body. "I do know," he said warmly. "In fact, Kamran was talking about how much film work is available here just before Lisa called. It hit me that I don't *need* to be in LA. I could get just as much steady work here, if not more, so I'd have to travel less."

Jay looked up at him, hardly daring to believe one person could get to be so happy. "Do you want to move in with me?" he asked tentatively.

Angel snorted and kissed him through his grin. "No, I thought I'd move in with my *other* amazing, gorgeous boyfriend. He has this adorable corgi, you see, so – ow."

He grinned harder as Jay thumped him gently.

"Shut up," Jay grumbled. "No other boyfriends, please."

"None, I swear," Angel said, kissing him sweetly.

"Hey, Mr. Hero," Detective Padilla called out as she approached, giving Jay and Angel time to pull apart. "Look what one of my guys found. I assume it's yours?"

"My phone!" Jay cried. It showed how tired he was that tears sprung into his eyes. "I thought I'd lost it. Is it totally smashed?" He didn't really mind. If he could rescue the SIM card, he could save all his photos and contacts.

But Padilla shook her head and offered it to him. "That's a good case you've got on it. Or you're just really lucky. One crack, not even a big one. The universe is thanking you for catching Mr. Brooker in the act. He's got a long list of charges facing him now."

"Hey, Detective?" Angel said, frowning up at her as Jay saw for himself that his phone was really okay. "Would adding attempted murder add much to the charges, considering he already fessed up to planting the bomb?"

Jay dropped his phone in his lap and looked at Angel with curiosity. Padilla's eyebrows rose as she considered Angel intently. "It depends on what you mean."

Angel shook his head. "I don't know...something Kenny

said when I pulled him off Jay. Something about me crashing the car. I thought I remembered something."

"From the accident?" Jay asked.

Angel nodded at him. "It's still mostly a blank, but I got this flash of feeling, like half a memory." He turned back to Padilla. "I'm pretty sure someone cut the brake lines. I remember hitting the pedal and nothing happening. Maybe the investigator looking at the wreck could check that out specifically?"

"Oh my god, Angel," Jay said, horror washing over him all over again. "You could have died."

Padilla thought for a moment, then nodded. "We can certainly ask the investigator to look into that. But what makes you think Kenny was involved?"

"He was on set just before the accident," said Jay, answering on Angel's behalf, seeing as he still had all his memories from that night. Anger burned in him like a fire. "And his cousin is a mechanic – he works at the same garage as my brother's boyfriend, Dair Epping. We know that Kenny used a distraction tonight with those people chaining themselves to the trees. What if *Kenny* was the distraction the other night while his cousin cut the brake lines?"

Padilla exhaled loudly and rubbed the back of her head under her ponytail. "Fuck *me*. I mean…that's definitely something we can look into." She cleared her throat. "Thank you, Mr. Shields. And, Mr. Coal. I'll have someone come take another statement in a sec. Don't, uh, go anywhere, okay?"

"We'll be right here," Angel promised. Padilla hurried off with purpose, muttering about lunatics.

"I'll kill him," Jay whispered, rage coursing through him as he clung to Angel's jacket. "If he…he could have…"

"Hey, shh, it's okay," Angel said soothingly.

Jay shuddered and looked into Angel's eyes. "He could

have *killed* you. He could have taken you away from me before you were ever really mine!"

Angel smiled sweetly at him and carded his fingers through his hair. "I was always yours in some way," he said fondly. "But it doesn't matter. None of that happened. We're here and we're fine, and Kenny is probably going to jail. If I'm right and someone tampered with the car, then I won't lose my job or damage my reputation, either. I just hope what I think I remember is right."

Jay took a shaky breath and nodded, rubbing Angel's chest. "You must have been so scared."

But sighed and rested their foreheads together. "I don't remember anything more than a jolt of panic. Just a second. Do you know what I *do* remember?" Jay shook his head. "I remember waking up and seeing you there beside my bed. I remember your face lighting up with a smile, and I knew everything was going to be okay. I remember thinking I was *home*."

"Oh, Angel," Jay said softly as they hugged tightly. "You're my home."

He'd been Jay's home almost his whole life. But now they were going to get to *share* a home, to build their lives together.

Despite being cold and exhausted to the bone, Jay felt a deep contentment wash over him.

He had his Angel, and everything was going to be all right.

22

JAY

By the time the cops said they could leave, it was past midnight. Jay's phone was definitely working again, as he'd received approximately one thousand messages from all his friends. They had started by asking about his phone call from Lisa and whether Angel had found him yet, then very quickly moved on to 'WTF DO YOU MEAN A BOMB?!'

And of course, the most important messages:

BEN: Angel told us the great news! Congrats, hon!

ROBIN: I really hoped you guys would get here eventually. Love you, bro.

ELIAS: You guys make a lovely couple.

SWIFT: Told you so.

AVA: Awesome work, baby bro. Don't even think about asking me to be a bridesmaid. I already told Swift no.

EMERY: OH EM GEE FINALLY!!!!

KAMRAN: I knew you crazy kids would figure it out in the end. Tell Angel to look after my damn car as if your firstborn was inside.

Angel had felt bad about accidentally spilling the beans, but Jay hadn't minded in the slightest. After all his doubts and insecurities, he kind of loved that the news had spread naturally, without a big announcement from them. It seemed his friends had been rooting for them for longer than he'd realized, and he should have accepted the truth sooner.

He and Angel were destined to be together.

Jay wasn't going to let himself get rattled again like he had with Lisa if he could help it. What he and Angel had was *strong*. It had already survived so much, and Jay was finally ready to believe that it wasn't all going to fall apart like a house of cards in a stiff breeze.

Still, it was hard to part ways so soon. However, they each had a car to drive off the bridge back into town. "See you in a minute," he said as he kissed Angel before they parted. "Drive safe." Then he blinked and looked at Kamran's car.

Angel had explained how he'd borrowed it in his haste to reach Jay, and from Kamran's increasingly frequent, drunken, and anxious texts, he was quite eager to get it back. Jay suspected that if Kamran wasn't reunited with his baby soon, he was going to have a breakdown.

But there was something else Jay only just realized in that moment.

"You drove," he said, looking between Angel and the car.

Angel frowned with a smile. "Yeah, hence the car," he said slowly.

But Jay shook his head. "You *drove*. You haven't been behind the wheel since the accident, have you?"

Angel's eyebrows crept up toward his hairline. "Oh, wow. You're right. I didn't even realize." But then he laughed and leaned over to kiss Jay again. "I guess I just needed something really, *really* important to help me. Like, say, thinking my boyfriend was in trouble." He sighed and cupped the side of Jay's face with his cold hand. "I'm actually glad Lisa called when she did. Otherwise I might not have come looking for you. When you weren't at your apartment, I just had this strange feeling that you'd be here. It was like the universe was talking to me."

"Maybe on some level, you knew this was where I fell in love with you," Jay said, rubbing Angel's back.

"I think so," Angel agreed with a happy sigh, resting his forehead against Jay's for a second. "Okay, right. Let's get into the warm. I'll see you back at your place – no – back *home*," he corrected himself with a grin. "I'll drop Kamran's car at his place, then grab an Uber."

Jay chewed his lip. "Wait, an Uber doesn't make sense. I could follow you to Kamran's apartment and—"

"No," said Angel firmly. "I want you home and safe as soon as possible. Kamran's place is on the other side of town from yours, and you have work in the morning. Get yourself back to Button and snuggle up. I'll be there soon."

Warmth spread through Jay just from Angel's words. "You've always looked after me," he said with such love he could barely contain it.

Angel sighed and nodded. "And I always will, I promise. Now go before we spend the whole night out on this bridge."

Jay shivered and had to agree it was definitely time to leave. Even with the blanket he'd been huddling in, he was frozen, and he took a minute to just sit in his car (having retrieved the keys from underneath it) and blasted the heat. He rubbed his hands and waited for the air to warm up before he began the drive home.

As much as he hadn't wanted to be away from Angel for even a minute, after everything they'd been through that day, it was probably good that he had some time alone with his thoughts. The happy ones, not the tortured ones that had driven him to the railway bridge in the first place.

Angel was really his boyfriend. Angel was going to move in with him.

It had taken sixteen years, but it had been worth the wait.

As much as Jay would have liked to have skipped over some of the past decade's heartache, he also firmly believed that he and Angel hadn't been ready to be together until now. They weren't done baking, like Ben's spiced apple muffins that were sitting waiting at home for them. They had to stay in the oven for long enough until they were perfect. Besides, what use were regrets? Jay only wanted to look to the future.

When he unlocked the apartment door, he was met by a frantic Button, who had obviously become convinced that Jay had gone and died on her and was never, ever coming back. He laughed in relief as he fussed over her. "You have no idea how close things got, baby girl," he muttered as he hugged her wriggling body. "Okay, it's all right. Yes, I'm here."

Eventually, she settled, and Jay stood again, evaluating the apartment.

He and Angel had tidied away the rose petals and candles that morning. That seemed like a week ago, not a few hours. But Jay wanted to make Angel feel even more welcome when he got back. Because he was coming *home* for the first time.

So Jay got to tidying away some of his grading and emptied the dishwasher, but that didn't feel like enough. He chewed his lip and wandered into the bedroom, looking at Angel's suitcase and the various clothes and toiletries lying around the place.

Suddenly, he knew exactly what to do.

He'd only just finished as he heard Angel's keys jangle in the door. As he stepped inside, they went through the whole song and dance with Button again, but Angel didn't seem to mind at all. Eventually, when Button was satisfied neither her dad nor his boyfriend was dead, she flopped at their feet and allowed the humans to greet each other. Angel stood and smiled at Jay, opening his arms to envelop Jay and kiss the top of his head tenderly.

"It's good to be home," he said with a happy sigh, and Jay's chest filled with warmth again.

Wordlessly, he took Angel's hand and led him into his bedroom – *their* bedroom now. Jay had no hesitation about opening up his space for Angel. He wanted his boyfriend to stamp his mark in every room and feel completely at home.

Starting tonight.

"Notice anything different?" Jay asked coyly. He watched Angel look around the room.

"Oh," said Angel as he noticed what was missing. "My suitcase is gone. Did you put it in the closet?"

"No," said Jay, shaking his head with a laugh. "No more closets for you. The case is under the bed. Everything that was *inside* the case is now…"

He reached over and opened the top drawer of one of his chests. Angel's eyebrows shot up. "That's my stuff," he said, very cutely stating the obvious. "Oh wow, I have a drawer?"

"You can have as many drawers as you need," Jay said, slipping his arms around Angel's waist and looking into his blue-gray eyes. "You can move in as soon as you want."

Angel blinked and looked around the room. "*Yeeaah*, right now seems like a pretty good time, don't you think? That works with my schedule. How about I just don't leave?"

Jay snorted. He knew that Angel would have to leave eventually for work. And there was the small matter of his apartment in LA which he'd have to empty and negotiate breaking the lease early. But Jay appreciated his enthusiasm.

"Sounds good to me. I think we should celebrate."

"In bed?" Angel asked, waggling his eyebrows.

Jay laughed and kissed him. "Sure. But hot chocolate first. And I think it's about time we finally ate those spiced apple muffins."

Angel groaned. "Breakfast for dinner, hell yeah."

Jay slapped his ass as Angel moved to get under the

covers, the both of them laughing happily. Jay had been back for half an hour, and he was still cold, so he hurried to make the hot chocolate so he could join his boyfriend back in bed with their tasty treats.

Snuggled up next to Angel, Jay blew on his hot chocolate, watching the marshmallows bob in the steaming cup. He and Angel talked back and forth, mostly going over the unbelievable events of the day, but then the conversation drifted to the future. Angel reckoned he didn't actually have much stuff to bring up from LA. His rented apartment was pre-furnished, as the wicked witch had kept most of their things in the break-up. He seemed pretty confident that he'd be able to get the small items to Pine Cove in one carload. Then the big things such as his treadmill could be moved with a U-Haul.

"Mind you, I'll probably want to run more in the woods," Angel said thoughtfully. "It's so beautiful here. It feels amazing to be coming home."

"Tell me about it," said Jay as he placed his now empty mug on the nightstand.

As he started kissing Angel's jaw, Angel got the hint and discarded his own cup, pulling Jay farther down under the covers. Jay's kisses found Angel's lips as his (finally warm) hands slipped under Angel's shirt. His lips tasted so sweet from the hot chocolate with a zing of cinnamon from the muffin. Jay hummed as he lapped it up.

"How do you feel after all that driving?" he asked, running his hand down Angel's arm.

Angel dropped his head back and laughed. "If you're asking if I feel well enough for sex, the answer is 'yes.'" He nuzzled his nose against Jay's. "It's always 'yes' for you, handsome."

Jay chuckled, not minding getting busted in the slightest.

"It's always 'yes' for you too, baby," he said, the word 'baby' dancing on his tongue like a delightful spell.

Button got the hint pretty quickly that there wasn't going to be much room for her with two sets of legs kicking around, so she trotted off the bed and down her stairs with a grumble. "You can come back later, baby girl," Angel promised with a grin. "Once I'm done with your dad."

Jay groaned and started undoing Angel's jeans. He wondered when the novelty of finally getting to see his best friend naked would wear off.

Never, he decided as he slipped his hand over Angel's already hard length, feeling him through his underwear. Angel moaned and kissed Jay with increasing hunger.

"I want to be inside you again," he said breathlessly into Jay's mouth. "Is it too soon?"

Jay shook his head. "Not if we take it slowly. Gently."

Angel growled and nipped at Jay's collarbone. "Gonna make love to my baby," he said, making Jay's heart swell.

They took their time kissing and pulling each other's clothes off. This was definitely the best way to warm up, Jay concluded. By the time they were down to their underwear, they'd thrown the covers off completely and were panting as their briefs hit the floor. Jay grabbed another condom and the bottle of lube for them.

"Can we do it this way tonight?" Angel asked him as he hovered above Jay. He ran his hand down Jay's side and kissed his lips reverently. "Face-to-face. I want to see you."

Jay swallowed and nodded, doing his best not to feel overcome by the moment. "That sounds perfect," he said, caressing the side of Angel's face.

He reached over and grabbed a pillow from the other side of the bed and shoved it under his hips to help with the angle. As he lay back down, Angel captured his lips for a sweet kiss. He was kneeing between Jay's legs, and within a few seconds, Jay felt his fingers slip between his cheeks to rub his hole.

He was so hot by now he didn't even mind the coolness of the lube. All he cared about was the delicious burn of Angel's finger pushing inside him. He was still a little sore from the ravishing he'd taken before, but it was okay. In fact, he almost preferred the extra sensitivity that grounded him in the moment. He wanted to feel every second with Angel, to remind him that this was real and quite possibly forever.

They cuddled and kissed as Angel stretched Jay out, ready to accept him inside. There was so much damp skin pressed together Jay loved it. He felt enveloped by Angel, even though Angel was going to be the one inside him. Angel was everywhere, filling Jay's world.

"Baby," Angel murmured into his mouth as he reached for the condom.

Jay raked his fingers down Angel's back. "Oh, baby," he whispered back. "I'm ready for you. Please, Angel. *Please.*"

After applying more lube, Angel lined himself up and pushed against Jay's hole. It really was a bit too much, and Jay whimpered as he clung to Angel's shoulders.

"Jay?" Angel asked, stilling.

His golden skin shone with perspiration, and Jay hugged him tightly as he panted, relaxing into the intrusion.

"I'm okay," he promised, his voice hoarse. "Just take it slow. But you feel amazing. I need you."

Angel kissed Jay's throat and stroked his hair back. "You've got me, baby. I'm right here, and I'm not going anywhere, okay?"

Jay got the feeling they were talking about more than sex in that moment.

He nodded. "I know," he said sincerely as Angel pushed a little farther inside him. His heart was racing, and his cock was hard between them, leaking on their bellies. "You're my Angel, sent from above."

Angel laughed and nibbled Jay's earlobe, making Jay moan and squirm.

"You are so cheesy," said Angel. "I love it."

"I love *you*," Jay said, gazing into his eyes. "For so long. In so many different ways."

Angel kissed his lips, closing his eyes as he rested his forehead on Jay's. "I'm glad you don't have to love alone anymore."

Jay pushed up against Angel, encouraging him farther inside. "Yes, it's definitely better with two people," he agreed.

Angel snorted. "You filthy minx," he growled. "I'll show you 'better.'"

"Please do," Jay begged with no sense of irony.

He was excited that Angel was up for being versatile and switching positions in the future, but in that moment, Jay was thoroughly content to be claimed by his man. They were both so eager they didn't take it as slowly as they'd said they would, but Jay didn't mind. In fact, he couldn't really think of anything other than the primal need for Angel to push as deep in him as possible. His hard cock was perfect as it tagged Jay's prostate, sending beautiful electricity all through his body.

They rocked as they kissed. This wasn't like the dizzy excitement of the night before. It was more tender and slower as they stared into each other's eyes, gently rising to their joint climax. "Touch me," Jay pleaded as he felt himself getting close. He gripped the back of Angel's neck as they thrust together, Angel's strong hand feeling so incredibly good around Jay's throbbing cock. "I'm close."

"Me, too, handsome," Angel grunted.

Sweat was running off him, helping their hot bodies slide

against each other. The sound of their slapping skin and desperate gasps filled the room, urging Jay to his orgasm.

"Angel!" Jay cried in warning, just as he clenched and his cum began shooting all over Angel's hand and his own belly. He moaned and bit Angel's shoulder as Angel continued to stroke him to completion, Angel's cock thrusting deep inside as he chased his own release. Mere moments later, he bellowed Jay's name and arched his back. Jay felt him pulsing inside him as they clung to each other like life rafts.

After what felt like minutes, Angel eventually took a deep breath, then lowered himself down, gathering Jay up in his arms to hug him tightly and smatter kisses all over his face. "I love you, Jay Coal," he said gruffly, and Jay squeezed his eyes shut tightly as the happy tears threatened to fall.

"I love you, too, Angel Shields. Now and forever."

Angel hummed, rubbing Jay's back and stroking his hair. "I like the sound of forever, handsome. I mean, technically, I already proposed to you like two or three times, so, you know…"

Jay laughed and shook his head. "I am not accepting a proposal spurred on by amnesia and morphine, sorry. You'll have to do better than that."

Angel waggled his eyebrows. "I'm sure one day I will," he said.

Jay knew they were just joking.

Sort of.

He also knew that one day he was sure he'd say yes.

EPILOGUE – TWO MONTHS LATER

ANGEL

"Is that the last of it?" Dair asked, shuffling into the apartment with a box so large his head and torso were totally lost behind it.

"Please *god*, let it be the last of it," Emery said with a whimper as he followed with a box half the size of Dair's.

His fiancé, Scout, brought up the procession with a laugh and another of the large boxes. "You're the one who insisted on doing heavy lifting. You could have been organizing the closet if you weren't so stubborn."

"Because I am a strong, independent woman, and I refuse to conform to gender stereotypes!" Emery cried, dumping his box in the living room with all the rest of Angel's stuff. He breathed in a few deep breaths, then scowled at his hand. "Oh, I broke a nail."

Scout chuckled and – after placing his own box down carefully – went and kissed Emery's finger. "Oh, no. How sad," he gently teased.

Angel wrapped his arms around Jay from where they were reorganizing the kitchen with Robin, and smiled at their friends. "Thanks, guys," he said with genuine appreciation. "Yes, if the car is empty, that's the last of it."

Dair winked at him and tossed him his car keys. "There we go, then," he said brightly. "You're officially a resident of Pine Cove again. How does it feel?"

Angel smiled down at Jay and kissed his boyfriend as happiness threatened to burst through his every pore. "Pretty damn awesome," he admitted.

"Oh, yay," said Emery, clapping and spinning around. Apparently, he was already recovered from his box-carrying ordeal. "So now we can go party, yes?"

"Oh, I don't know," said Angel, looking around at all the boxes that Button was currently running around and sniffing. "We should probably—"

"Come party, yes!" Emery agreed, bouncing across the room to where he'd left a bag of his own. "We're all Ubering to the Coals' house, yes? Great! Jay, where are your shot glasses?" He pulled out a frighteningly green bottle with a flourish, and the room collectively gasped.

"Oh, no, babe," Scout protested, waving his hands. "Let's at least eat something first, okay?"

"What! Come on," Emery pleaded. But Scout knew how to deal with him.

He wrapped his arms around Emery's waist and kissed his cheek. "We can do shots later, I promise. And then we can…" He whispered something into Emery's ear that made him blush. Angel had to grin, imagining what filthy things Scout was promising his fiancé that they could also do later.

Emery giggled, then composed himself and made a big deal of sighing and pouting as he put the bottle away again. "Fine. But if Kamran were here, he'd have agreed."

"Has anyone heard from him?" Dair asked with a frown.

"I've had a few texts," said Scout. "All vague."

"Me, too," Angel agreed.

"He just keeps insisting he's okay and not to worry," added Robin.

"No one knows where he is despite all these assurances that he's fine." Jay shook his head. "And recently, he's dropped completely off the grid. I wouldn't mind, if only he'd explained why."

Angel frowned. Things had been a little off since that night Kamran had acted weird at Aquarium – the night of Kenny Brooker's arrest – but now no one had seen him in a week.

"Oh, don't worry," Emery said as he skipped over to one of the mirrors on the wall and applied a fresh coat of glittery lip gloss. "I'm almost certain he's found himself a *man*. I have a hunch. He's probably just all loved up and forgotten about his friends. You know how it goes."

Angel had to laugh as he hugged Jay tighter and kissed him again. "No, but I intend to," he said with a grin.

Emery was probably right. If Kamran wanted to lock himself away and have a sexy marathon with a new someone – or some*ones* – that was totally up to him. Angel trusted Kamran would let him and their friends know if something was actually wrong.

It gave Angel a thrill to count himself among the Pine Cove gang. And like Dair said, now that all his stuff was moved in, it was official.

He was a Pine Covian. Not that there was such a term as that, but Angel was so giddy with happiness he wondered if he could make it a thing.

His lease on his place in LA had only just ended. However, Angel had been true to his word and essentially moved in with Jay the night of Kenny's arrest. But that hadn't meant he'd been able to spend as much time here as he'd wanted, not by a long shot. Production on Fallen Angels Club 2 had only just wrapped last week, and Angel had spent most of his time over the last several weeks traveling all over the country and parts of Europe too.

But now he was home, and although everything was in chaos, he also felt a kind of inner peace he hadn't experienced in years. Possibly ever. Things were just better when he was with Jay, and now they were going to wake up next to each other every day Angel wasn't away for work.

Before even starting on Fallen Angels, he'd already had another movie lined up that would begin filming in a couple of weeks. But after that, he'd started booking the majority of his work locally, like Kamran did. Except Angel was more qualified in more fields than Kamran, so his schedule was already looking pretty full.

This was his life now. Living and working in Pine Cove alongside his gorgeous boyfriend, whose generous parents were hosting a welcome home party for him in their back yard this afternoon. He wasn't sure how it could get much better than this.

But he had a few ideas. Someday. His memory was pretty good these days, but he'd never forgotten the feeling of thinking he was engaged to Jay Coal.

Someday, he was going to recreate that feeling for real.

One rather crowded Uber journey later, Angel found himself back at the Coal family home. There were a few cars in the long driveway, but Angel had a sneaking suspicion that they weren't the only ones who were planning on drinking and had taken a cab.

But even so, he wasn't prepared.

Robin led the six of them (plus Button, who they'd had to get a special Uber to accommodate for) around the side of the large property directly out into the back yard. As they rounded the last corner, Robin and Dair stepped to the left, and Scout and Emery to the right, parting to leave Angel and Jay in the middle.

"SURPRISE!" about thirty or forty people yelled.

Button barked at every single one of them, of course. But Angel's mouth dropped open, and he laughed as people continued to clap and cheer, pulling party poppers and wolf-whistling.

"Did you...?" he began to ask Jay, but his boyfriend shook his head.

"Not me," he said, his eyebrows lost under his dark curls. "Mom, Dad?"

The Coals came forward to embrace Jay and Angel. "We just wanted Angel to know he was welcome," said Jay's mom.

"So he won't leave again like a dufus!" Kestrel cried, skipping up to them with little Imogen in tow as Jay's parents let them go. Both the girls held extremely glittery 'Welcome Home!' signs that were leaving a sparkling trail in the grass behind them.

"See," said Imogen, pushing her glasses up her nose and grinning triumphantly. "I told you you'd make a good boyfriend for Jay, Angel. And, Jay? Angel is very good at playing mermaid pirates, just so you know."

Jay laughed and hugged Angel to his side. "Is he now?"

"We are *not* playing that in the bedroom," Angel murmured into Jay's ear so that no one else could hear, making Jay snort very inelegantly.

The two of them soon had glasses of Champagne pressed into their hands that Angel dutifully drank before switching to the beer he preferred. He and Jay mingled through the crowd, with Jay introducing Angel to anyone he didn't already know or hadn't seen in a long time.

Half the guests were the Perkins family. Angel already knew Imogen, obviously, and had met Micha Perkins – Swift's fiancé – at the last lunch they'd had at this house. But apparently, the two families celebrated most things together these days, so Micha's four siblings, their other halves, and

263

their kids were all here. There were also numerous friends of the two families as well, like Ben and Elias and of course Emery and Scout.

"Nice to see you again, dude," said Robin's best friend, Peyton, as she clinked her beer bottle with Angel's. "You left in rather a dramatic fashion when I last saw you at Aquarium. I heard things turned out pretty okay, though, all things considered."

Angel looked over to where Jay was talking animatedly with Robin and Dair. "It really did," said Angel warmly. "Perfectly, you might say."

True to their word, Jay and Angel had systematically blocked Lisa from their phones and all social media platforms. If she really wanted to, Angel knew she could try and spy on them in other ways, but he hoped she'd have enough dignity to move on with her life and not try any funny business again.

And not only had Kenny been arrested and charged for his many crimes, but so had several other of the protesters. Angel knew Jay had been worried about an undercurrent of discontent brewing in Pine Cove, but membership of the Pine Cove High Gay-Straight Alliance had almost doubled since the incident. When the kids had come to do their extras work for the film, a lot of their parents had come to chaperone at the shoot and make their support well and truly known.

Bryce Brooker – Kenny's dad – had also come to visit Jay personally to apologize for his son and nephew's behavior. Kenny's cousin was in just as much hot water for cutting the brake lines of the movie's car and almost killing Angel. Bryce had made it very clear that the rest of the family did *not* share the same bigoted opinions as the two men, and offered Jay and Angel discounted service at all the Brooker businesses in town for life.

So Angel had kept reminding Jay of all these things when Jay got worried that his hometown wasn't as welcoming as he used to think. Besides, looking at this happy throng of people, Jay had to know he was loved and supported by those who mattered, didn't he?

Angel caught his eye across the crowd, and for a second, all the music and chatter and sizzling from the barbecue faded away.

Jay was Angel's whole world now, and he couldn't be happier.

There were still gaps in his memory, but Angel knew enough. He'd remembered the crucial moment of the accident so the investigation team had known what they were looking for to charge Kenny and his cousin. But way more important than that, his temporary blank slate had enabled him to see Jay with fresh new eyes.

And to fall in love with him.

"So, I take it you haven't heard from Kamran either?" Peyton asked, snapping Angel from his reverie.

He blinked at her. "Oh, no, well, not the past few days. Before that, he told several of us that he was okay, just taking a break from things." Whatever that meant. But Emery was probably right. He was most likely just loved up. "Why do you ask?"

Peyton sighed. "Apparently, Sabina Max wanted to give me her phone number." She let out a little squeak of excitement, and Angel couldn't say he blamed her.

"Wow, that's amazing," he said.

But Peyton shrugged, her face dropping. "But Kamran never passed it on."

Angel grinned at her. "Well, today's your lucky day! I *also* happen to have her number. I'd like to check with her quickly first, but if she says it's okay, I could totally give it to you."

"Oh yes, please, thank you," said Peyton happily.

"NO!"

The party stalled. Even the music dropped in sound as one song finished, and another waited to start.

Ava Coal had dropped her bottle of beer to the ground and was looking at Angel and Peyton in horror.

Or, more specifically, she was looking at Peyton like she'd just told her Christmas was canceled.

Forever.

"Ava?" said Peyton, and Angel took a step back, looking between them. In fact, *everyone* seemed to be looking at them both, some with mouths open or eyebrows raised or hands clasped in front of their chests.

"I, uh..." said Ava, her hands twitching and her feet jerking like she was very much resisting the urge to run away.

Angel almost jumped as Jay materialized by his side, slipping his hand into Angel's. "Oh my god," he whispered. "Is Ava actually *talking* to Peyton?"

Angel shook his head, not wanting to say anything in case they spooked Ava, like she was a wild horse.

Ava cleared her throat, her wide eyes looking around at everyone staring. Peyton hugged her beer bottle to her chest, biting her lip. There was maybe a dozen feet between them, and the group of party-goers had fanned out so there was no one standing in their way.

"I-is there something you wanted to say to me?" Peyton asked.

Ava blinked, and for a second, Angel thought she was going to bolt. She always ran away from Peyton, according to Jay and everyone else.

But not today, apparently.

"You can totally swap numbers with Sabina Max if you want," Ava finally blurted out, clenching her hands in fists and swaying on the spot like she was going to pass out. "She's – like – a super hot Hollywood star. But you should know that she'd be lucky to have *you*. Because there are other people who think you're amazing...and kind and funny and really cute. But...but these people might have been really, *really* dumb and not spoken up about how amazing they think you are until, well, right now."

She swallowed and closed her eyes.

"It's me. *I* think you're amazing. And I only have myself to blame if you go and fall in love with Sabina fucking Max. But if I don't tell you now, I really won't ever forgive myself, and I know it shouldn't have taken an A-list celebrity for me to get some fucking courage, but if you want, I—"

She stopped her increasingly frantic monologue. Probably because Peyton had also dropped *her* beer bottle and sprinted across the several feet between them, crashing into Ava, flinging her arms around her, and kissing her like Christmas had just been un-canceled.

"Oh, *Ava*," she moaned, sounding equally frustrated and ecstatic. *"Finally!"*

"WOOHOO!" Emery bellowed, breaking the spell that had hushed the party, and suddenly everyone was whooping and clapping again.

"Oh, wow," said Jay, half turning away with a giggle and clinging to Angel. "She is *really* kissing my sister."

Angel laughed and ruffled Jay's hair, hugging him close. "I guess we weren't the only ones who needed a little help to see what was right in front of them."

Jay seemed to forget all about Peyton and Ava at that, turning to give Angel all his attention as he slipped his arms around Angel's neck. He smiled so sweetly as he leaned in to kiss Angel on the lips. It wasn't as earth shattering as the kiss they'd just witnessed, but to Angel, it was perfect.

"I'm glad I finally saw that everything I ever wanted was just here, waiting for me," he said, shaking his head.

They swayed back and forth as the party came back to life around them. Angel was aware of people crowding around Ava and Peyton, but as far as he was concerned, it was just him and Jay in that moment.

How many moments would they get like this now? How many years of happiness were stretched out before them? All because Angel had finally been given the chance to spread his wings and discover who he really was.

And who he was meant to be with.

There might be some parts of his memory that he'd never get back, but he had Jay to fill in the gaps for him. They had all the time in the world to make new memories, back home in the place where they'd grown up together.

Angel had never imagined wedding bells or the pitter-patter of little feet with his ex, despite everyone telling them that was their destiny. But with Jay, he had no doubt that was what their future held.

This was it for Angel. He'd found his person when they'd been in kindergarten. He'd just had to wait until he was thirty to realize.

And now he was never going to forget it.

Thank you for reading Jay and Angel's story! If you want to discover what's going on with Kamran, make sure you pre-order Pine Cove #6 Thin Ice today! Coming May 7th.

Go back to the beginning of Pine Cove:

#2 – Troubled Waters – Emery and Scout

#3 – Homeward Bound – Micha and Swift

#4 – Bright Horizon – Ben and Elias

#4.5 – Crossed Paths – Raj and Antoni (a Bright Horizon companion)

#5.05 – Midnight Sky – Taylan and Hudson

FOR GIVEAWAYS, sneak peeks, ARC opportunities and general fun times, please join my Facebook group! Helen's Jewels. We're very friendly! For more of my books, take a look below...

HOMECOMING HEARTS

WANT MORE FROM HJ WELCH? How about a whole box set?! All five Homecoming Hearts books are available in one place along with two extra short stories. Follow the former members of boy band Below Zero as they return home and find their true loves!

- Homecoming Heart Complete Box Set

SHARED UNIVERSES

HJ Welch has written in two shared universes with multiple authors to create incredible worlds! You can find the links to her contributions below:

HIDDEN CREEK

Welcome to Hidden Creek, Texas, where the heart knows what it wants, and where true love lives happily ever after. Every Men of Hidden Creek novel can be read on its own, but keep an eye out for familiar faces around town!

- Season 1: Storm
- Season 2: Ashes
- Season 3: Masterpiece
- Season 4: Reveal

ROSAVIA ROYALS

Welcome to the tiny European country of Rosavia, where roses ramble over alpine slopes and princes fall for the men of their dreams. Every Rosavia Royals book happens simultaneously, so books can be read on their own, or in any order... but keep an eye out for familiar faces around the palace!

- Reign or Shine

ACKNOWLEDGMENTS

Cheerleaders: Ed, Amelia, Conrad, Mum, Hubby, kitty cats
    Cover Artist: AngstyG
    Beta Reading: Amy Pittel
    Editing: Meg Cooper
    Proof Reading: Tanja Ongkiehong

ABOUT THE AUTHOR

HJ Welch is a contemporary MM romance author living in London with her husband and two balls of fluff that occasionally pretend to be cats. She began writing at an early age, later honing her craft online in the world of fanfiction on sites like Wattpad. Fifteen years and over a million words later, she sought out original MM novels to read. By the end of 2016 she had written her first book of her own, and in 2017 she fulfilled her lifelong dream of becoming a fulltime author.

She also writes contemporary British MM romance as Helen Juliet.

You can contact HJ Welch via social media:

Website – http://www.hjwelch.com/

Newsletter – https://www.subscribepage.com/helenjuliet

Facebook Group – Helen's Jewels

Facebook Page – @HJWelchAuthor

Instagram – @helenjwrites

Twitter – @helenjwrites

Email – helenjulietauthor@gmail.com